METAMORPHOSIS

Piri dived flat to the water, sliced neatly under a wave, and paddled out to waist-height. He paused there. He held his nose and worked his arms up and down, blowing air through his mouth and swallowing at the same time. What looked like long, hairline scars between his lower ribs came open. Red-orange fringes became visible inside them, and gradually lowered. He was no longer an air-breather.

He dived again, mouth open, and this time he did not come up. His esophagus and trachea closed and a new valve came into operation. It would pass water in only one direction, so his diaphragm now functioned as a pump pulling water through his mouth and forcing it out through the gill-slits. The water flowing through this lower chest area caused his gills to engorge with blood, turning them purplish-red and forcing his lungs to collapse upward into his chest cavity. Bubbles of air trickled out his sides, then stopped. His transition was complete . . .

—from John Varley's
Good-Bye, Robinson Crusoe

Isaac Asimov's Solar System

Edited by
Gardner Dozois
and
Sheila Williams

ACE BOOKS, NEW YORK

ISAAC ASIMOV'S SOLAR SYSTEM

An Ace Book / published by arrangement with
Dell Magazines

PRINTING HISTORY
Ace edition / December 1999

All rights reserved.
Copyright © 1999 by Dell Magazines.
Cover art by Danilo Ducak.
This book may not be reproduced in whole or in part,
by mimeograph or any other means, without permission.
For information address: The Berkley Publishing Group,
a division of Penguin Putnam, Inc.
375 Hudson Street, New York, New York 10014.

The Penguin Putnam Inc. World Wide Web site address is
http://www.penguinputnam.com

Check out the ACE Science Fiction & Fantasy newsletter
and much more on the Internet at Club PPI!

ISBN: 0-441-00698-1

ACE®
Ace Books are published
by The Berkley Publishing Group,
a division of Penguin Putnam Inc.,
375 Hudson Street, New York, New York 10014.
ACE and the "A" design are trademarks
belonging to Penguin Putnam Inc.

PRINTED IN THE UNITED STATES OF AMERICA

10 9 8 7 6 5 4 3 2 1

For Kristin L. Korn

CONTENTS

THE SUN SPIDER

Lucius Shepard

*"The Sun Spider" appeared in the April 1987 issue
of* Asimov's *with a cover illustration by Bob Eg-
gleton and an interior illustration by J. K. Potter.
It was one of a long string of Shepard stories—
more than a dozen sales to* Asimov's Science Fiction *magazine since his debut sale here in 1984—
that have made him one of the mainstays of the
magazine. In it, he takes us to a very exotic locale—
Helios Station, a research facility in orbit around
the south pole of the Sun, at the very center of the
Solar System—for a passionate tale of love, in-
trigue, betrayal, and transcendence.*

*Lucius Shepard was one of the most popular, in-
fluential, and prolific of the new writers of the '80s,
and that decade and the decade that followed would
see a steady stream of bizarre and powerfully compelling stories by Shepard, stories such as the land-
mark novella "R&R," which won him a Nebula
Award in 1987, "The Jaguar Hunter," "Black
Coral," "A Spanish Lesson," "The Man Who
Painted the Dragon Griaule," "Shades," "A Trav-
eler's Tale," "Human History," "How the Wind
Spoke at Madaket," "Beast of the Heartland,"
"The Scalehunter's Beautiful Daughter," and
"Barnacle Bill the Spacer," which won him a*

Hugo Award in 1993. In 1988, he picked up a World Fantasy Award for his monumental short-story collection The Jaguar Hunter, *following it in 1992 with a second World Fantasy Award for his second collection,* The Ends of the Earth. *Shepard's other books include the novels* Green Eyes, Kalimantan, *and* The Golden. *His most recent book is a new collection,* Barnacle Bill the Spacer, *and he's currently at work on a mainstream novel,* Family Values. *Born in Lynchberg, Virginia, he now lives in Seattle, Washington.*

". . . In Africa's Namib Desert, one of the most hostile environments on the face of the earth, lives a creature known as the sun spider. Its body is furred pale gold, the exact color of the sand beneath which it burrows in search of its prey, disturbing scarcely a grain in its passage. It emerges from hiding only to snatch its prey, and were you to look directly at it from an inch away, you might never notice its presence. Nature is an efficient process, tending to repeat elegant solutions to the problem of survival in such terrible places. Thus, if—as I posit—particulate life exists upon the Sun, I would not be startled to learn it has adopted a similar form."

from *Alchemical Diaries*
by Reynolds Dulambre

I
Carolyn

My husband Reynolds and I arrived on Helios Station following four years in the Namib, where he had delivered himself of the *Diaries*, including the controversial Solar Equations, and where I had become adept in the uses of boredom. We were met at the docking arm by the administrator of the Physics Section, Dr. Davis Brent, who es-

corted us to a reception given in Reynolds' honor, held
in one of the pleasure domes that blistered the skin of the
station. Even had I been unaware that Brent was one of
Reynolds' chief detractors, I would have known the two
of them for adversaries: in manner and physicality, they
were total opposites, like cobra and mongoose. Brent was
pudgy, of medium stature, with a receding hairline, and
dressed in a drab standard-issue jumpsuit. Reynolds—at
thirty-seven, only two years younger—might have been
ten years his junior. He was tall and lean, with chestnut
hair that fell to the shoulders of his cape, and possessed
of that craggy nobility of feature one associates with a
Shakespearean lead. Both were on their best behavior, but
they could barely manage civility, and so it was quite a
relief when we reached the dome and were swept away
into a crowd of admiring techs and scientists.

Helios Station orbited the south pole of the Sun, and
through the ports I had a view of a docking arm to which
several of the boxy ships that journeyed into the coronosphere were moored. Leaving Reynolds to be lionized, I
lounged beside one of the ports and gazed toward Earth,
pretending I was celebrating Nation Day in Abidjan rather
than enduring this gathering of particle pushers and in-
ductive reasoners, most of whom were gawking at Reynolds, perhaps hoping he would live up to his reputation
and perform a drugged collapse or start a fight. I watched
him and Brent talking. Brent's body language was toad-
ying, subservient, like that of a dog trying to curry favor;
he would clasp his hands and tip his head to the side when
making some point, as if begging his master not to strike
him. Reynolds stood motionless, arms folded across his
chest.

At one point Brent said, "I can't see what purpose you
hope to achieve in beaming protons into coronal holes,"
and Reynolds, in his most supercilious tone, responded by

saying that he was merely poking about in the weeds with a long stick.

I was unable to hear the next exchange, but then I did hear Brent say, "That may be, but I don't think you understand the openness of our community. The barriers you've erected around your research go against the spirit, the . . ."

"All my goddamned life," Reynolds cut in, broadcasting in a stagey baritone, "I've been harassed by little men. Men who've carved out some cozy academic niche by footnoting my work and then decrying it. Mousey little bastards like you. And that's why I maintain my privacy . . . to keep the mice from nesting in my papers."

He strode off toward the refreshment table, leaving Brent smiling at everyone, trying to show that he had not been affected by the insult. A slim brunette attached herself to Reynolds, engaging him in conversation. He illustrated his points with florid gestures, leaning over her, looking as if he were about to enfold her in his cape, and not long afterward they made a discreet exit.

Compared to Reynolds' usual public behavior, this was a fairly restrained display, but sufficient to make the gathering forget my presence. I sipped a drink, listening to the chatter, feeling no sense of betrayal. I was used to Reynolds' infidelities, and, indeed, I had come to thrive on them. I was grateful he had found his brunette. Though our marriage was not devoid of the sensual, most of our encounters were ritual in nature, and after four years of isolation in the desert, I needed the emotional sustenance of a lover. Helios would, I believed, provide an ample supply.

Shortly after Reynolds had gone, Brent came over to the port, and to my amazement, he attempted to pick me up. It was one of the most inept seductions to which I have ever been subject. He contrived to touch me time and again as if by accident, and complimented me several times on the largeness of my eyes. I managed to turn the conversation into harmless channels, and he got off into politics, a topic on which he considered himself expert.

"My essential political philosophy," he said, "derives from a story by one of the masters of twentieth century speculative fiction. In the story, a man sends his mind into the future and finds himself in a utopian setting, a green-sward surrounded by white buildings, with handsome men and beautiful women strolling everywhere . . ."

I cannot recall how long I listened to him, to what soon became apparent as a ludicrous Libertarian fantasy, before bursting into laughter. Brent looked confused by my re-action, but then masked confusion by joining in my laugh-ter. "Ah, Carolyn," he said. "I had you going there, didn't I? You thought I was serious!"

I took pity on him. He was only a sad little man with an inflated self-opinion; and, too, I had been told that he was in danger of losing his administrative post. I spent the best part of an hour in making him feel important; then, scraping him off, I went in search of a more suitable companion.

My first lover on Helios Station, a young particle physicist named Thom, proved overweening in his affections. The sound of my name seemed to transport him; often he would lift his head and say, "Carolyn, Carolyn," as if by doing this he might capture my essence. I found him ab-surd, but I was starved for attention, and though I could not reciprocate in kind, I was delighted in being the object of his single-mindedness. We would meet each day in one of the pleasure domes, dance to drift, and drink paradi-siacs—I developed quite a fondness for Amouristes—and then retire to a private chamber, there to make love and watch the sunships return from their fiery journeys. It was Thom's dream to be assigned someday to a sunship, and he would rhapsodize on the glories attendant upon swoop-

ing down through layers of burning gasses. His fixation
with the scientific adventure eventually caused me to
break off the affair. Years of exposure to Reynolds' work
had armored me against any good opinion of science, and
further I did not want to be reminded of my proximity to
the Sun: sometimes I imagined I could hear it hissing,
roaring, and feel its flames tonguing the metal walls, pre-
paring to do us to a crisp with a single lick.

By detailing my infidelity, I am not trying to characterize my marriage as loveless. I loved Reynolds, though
my affections had waned somewhat. And he loved me in
his own way. Prior to our wedding, he had announced
that he intended our union to be "a marriage of souls."
But this was no passionate outcry, rather a statement of
scientific intent. He believed in souls, believed they were
the absolute expression of a life, a quality that pervaded
every particle of matter and gave rise to the lesser expressions of personality and physicality. His search for
particulate life upon the Sun was essentially an attempt to
isolate and communicate with the anima, and the "marriage of souls" was for him the logical goal of twenty-
first century physics. It occurs to me now that this search
may have been his sole means of voicing his deepest emotions, and it was our core problem that I thought he would
someday love me in a way that would satisfy me, whereas
he felt my satisfaction could be guaranteed by the appli-
cation of scientific method.

To further define our relationship, I should mention that
he once wrote me that the "impassive, vaguely oriental
beauty" of my face reminded him of "those serene coun-
tenances used to depict the solar disc on ancient sailing
charts." Again, this was not the imagery of passion: he
considered this likeness a talisman, a lucky charm. He was
a magical thinker, perceiving himself as more akin to the
alchemists than to his peers, and like the alchemists, he
gave credence to the power of similarities. Whenever he

made love to me, he was therefore making love to the Sun. To the great detriment of our marriage, every beautiful woman became for him the Sun, and thus a potential tool for use in his rituals. Given his enormous ego, it would have been out of character for him to have been faithful, and had he not utilized sex as a concentrative ritual, I am certain he would have invented another excuse for infidelity. And, I suppose, I would have had to contrive some other justification for my own.

During those first months I was indiscriminate in my choice of lovers, entering into affairs with both techs and a number of Reynolds' colleagues. Reynolds himself was no more discriminating, and our lives took separate paths. Rarely did I spend a night in our apartment, and I paid no attention whatsoever to Reynolds' work. But then one afternoon as I lay with my latest lover in the private chamber of a pleasure dome, the door slid open and in walked Reynolds. My lover—a tech whose name eludes me— leaped up and began struggling into his clothes, apologizing all the while. I shouted at Reynolds, railed at him. What right did he have to humiliate me this way? I had never burst in on him and his whores, had I? Imperturbable, he stared at me, and after the tech had scurried out, he continued to stare, letting me exhaust my anger. At last, breathless, I sat glaring at him, still angry, yet also feeling a measure of guilt . . . not relating to my affair, but to the fact that I had become pregnant as a result of my last encounter with Reynolds. We had tried for years to have a child, and despite knowing how important a child would be to him, I had put off the announcement. I was no longer confident of his capacity for fatherhood.

"I'm sorry about this." He waved at the bed. "It was urgent I see you, and I didn't think."

The apology was uncharacteristic, and my surprise at it drained away the dregs of anger. "What is it?" I asked.

Contrary emotions played over his face. "I've got him," he said.

I knew what he was referring to: he always personified the object of his search, although before too long he began calling it "the Spider." I was happy for his success, but for some reason it had made me a little afraid, and I was at a loss for words.

"Do you want to see him?" He sat beside me. "He's imaged in one of the tanks."

I nodded.

I was sure he was going to embrace me. I could see in his face the desire to break down the barriers we had erected, and I imagined now his work was done, we would be as close as we had once hoped, that honesty and love would finally have their day. But the moment passed, and his face hardened. He stood and paced the length of the chamber. Then he whirled around, hammered a fist into his palm, and with all the passion he had been unable to direct toward me, he said, "I've got him!"

"I had been watching him for over a week without knowing it: a large low-temperature area shifting about in a coronal hole. It was only by chance that I recognized him; I inadvertently nudged the color controls of a holo tank, and brought part of the low-temperature area into focus, revealing a many-armed ovoid of constantly changing primary hues, the arms attenuating and vanishing: I have observed some of these arms reach ten thousand miles in length, and I have no idea what limits apply to their size. He consists essentially of an inner complex of ultracold neutrons enclosed by an intense magnetic field. Lately it has occurred to me that certain of the coronal holes may be no more than the attitude of his movements. Aside from these few facts and guesses, he remains a mystery, and I have begun to suspect that no matter how many elements of his nature are disclosed, he will always remain so.''

from *Collected Notes*
by Reynolds Dulambre

II
Reynolds

Brent's face faded in on the screen, his features composed into one of those fawning smiles. "Ah, Reynolds," he said. "Glad I caught you."

"I'm busy," I snapped, reaching for the off switch.

"Reynolds!"

His desperate tone caught my attention.

"I need to talk to you," he said. "A matter of some importance."

I gave an amused sniff. "I doubt that."

"Oh, but it is . . . to both of us."

An oily note had crept into his voice, and I lost patience. "I'm going to switch off, Brent. Do you want to say goodbye, or should I just cut you off in mid-sentence?"

"I'm warning you, Reynolds!"

"Warning me? I'm all aflutter, Brent. Are you planning to assault me?"

His face grew flushed. "I'm sick of your arrogance!" he shouted. "Who the hell are you to talk down to me? At least I'm productive . . . you haven't done any work for weeks!"

I started to ask how he knew that, but then realized he could have monitored my energy usage via the station computers.

"You think . . ." he began, but at that point I did cut him off and turned back to the image of the Spider floating in the holo tank, its arms weaving a slow dance. I had never believed he was more than dreams, vague magical images, the grandfather wizard trapped in flame, in golden light, in the heart of power. I'd hoped, I'd wanted to believe. But I hadn't been able to accept his reality until I came to Helios, and the dreams grew stronger. Even now I wondered if belief was merely an extension of madness. I have never doubted the efficacy of madness: it is my constant, my referent in chaos.

The first dream had come when I was . . . what? Eleven, twelve? No older. My father had been chasing me, and I had sought refuge in a cave of golden light, a mist of pulsing, shifting light that contained a voice I could not quite hear: it was too vast to hear. I was merely a word upon its tongue, and there had been other words aligned around me, words I needed to understand or else I would be cast out from the light. The Solar Equations—which seemed to have been visited upon me rather than a product of reason—embodied the shiftings, the mysterious principles I had sensed in the golden light, hinted at the arcane processes, the potential for union and dissolution that I had apprehended in every dream. Each time I looked at them, I felt tremors in my flesh, my spirit, as if signaling the onset of a profound change, and . . .

The beeper sounded again, doubtless another call from Brent, and I ignored it. I turned to the readout from the particle traps monitored by the station computers. When I had discovered that the proton bursts being emitted from the Spider's coronal hole were patterned—coded, I'm tempted to say—I had been elated, especially considering that a study of these bursts inspired me to create several addenda to the Equations. They had still been fragmentary, however, and I'd had the notion that I would have to get closer to the Spider in order to complete them . . . perhaps join one of the flights into the coronosphere. My next reaction had been fear. I had realized it was possible the Spider's control was such that these bursts were living artifacts, structural components that maintained a tenuous connection with the rest of his body. If so, then the computers, the entire station, might be under his scrutiny . . . if not his control. Efforts to prove the truth of this had proved inconclusive, but this inconclusiveness was in itself an affirmative answer: the computers were not capable of evasion, and it had been obvious that evasiveness was at work here.

The beeper broke off, and I began to ask myself questions. I had been laboring under the assumption that the Spider had in some way summoned me, but now an alternate scenario presented itself. Could I have stirred him to life? I had beamed protons into the coronal holes, hadn't I? Could I have educated some dumb thing . . . or perhaps brought him to life? Were all my dreams a delusionary system of unparalleled complexity and influence, or was I merely a madman who happened to be right?

These considerations might have seemed irrelevant to my colleagues, but when I related them to my urge to approach the Spider more closely, they took on extreme personal importance. How could I trust such an urge? I stared at the Spider, at its arms waving in their thousand-mile-long dance, their slow changes in configuration redolent of Kali's dance, of myths even more obscure. There were no remedies left for my fear. I had stopped work, drugged myself to prevent dreams, and yet I could do nothing to remove my chief concern: that the Spider would use its control over the computers (if, indeed, it did control them) to manipulate me.

I turned off the holo tank and headed out into the corridor, thinking I would have a few drinks. I hadn't gone fifty feet when Brent accosted me; I brushed past him, but he fell into step beside me. He exuded a false heartiness that was even more grating than his usual obsequiousness.

"Production," he said. "That's our keynote here, Reynolds."

I glowered at him.

"We can't afford to have dead wood lying around," he went on. "Now if you're having a problem, perhaps you need a fresh eye. I'd be glad to take a look . . ."

I gave him a push, sending him wobbling, but it didn't dent his mood.

"Even the best of us run up against stone walls," he said. "And in your case, well, how long has it been since your last major work. Eight years? Ten? You can only ride the wind of your youthful successes for so . . ."

My anxiety flared into rage. I drove my fist into his stomach, and he dropped, gasping like a fish out of water. I was about to kick him, when I was grabbed from behind by the black-clad arms of a security guard. Two more guards intervened as I wrenched free, cursing at Brent. One of the guards helped Brent up and asked what should be done with me.

"Let him go," he said, rubbing his gut. "The man's not responsible."

I lunged at him, but was shoved back. "Bastard!" I shouted. "You smarmy little shit, I'll swear I'll kill you if . . ."

A guard gave me another shove.

"Please, Reynolds," Brent said in a placating tone. "Don't worry . . . I'll make sure you receive due credit."

I had no idea what he meant, and was too angry to wonder at it. I launched more insults as the guards escorted him away.

No longer in the mood for a public place, I returned to the apartment and sat scribbling meaningless notes, gazing at an image of the Spider that played across one entire wall. I was so distracted that I didn't notice Carolyn had entered until she was standing close beside me. The Spider's colors flickered across her, making her into an incandescent silhouette.

"What are you doing?" she asked, sitting on the floor.

"Nothing." I tossed my notepad aside.

"Something's wrong."

"Not at all . . . I'm just tired."

She regarded me expressionlessly. "It's the Spider, isn't it?"

I told her that, Yes, the work was giving me trouble, but it wasn't serious. I'm not sure if I wanted her as much as it seemed I did, or if I was using sex to ward off more questions. Whatever the case, I lowered myself beside her, kissed her, touched her breasts, and soon we were in that heated secret place where—I thought—not even the Spider's eyes could pry. I told her I loved her in that rushed breathless way that is less an intimate disclosure than a form of gasping, of shaping breath to accommodate movement. That was the only way I have ever been able to tell her the best of my feeling, and it was because I was shamed by this that we did not make love more often.

Afterward I could see she wanted to say something important: it was working in her face. But I didn't want to hear it, to be trapped into some new level of intimacy. I turned from her, marshalling words that would signal my need for privacy, and my eyes fell on the wall where the image of the Spider still danced . . . danced in a way I had never before witnessed. His colors were shifting through a spectrum of reds and violets, and his arms writhed in a rhythm that brought to mind the rhythms of sex, the slow beginning, the furious rush to completion, as if he had been watching us and was now mimicking the act.

Carolyn spoke my name, but I was transfixed by the sight and could not answer. She drew in a sharp breath, and seconds later I heard her cross the room and make her exit. The Spider ceased his dance, lapsing into one of his normal patterns. I scrambled up, went to the controls and flicked the display switch to off. But the image did not fade. Instead, the Spider's colors grew brighter, washing from fiery red to gold and at last, to a white so brilliant, I had to shield my eyes. I could almost feel his heat on my skin, hear the sibilant kiss of his molten voice. I was certain he was in the room, I knew I was going to burn, to be swallowed in that singing heat, and I cried out for Carolyn, not wanting to leave unsaid all those things I had withheld from her. Then my fear reached such proportions that I collapsed and sank into a dream, not a nightmare as one might expect, but a dream of an immense city, where I experienced a multitude of adventures and met with a serene fate.

"... To understand Dulambre, his relationship with his father must be examined closely. Alex Dulambre was a musician and poet, regarded to be one of the progenitors of drift: a popular dance form involving the use of improvised lyrics. He was flamboyant, handsome, amoral, and these qualities, allied with a talent for seduction, led him on a twenty-five-year fling through the boudoirs of the powerful, from the corporate towers of Abidjan to the Gardens of Novo Sibersk, and lastly to a beach on Mozambique, where at the age of forty-four he died horribly, a victim of a neural poison that purportedly had been designed for him by the noted chemist Virginia Holland. It was Virginia who was reputed to be Reynolds' mother, but no tests were ever conducted to substantiate the rumor. All we know for certain is that one morning Alex received a crate containing an artificial womb and the embryo of his son. An attached folder provided proof of his paternity and a note stating that the mother wanted no keepsake to remind her of an error in judgment.''

''Alex felt no responsibility for the child, but liked having a relative to add to his coterie. Thus it was that Reynolds spent his first fourteen years globe-trotting, sleeping on floors, breakfasting off the remains of the previous night's party, and generally being ignored, if not rejected. As a defense against both this rejection and his father's charisma, Reynolds learned to mimick Alex's flamboyance and developed similar verbal skills. By the age of eleven he was performing regularly with his father's band, creating a popular sequence of drifts that detailed the feats of an all-powerful wizard and the trials of those who warred against him. Alex took pride in these performances; he saw himself as less father than elder brother, and he insisted on teaching Reynolds a brother's portion of the world. To this end he had one of his lovers seduce the boy on his twelfth birthday, and from then on Reynolds also mimicked his father's omnivorous sexuality. They did, indeed, seem brothers, and to watch Alex drape an arm over the boy's shoulders, the casual observer might have supposed them to be even closer. But there was no strong bond between them, only a history of abuse. This is not to say that Reynolds was unaffected by his father's death, an event to which he was witness. The sight of Alex's agony left him severely traumatized and with a fear of death bordering on the morbid. When we consider this fear in alliance with his difficulty in expressing love—a legacy of his father's rejections—we have gone far in comprehending both his marital problems and his obsession with immortality, with immortality in any form, even that of a child . . ."

from *The Last Alchemist*
by Russell E. Barrett

III
Carolyn

Six months after the implantation of Reynolds' daughter in an artificial womb, I ran into Davis Brent at a pleasure dome where I had taken to spending my afternoons, enjoying the music, writing a memoir of my days with Reynolds, but refraining from infidelity. The child and my concern for Reynolds' mental state had acted to make me conservative: there were important decisions to be made, disturbing events afoot, and I wanted no distractions.

This particular dome was quite small, its walls Maxfield Parrish holographs—alabaster columns and scrolled archways that opened onto rugged mountains drenched in the colors of a pastel sunset; the patrons sat at marble tables, their drab jumpsuits at odds with the decadence of the decor. Sitting there, writing, I felt like some sad and damaged lady of a forgotten age, brought to the sorry pass of autobiography by a disappointment at love.

Without announcing himself, Brent dropped onto the bench opposite me and stared. A smile nicked the corners of his mouth. I waited for him to speak, and finally asked what he wanted.

"Merely to offer my congratulations," he said.

"On what occasion?" I asked.

"The occasion of your daughter."

The implantation had been done under a seal of privacy, and I was outraged that he had discovered my secret.

Before I could speak, he favored me with an unctuous smile and said, "As administrator, little that goes on here escapes me." From the pocket of his jumpsuit he pulled a leather case of the sort used to carry holographs. "I have a daughter myself, a lovely child. I sent her back to Earth some months back." He opened the case, studied the contents, and continued, his words freighted with an odd tension. "I had the computer do a portrait of how she'll look in a few years. Care to see it?"

I took the case and was struck numb. The girl depicted was seven or eight, and was the spitting image of myself at her age.

"I never should have sent her back," said Brent. "It appears the womb has been misshipped, and I may not be able to find her. Even the records have been misplaced. And the tech who performed the implantation, he returned on the ship with the womb and has dropped out of sight."

I came to my feet, but he grabbed my arm and sat me back down. "Check on it if you wish," he said. "But it's the truth. If you want to help find her, you'd be best served by listening."

"Where is she?" A sick chill spread through me, and my heart felt as if it were not beating but trembling.

"Who knows? Sao Paolo, Paris. Perhaps one of the Urban Reserves."

"Please," I said, a catch in my voice. "Bring her back."

"If we work together, I'm certain we can find her."

"What do you want, what could you possibly want from me?"

He smiled again. "To begin with, I want copies of your husband's deep files. I need to know what he's working on."

I had no compunction against telling him; all my concern was for the child. "He's been investigating the possibility of life on the Sun."

The answer dismayed him. "That's ridiculous."

"It's true, he's found it!"

He gaped at me.

"He calls it the Sun Spider. It's huge . . . and made of some kind of plasma."

Brent smacked his forehead as if to punish himself for an oversight. "Of course! That section in the *Diaries*." He shook his head in wonderment. "All that metaphysical gabble about particulate life . . . I can't believe that has any basis in fact."

"I'll help you," I said. "But please bring her back!"

He reached across the table and caressed my cheek. I stiffened but did not draw away. "The last thing I want to do is hurt you, Carolyn. Take my word, it's all under control."

Under control.

Now it seems to me that he was right, and that the controlling agency was no man or creature, but a coincidence of possibility and wish such as may have been responsible for the spark that first set fire to the stars.

Over the next two weeks I met several times with Brent, on each occasion delivering various of Reynolds' files; only one remained to be secured, and I assured Brent I would soon have it. How I hated him! And yet we were complicitors. Each time we met in his lab, a place of bare metal walls and computer banks, we would discuss means of distracting Reynolds in order to perform my thefts, and during one occasion I asked why he had chosen Reynolds' work to pirate, since he had never been an admirer.

"Oh, but I am an admirer," he said. "Naturally I despise his personal style, the passing off of drugs and satyrism as scientific method. But I've never doubted his genius. Why, I was the one who approved his residency grant."

Disbelief must have showed on my face, for he went on to say, "It's true. Many of the board were inclined to reject him, thinking he was no longer capable of important work. But when I saw the Solar Equations, I knew he was still a force to reckon with. Have you looked at them?"

"I don't understand the mathematics."

"Fragmentary as they are, they're astounding, elegant. There's something almost mystical about their structure. You get the idea there's no need to study them, that if you keep staring at them they'll crawl into your brain and work some change." He made a church-and-steeple of his fingers. "I hoped he'd finish them here but ... well, maybe that last file."

We went back to planning Reynolds' distraction. He rarely left the apartment anymore, and Brent and I decided that the time to act would be during his birthday party the next week. He would doubtless be heavily drugged, and I would be able to slip into the back room and access his computer. The discussion concluded, Brent stepped to the door that led to his apartment, keyed it open and invited me for a drink. I declined, but he insisted and I preceded him inside.

The apartment was decorated in appallingly bad taste. His furniture was of a translucent material that glowed a sickly bluish-green, providing the only illumination. Matted under glass on one wall was a twentieth century poster of a poem entitled "Desiderata," whose verses were the height of mawkish romanticism. The other walls were hung with what appeared to be ancient tapestries, but which on close inspection proved to be pornographic counterfeits, depicting subjects such as women mating with stags. Considering these appointments, I found hypocritical Brent's condemnation of Reynolds' private life. He poured wine from a decanter and made banal small talk, touching me now and then as he had during our first meeting. I forced an occasional smile, and at last, thinking I had humored him long enough, I told him I had to leave.

"Oh, no," he said, encircling my waist with an arm. "We're not through."

I pried his arm loose: he was not very strong.

"Very well." He touched a wall control, and a door to the corridor slid open. "Go."

The harsh white light shining through the door transformed him into a shadowy figure and made his pronouncement seem a threat.

"Go on." He drained his wine. "I've got no hold on you."

God, he thought he was clever! And he was . . . more clever than I, perhaps more so than Reynolds. And though he was to learn that cleverness has its limits, particularly when confronted by the genius of fate, it was sufficient to the moment.

"I'll stay," I said.

". . . In the dance of the Spider, in his patterned changes in color, the rhythmic waving of his fiery arms, was a kind of language, the language that the Equations sought to clarify, the language of my dreams. I sat for hours watching him; I recorded several sequences on pocket holographs and carried them about in hopes that this propinquity would illuminate the missing portions of the Equations. I made some progress, but I had concluded that a journey sunwards was the sort of propinquity I needed—I doubted I had the courage to achieve it. However, legislating against my lack of courage was the beauty. I had begun to perceive in the Spider's dance, the hypnotic grace: like that of a Balinese dancer, possessing a similar allure. I came to believe that those movements were signaling all knowledge, infinite possibility. My dreams began to be figured with creatures that I would have previously considered impossible—dragons, imps, men with glowing hands or whose entire forms were glowing, all a ghostly, grainy white; now these creatures came to seem not only possible but likely inhabitants of a world that was coming more and more into focus, a world to which I was greatly attracted. Sometimes I would lie in bed all day, hoping for more dreams of that world, of the wizard who controlled it. It may be that I was using the dreams to escape confronting a difficult and frightening choice. But in truth I have lately doubted that it is even mine to make.''

from *Collected Notes*
by Reynolds Dulambre

IV
Reynolds

I remember little of the party, mostly dazed glimpses of breasts and thighs, sweaty bodies, lidded eyes. I remember the drift, which was performed by a group of techs. They played Alex's music as an *hommage*, and I was taken back to my years with the old bastard-maker, to memories of beatings, of walking in on him and his lovers, of listening to him pontificate. And, of course, I recalled that night in Mozambique when I watched him claw at his eyes, his face. Spitting missiles of blood, unable to scream, having bitten off his tongue. Sobered, I got to my feet and staggered into the bedroom, where it was less crowded, but still too crowded for my mood. I grabbed a robe, belted it on and keyed my study door.

As I entered, Carolyn leaped up from my computer. On the screen was displayed what looked to be a page from my deep files. She tried to switch off the screen, but I caught her arm and checked the page: I had not been mistaken. "What are you doing?" I shouted, yanking her away from the computer.

"I was just curious." She tried to jerk free.

Then I spotted the microcube barnacled to the computer: she had been recording. "What's that?" I asked, forcing her to look at it. "What's that? Who the hell are you working for?"

She began to cry, but I wasn't moved. We had betrayed each other a thousand times, but never to this degree.

"Damn you!" I slapped her. "Who is it?"

She poured out the story of Brent's plan, his demands on her. "I'm sorry," she said, sobbing. "I'm sorry."

I felt so much then, I couldn't characterize it as fear or anger or any specific emotion. In my mind's eye I saw the child, that scrap of my soul, disappearing down some earthly sewer. I threw off my robe, stepped into a jumpsuit.

"Where are you going?" Carolyn asked, wiping away tears.

I zipped up the jumpsuit.

"Don't!" Carolyn tried to haul me back from the door. "You don't understand!"

I shoved her down, locked the door behind me, and went storming out through the party and into the corridor. Rage flooded me. I needed to hurt Brent. My reason was so obscured that when I reached his apartment, I saw nothing suspicious in the fact that the door was open . . . though I later realized he must have had a spy at the party to warn him of anything untoward. Inside, Brent was lounging in one of those ridiculous glowing chairs, a self-satisfied look on his face, and it was that look more than anything, more than the faint scraping at my rear, that alerted me to danger. I spun around to see a security guard bringing his laser to bear on me. I dove at him, feeling a discharge of heat next to my ear, and we went down together. He tried to gouge my eyes, but I twisted away, latched both hands in his hair and smashed his head against the wall. The third time his head impacted, it made a softer sound than it had the previous two, and I could feel the skull shifting beneath the skin like pieces of broken tile in a sack. I rolled off the guard, horrified, yet no less enraged. And when I saw that Brent's chair was empty, when I heard him shouting in the corridor, even though I knew his shouts would bring more guards, my anger grew so great that I cared nothing for myself, I only wanted him dead.

By the time I emerged from the apartment, he was sprinting around a curve in the corridor. My laser scored the metal wall behind him the instant before he went out of sight. I ran after him. Several of the doorways along the corridor slid open, heads popped out, and on seeing me, ducked back in. I rounded the curve, spotted Brent, and fired again . . . too high by inches. Before I could correct my aim, half a dozen guards boiled out of a side corridor and dragged him into cover. Their beams drew smouldering lines in the metal by my hip, at my feet, and I retreated, firing as I did, pounding on the doors, thinking that I would barricade myself in one of the rooms and try to debunk Brent's lies, to reveal his deceit over the intercom. But none of the doors opened, their occupants having apparently been frightened by my weapon.

Two guards poked their heads around the curve, fired, and one of the beams came so near that it torched the fabric of my jumpsuit at the knee. I beat out the flames and ran full tilt. Shouts behind me, beams of ruby light skewering the air above my head. Ahead, I made out a red door that led to a docking arm, and having no choice, I keyed it open and raced along the narrow passageway. The first three moorings were empty, but the fourth had a blue light glowing beside the entrance hatch, signaling the presence of a ship. I slipped inside, latched it, and moved along the tunnel into the airlock; I bolted that shut, then went quickly along the mesh-walled catwalk toward the control room, toward the radio. I was on the point of entering the room, when I felt a shudder go all through the ship and knew it had cast loose, that it was headed sunwards.

Panicked, I burst into the control room. The chairs fronting the instrument panel were empty, the panel itself aflicker with lights; the ship was being run by computer. I sat at the board, trying to override, but no tactic had any effect. Then Brent's voice came over the speakers. "You've bought yourself a little time, Reynolds," he said. "That's all. When the ship returns, we'll have you."

I laughed.

It had been my hope that he had initiated the ship's flight, but his comments made clear that I was now headed toward the confrontation I had for so long sought to avoid, brought to this pass by a computer under the control of the creature for whom I had searched my entire life, a creature of fire and dreams, the stuff of souls. I knew I would not survive it. But though I had always dreaded the thought of death, now that death was hard upon me, I was possessed of a strange confidence and calm . . . calm enough to send this transmission, to explore the confines of this my coffin, even to read the manuals that explain its operation. I had never attempted to understand the workings of the sunships, and I was interested to read of the principles that underlie each flight. As the ship approaches the Sun, it will monitor the magnetic field direction and determine if the Archimedean spiral of the solar wind is oriented outward.

If all is as it should be, it will descend to within one A.U. and will skip off the open-diverging magnetic field of a coronal hole. It will be traveling at such a tremendous speed, its actions will be rather like those of a charged particle caught in a magnetic field, and as the field opens out, it will be flung upward, back toward Helios . . . that is, it will be flung up and out if a creature who survives by stripping particles of their charge does not inhabit the coronal hole in question. But there is little chance of that.

I wonder how it will feel to have my charge stripped. I would not care to suffer the agonies of my father.

The closer I come to the Sun, the more calm I become. My mortal imperfections seem to be flaking away. I feel clean and minimal, and I have the notion that I will soon be even simpler, the essential splinter of a man. I have so little desire left that only one further thing occurs to me to say.

Carolyn, I . . .

". . . A man walking in a field of golden grass under a bright sky, walking steadfastly, though with no apparent destination, for the grasslands spread to the horizon, and his thoughts are crystal-clear, and his heart, too, is clear, for his past has become an element of his present, and his future—visible as a sweep of golden grass carpeting the distant hills, beyond which lies a city sparkling like a glint of possibility—is as fluent and clear as his thought, and he knows his future will be shaped by his walking, by his thought and the power in his hands, especially by that power, and of all this he wishes now to speak to a woman whose love he denied, whose flesh had the purity of the clear bright sky and the golden grasses, who was always the heart of his life even in the country of lies, and here in the heartland of the country of truth is truly loved at last . . ."

from *The Resolute Lover*
part of The White Dragon Cycle

V
Carolyn

After Reynolds had stolen the sunship—this, I was informed, had been the case—Brent confined me to my apartment and accused me of conspiring with Reynolds to kill him. I learned of Reynolds' death from the security guard who brought me supper that first night; he told me that a prominence (I pictured it to be a fiery fishing lure) had flung itself out from the Sun and incinerated the ship. I wept uncontrollably. Even after the computers began to translate the coded particle bursts emanating from the Spider's coronal hole, even when these proved to be the completed Solar Equations, embodied not only in mathematics but in forms comprehensible to a layman, still I wept. I was too overwhelmed by grief to realize what they might portend.

I was able to view the translations on Reynolds' computer, and when the stories of the White Dragon Cycle came into view, I understood that whoever or whatever had produced them had something in particular to say to me. It was *The Resolute Lover*, the first of the cycle, with its numerous references to a wronged beautiful woman, that convinced me of this. I read the story over and over, and in so doing I recalled Brent's description of the feelings he had had while studying the equations. I felt in the focus of some magical lens, I felt a shimmering in my flesh, confusion in my thoughts . . . not a confusion of motive but of thoughts running in new patterns, colliding with each other like atoms bred by a runaway reactor. I lost track of time, I lived in a sweep of golden grasses, in an exotic city where the concepts of unity and the divisible were not opposed, where villains and heroes and beasts enacted ritual passions, where love was the ordering pulse of existence.

One day Brent paid me a visit. He was plumped with self-importance, with triumph. But though I hated him, emotion seemed incidental to my goal—a goal his visit helped to solidify—and I reacted to him mildly, watching as he moved about the room, watching me and smiling.

"You're calmer than I expected," he said.

I had no words for him, only calm. In my head the Resolute Lover gazed into a crystal of Knowledge, awaiting the advent of Power. I believe that I, too, smiled.

"Well," he said. "Things don't always work out as we plan. But I'm pleased with the result. The Spider will be Reynolds' great victory . . . no way around that. Still, I've managed to land the role of Sancho Panza to his Don Quixote, the rationalist who guided the madman on his course."

My smile was a razor, a knife, a flame.

"Quite sufficient," he went on, "to secure my post . . . and perhaps even my immortality."

I spoke to him in an inaudible voice that said Death.

His manner grew more agitated; he twitched about the room, touching things. "What will I do with you?" he said. "I'd hate to send you to your judgment. Our nights together . . . well, suffice it to say I would be most happy if you'd stay with me. What do you think? Shall I testify on your behalf, or would you prefer a term on the Urban Reserves?"

Brent, Brent, Brent. His name was a kind of choice.

"Perhaps you'd like time to consider?" he said.

I wished my breath was poison.

He edged toward the door. "When you reach a decision, just tell the guard outside. You've two months 'til the next ship. I'm betting you'll choose survival."

My eyes sent him a black kiss.

"Really, Carolyn," he said. "You were never a faithful wife. Don't you think this pose of mourning somewhat out of character?"

Then he was gone, and I returned to my reading.

Love.

What part did it play in my desire for vengeance, my furious calm? Sorrow may have had more a part, but love was certainly a factor. Love as practiced by the Resolute Lover. This story communicated this rigorous emotion, and my heartsickness translated it to vengeful form. My sense of unreality, of tremulous being, increased day by day, and I barely touched my meals.

I am not sure when the Equations embodied by the story began to take hold, when the seeded knowledge became power. I believe it was nearly two weeks after Brent's visit. But though I felt my potential, my strength, I did not act immediately. In truth, I was not certain I could act or that action was to be my course. I was mad in the same way Reynolds had been: a madness of self-absorption, a concentration of such intensity that nothing less intense had the least relevance.

One night I left off reading, went into my bedroom and put on a sheer robe, then wrapped myself in a cowled cloak. I had no idea why I was doing this. The seductive rhythms of the story were coiling through my head and preventing thought. I walked into the front room and stood facing the door. Violent tremors shook my body. I felt frail, insubstantial, yet at the same time possessed of fantastic power. I knew that nothing could resist me . . . not steel or flesh or fire. Inspired by this confidence, I reached out my right hand to the door. The hand was glowing a pale white, its form flickering, the fingers lengthening and attenuating, appearing to ripple as in a graceful dance. I did not wonder at this. Every thing was as it should be. And when my hand slid into the door, into the metal, neither did I consider that remarkable. I could feel the mechanisms of the lock, I—or rather my ghostly fingers—seemed to know the exact function of every metal bit, and after a moment the door hissed open.

The guard peered in, startled, and I hid the hand behind me. I backed away, letting the halves of my cloak fall apart. He stared, glanced left and right in the corridor, and entered. "How'd you do the lock?" he asked.

I said nothing.

He keyed the door, testing it, and slid it shut, leaving the two of us alone in the room. "Huh," he said. "Must have been a computer foul-up."

I came close beside him, my head tipped back as if to receive a kiss, and he smiled, he held me around the waist. His lips mashed against mine, and my right hand, seeming almost to be acting on its own, slipped into his side and touched something that beat wildly for a few seconds, and then spasmed. He pushed me away, clutching his chest, his face purpling, and fell to the floor. Emotionless, I stepped over him and went out into the corridor, walking at an unhurried pace, hiding my hand beneath the cloak.

On reaching Brent's apartment, I pressed the bell, and a moment later the door opened and he peered forth, looking sleepy and surprised. "Carolyn!" he said. "How did you get out?"

"I told the guard I planned to stay with you," I said, and as I had done with the guard, I parted the halves of my cloak.

His eyes dropped to my breasts. "Come in," he said, his voice blurred.

Once inside, I shed the cloak, concealing my hand behind me. I was so full of hate, my mind was heavy and blank like a stone. Brent poured some wine, but I refused the glass. My voice sounded dead, and he shot me a searching look and asked if I felt well. "I'm fine," I told him.

He set down the wine and came toward me, but I moved away.

"First," I said, "I want to know about my daughter."

That brought him up short. "You have no daughter," he said after a pause. "It was all a hoax."

"I don't believe you."

"I swear it's true," he said. "When you went for an exam, I had the tech inform you of a pregnancy. But you weren't pregnant. And when you came for the implantation procedure, he anesthetized you and simply stood by until you woke up."

It would have been in character, I realized, for him to have done this. Yet he also might have been clever enough to make up the story, and thus keep a hold on me, one he could inform me of should I prove recalcitrant.

"But you can have a child," he said, sidling toward me. "Our child, Carolyn. I'd like that, I'd like it very much." He seemed to be having some difficulty in getting the next words out, but finally they came: "I love you."

What twisted shape, I wondered, did love take in his brain?

"Do you?" I said.

"I know it must be hard to believe," he said. "You can't possibly understand the pressure I've been under, the demands that forced my actions. But I swear to you, Carolyn, I've always cared for you. I knew how oppressed you were by Reynolds. Don't you see? To an extent I was acting on your behalf. I wanted to free you."

He said all this in a whining tone, edging close, so close I could smell his bitter breath. He put a hand on my breast, lifted it . . . Perhaps he did love me in his way, for it seemed a treasuring touch. But mine was not. I laid my palely glowing hand on the back of his neck. He screamed, went rigid, and oh, how that scream made me feel! It was like music, his pain. He stumbled backward, toppled over one of the luminous chairs, and lay writhing, clawing his neck.

"Where is she?" I asked, kneeling beside him.

Spittle leaked between his gritted teeth. "I'll . . . find her, bring her . . . oh!"

I saw I could never trust him. Desperate, he would say anything. He might bring me someone else's child. I touched his stomach, penetrating the flesh to the first joint of my fingers, then wiggling them. Again he screamed. Blood mapped the front of his jumpsuit.

"Where is she?" I no longer was thinking about the child: she was lost, and I was only tormenting him.

His speech was incoherent, he tried to hump away. I showed him my hand, how it glowed, and his eyes bugged.

"Do you still love me?" I asked, touching his groin, hooking my fingers and pulling at some fiber.

Agony bubbled in his throat, and he curled up around his pain, clutching himself.

I could not stop touching him. I orchestrated his

screams, producing short ones, long ones, ones that held a strained hoarse chord. My hatred was a distant emotion. I felt no fury, no glee. I was merely a craftsman, working to prolong his death. Pink films occluded the whites of his eyes, his teeth were stained to crimson, and at last he lay still.

I sat beside him for what seemed a long time. Then I donned my cloak and walked back to my apartment. After making sure no one was in the corridor, I dragged the dead guard out of the front room and propped him against the corridor wall. I reset the lock, stepped inside, and the door slid shut behind me. I felt nothing. I took up *The Resolute Lover*, but even my interest in it had waned. I gazed at the walls, growing thoughtless, remembering only that I had been somewhere, done some violence; I was perplexed by my glowing hand. But soon I fell asleep, and when I was waked by the guards unlocking the door, I found that the hand had returned to normal.

"Did you hear anything outside?" asked one of the guards.

"No," I said. "What happened?"

He told me the gory details, about the dead guard and Brent. Like everyone else on Helios Station, he seemed more confounded by these incomprehensible deaths than by the fantastic birth that had preceded them.

"The walls of the station have been plated with gold, the corridors are thronged with tourists, with students come to study the disciplines implicit in the Equations, disciplines that go far beyond the miraculous transformation of my hand. Souvenir shops sell holos of the Spider, recordings of The White Dragon Cycle (now used to acclimate children to the basics of the equations), and authorized histories of the sad events surrounding the Spider's emergence. The pleasure domes reverberate with Alex Dulambre's drifts, and in an auditorium constructed for this purpose, Reynolds' clone delivers daily lectures on the convoluted circumstances of his death and triumph. The place is half amusement park, half shrine. Yet the greatest memorial to Reynolds' work is not here; it lies beyond the orbit of Pluto and consists of a vast shifting structure of golden light wherein dwell those students who have mastered the disciplines and overcome the bonds of corporeality. They are engaged, it is said, in an unfathomable work that may have taken its inspiration from Reynolds' metaphysical flights of fancy, or—and many hold to this opinion—may reflect the Spider's design, his desire to rid himself of the human nuisance by setting us upon a new evolutionary course. After Brent's death I thought to join in this work. But my mind was not suited to the disciplines; I had displayed all the mastery of which I was capable in dispensing with Brent.

"I have determined to continue the search for my daughter. It may be—as Brent claimed—that she does not exist, but it is all that is left to me, and I have made my resolve accordingly. Still, I have not managed to leave the station, because I am drawn to Reynolds' clone. Again and again I find myself in the rear of the auditorium, where I watch him pace the dias, declaiming in his most excited manner. I yearn to approach him, to learn how like Reynolds he truly is. I am certain he has spotted me on several occasions, and I wonder what he is thinking, how it would be to speak to him, touch him. Perhaps this is perverse of me, but I cannot help wondering . . ."

from *Days In The Sun*
by Carolyn Dulambre

VI
Carolyn/Reynolds

I had been wanting to talk with her since . . . well, since this peculiar life began. Why? I loved her, for one thing. But there seemed to be a far more compelling reason, one I could not verbalize. I suppressed the urge for a time, not wanting to hurt her; but seeing that she had begun to appear at the lectures, I finally decided to make an approach.

She had taken to frequenting a pleasure dome named Spider's. Its walls were holographic representations of the Spider, and these were strung together with golden webs that looked molten against the black backdrop, like seams of unearthly fire. In this golden dimness the faces of the patrons glowed like spirits, and the glow seemed to be accentuated by the violence of the music. It was not a place to my taste, nor—I suspect—to hers. Perhaps her patronage was a form of courage, of facing down the creature who had caused her so much pain.

I found her seated in a rear corner, drinking an Amouriste, and when I moved up beside her table, she paid me no mind. No one ever approached her; she was as much a memorial as the station itself, and though she was still a beautiful woman, she was treated like the wife of a saint. Doubtless she thought I was merely pausing by the table, looking for someone. But when I sat opposite her, she glanced up and her jaw dropped.

"Don't be afraid," I said.

"Why should I be afraid?"

"I thought my presence might . . . discomfort you."

She met my eyes unflinchingly. "I suppose I thought that, too."

"But . . . ?"

"It doesn't matter."

A silence built between us.

She wore a robe of golden silk, cut to expose the upper swells of her breasts, and her hair was pulled back from her face, laying bare the smooth serene lines of her beauty, a beauty that had once fired me, that did so even now.

"Look," I said. "For some reason I was drawn to talk to you, I feel I have . . ."

"I feel the same." She said this with a strong degree of urgency, but then tried to disguise the fact. "What shall we talk about?"

"I'm not sure."

She tapped a finger on her glass. "Why don't we walk?"

Everyone watched as we left, and several people followed us into the corridor, a circumstance that led me to suggest that we talk in my apartment. She hesitated, then signalled agreement with the briefest of nods. We moved quickly through the crowds, managing to elude our pursuers, and settled into a leisurely pace. Now and again I caught her staring at me, and asked if anything was wrong.

"Wrong?" She seemed to be tasting the word, trying it out. "No," she said. "No more than usual."

I had thought that when I did talk to him I would find he was merely a counterfeit, that he would be nothing like Reynolds, except in the most superficial way. But this was not the case. Walking along that golden corridor, mixing with the revelers who poured between the shops and bars, I felt toward him as I had on the day we had met in the streets of Abidjan: powerfully attracted, vulnerable, and excited. And yet I did perceive a difference in him. Whereas Reynolds' presence had been commanding and intense, there had been a brittleness to that intensity, a sense that his diamond glitter might easily be fractured.

With this Reynolds, however, there was no such inconstancy. His presence—while potent—was smooth, natural, and unflawed.

Everywhere we walked we encountered the fruits of the Equations: matter transmitters; rebirth parlors, where one could experience a transformation of both body and soul; and the omnipresent students, some of them half-gone into a transcorporeal state, cloaked to hide this fact, but their condition evident by their inward-looking eyes. With Reynolds beside me, all this seemed comprehensible, not—as before—a carnival of meaningless improbabilities. I asked what he felt on seeing the results of his work, and he said, "I'm really not concerned with it."

"What are you concerned with?"

"With you, Carolyn," he said.

The answer both pleased me and made me wary. "Surely you must have more pressing concerns," I said.

"Everything I've done was for you." A puzzled expression crossed his face.

"Don't pretend with me!" I snapped, growing angry. "This isn't a show, this isn't the auditorium."

He opened his mouth, but bit back whatever he had been intending to say, and we walked on.

"Forgive me," I said, realizing the confusion that must be his. "I . . ."

"No need for forgiveness," he said. "All our failures are behind us now."

I didn't know from where these words were coming. They were my words, yet they also seemed spoken from a place deep inside myself, one whose existence had been hidden until now, and it was all I could do to hold them back. We passed into the upper levels of the station, where the permanent staff was quartered, and as we rounded a curve, we nearly ran into a student standing motionless, gazing at the wall: a pale young man with black hair, a thin mouth, and a gray cape. His eyes were dead-looking, and his voice sepulchral. "It awaits," he said.

They are so lost in self-contemplation, these students, that they are likely to say anything. Some fancy them oracles, but not I: their words struck me as being random, sparks from a frayed wire.

"What awaits?" I asked, amused.

"Life . . . the city."

"Ah," I said. "And how do I get there?"

"You . . ." He lapsed into an open-mouthed stare.

Carolyn pulled at me, and we set off again. I started to make a joke about the encounter, but seeing her troubled expression, I restrained myself.

When we entered my apartment, she stopped in the center of the living room, transfixed by the walls. I had set them to display the environment of the beginning of *The Resolute Lover*: an endless sweep of golden grasses, with a sparkling on the horizon that might have been the winking of some bright tower.

"Does this bother you?" I asked, gesturing at the walls.

"No, they startled me, that's all." She strolled along, peering at the grasses, as if hoping to catch sight of someone. Then she turned, and I spoke again from that deep hidden place, a place that now—responding to the sight of her against those golden fields—was spreading all through me.

"Carolyn, I love you," I said . . . and this time I knew who it was that spoke.

He had removed his cloak, and his body was shimmering, embedded in that pale glow that once had made a weapon of my right hand. I backed away, terrified. Yet even in the midst of fear, it struck me that I was not as terrified as I should have been, that I was not at the point of screaming, of fleeing.

"It's me, Carolyn," he said.

"No," I said, backing farther away.

"I don't know why you should believe me." He looked at his flickering hand. "I didn't understand it myself until now."

"Who are you?" I asked, gauging the distance to the door.

"You know," he said. "The Spider . . . he's all through the station. In the computer, the labs, even in the tanks from which my cells were grown. He's brought us together again."

He tried to touch me, and I darted to the side.

"I won't hurt you," he said.

"I've seen what a touch can do."

"Not my touch, Carolyn."

I doubted I could make it to the door, but readied myself for a try.

"Listen to me, Carolyn," he said. "Everything we wanted in the beginning, all the dreams and fictions of love, they can be ours."

"I never wanted that," I said. "You did! I only wanted normalcy, not some . . ."

"All lovers want the same thing," he said. "Disillusionment leads them to pretend they want less." He stretched out his hands to me. "Everything awaits us, everything is prepared. How this came to be, I can't explain. Except that it makes a funny kind of sense for the ultimate result of science to be an incomprehensible magic."

I was still afraid, but my fear was dwindling, lulled by the rhythms of his words, and though I perceived him to be death, I also saw clearly that he was Reynolds, Reynolds made whole.

"This was inevitable," he said. "We both knew something miraculous could happen . . . that's why we stayed together, despite everything. Don't be afraid. I could never hurt you more than I have."

''What's inevitable?'' I asked. He was too close for me to think of running, and I thought I could delay him, put him off with questions.

''Can't you feel it?'' He was so close, now, I could feel his heat. ''I can't tell you what it is, Carolyn, only that it is, that it's life . . . a new life.''

''The Spider,'' I said. ''I don't understand, I . . .''

''No more questions,'' he said, and slipped the robes from my shoulders.

His touch was warmer than natural, making my eyelids droop, but causing no pain. He pulled me down to the floor, and in a moment he was inside me, we were heart to heart, moving together, enveloped in that pale flickering glow, and amidst the pleasure I felt, there was pain, but so little it did not matter . . .

. . . and I, too, was afraid, afraid I was not who I thought, that flames and nothingness would obliterate us, but in having her once again, in the consummation of my long wish, my doubts lessened . . .

. . . and I could no longer tell whether my eyes were open or closed, because sometimes when I thought them closed, I could see him, his face slack with pleasure, head flung back . . .

. . . and when I thought they were open I would have a glimpse of another place wherein she stood beside me, glimpses at first too brief for me to fix them in mind . . .

. . . and everything was whirling, changing, my body, my spirit, all in flux, and death—if this was death—was a long decline, a sweep of golden radiance, and behind me I could see the past reduced to a plain and hills carpeted with golden grasses . . .

• • •

. . . and around me golden towers, shimmering, growing more stable and settling into form moment by moment, and people shrouded in golden mist who were also becoming more real, acquiring scars and rags and fine robes, carrying baskets and sacks . . .

. . . and this was no heaven, no peaceful heaven, for as we moved beneath those crumbling towers of yellow stone, I saw soldiers with oddly shaped spears on the battlements, and the crowds around us were made up of hard-bitten men and women wearing belted daggers, and old crones bent double under the weight of sacks of produce, and younger women with the look of ill-usage about them, who leaned from the doors and windows of smoke-darkened houses and cried out their price . . .

. . . and the sun overhead seemed to shift, putting forth prominences that rippled and undulated as in a dance, and shone down a ray of light to illuminate the tallest tower, the one we had sought for all these years, the one whose mystery we must unravel . . .

. . . and the opaque image of an old man in a yellow robe was floating above the crowd, his pupils appearing to shift, to put forth fiery threads as did the sun, and he was haranguing us, daring us all to penetrate his tower, to negotiate his webs and steal the secrets of time . . .

. . . and after wandering all day, we found a room in an inn not half a mile from the wizard's tower, a mean place with grimy walls and scuttlings in the corners and a straw mattress that crackled when we lay on it. But it was so much more than we'd had in a long, long time, we were delighted, and when night had fallen, with moonlight streaming in and the wizard's tower visible through a window against the deep blue of the sky, the room seemed palatial. We made love until well past midnight, love as we had never practiced it: trusting, unfettered by inhibition. And afterward, still joined, listening to the cries and music of the city, I suddenly remembered my life in that other world, the Spider, Helios Station, everything, and from the tense look on Carolyn's face, from her next words, I knew that she, too, had remembered.

"Back at Helios," she said, "we were making love, lying exactly like this, and . . ." She broke off, a worry line creasing her brow. "What if this is all a dream, a moment between dying and death?"

"Why should you think that?"

"The Spider . . . I don't know. I just felt it was true."

"It's more reasonable to assume that everything is a form of transition between the apartment and this room. Besides, why would the Spider want you to to die?"

"Why has he done any of this? We don't even know what he is . . . a demon, a god."

"Or something of mine," I said.

"Yes, that . . . or death."

I stroked her hair, and her eyelids fluttered down.

"I'm afraid to go to sleep," she said.

"Don't worry," I said. "I think there's more to this than death."

"How do you know?"

"Because of how we are."

"That's why I think it *is* death," she said. "Because it's too good to last."

"Even if it is death," I told her, "in this place death might last longer than our old lives."

Of course I was certain of very little myself, but I managed to soothe her, and soon she was asleep. Out the window, the wizard's tower—if, indeed, that's what it was—glowed and rippled, alive with power, menacing in its brilliance. But I was past being afraid. Even in the face of something as unfathomable as a creature who has appropriated the dream of a man who may have dreamed it into existence and fashioned thereof either a life or a death, even in a world of unanswerable questions, when love is certain—love, the only question that is its own answer—everything becomes quite simple, and, in the end, a matter of acceptance.

"We live in an old chaos of the sun."
Wallace Stevens

CILIA-OF-GOLD

Stephen Baxter

*"Cilia-of-Gold" appeared in the August 1994 issue
of* Asimov's, *with an illustration by Ron Chironna,
one of a half-dozen or more vivid, inventive stories
the author's had here in recent years. British writer
Stephen Baxter made his first sale to* Interzone *in
1987, and since then has become one of that magazine's most frequent contributors, as well as making sales to* Asimov's Science Fiction, Science
Fiction Age, Zenith, New Worlds, *and elsewhere.
He's one of the most prolific of the new writers of
the '90s, and is rapidly becoming one of the most
popular and acclaimed of them as well. His books
include the novels* Raft, Timelike Infinity, Anti-Ice,
Flux, *and the H. G. Wells pastiche—a sequel to* The
Time Machine—The Time Ships, *which won both
the Arthur C. Clarke Award and the Philip K. Dick
Award. His most recent books are the novels* Voyage, Titan, *and* Moonseed, *and the collections* Vacuum Diagrams: Stories of the Xeelee Sequence *and*
Traces. *Upcoming is a new novel,* Manifold: Time.*

*Here he takes us to a mining colony on Mercury,
first planet out from the sun, in company with a
trouble-shooting mission that runs into troubles
considerably more bizarre than anyone could ever
have anticipated having to deal with . . .*

The people—though exhausted by the tunnel's cold—had rested long enough, Cilia-of-Gold decided.

Now it was time to fight.

She climbed up through the water, her flukes pulsing, and prepared to lead the group farther along the Ice-tunnel to the new Chimney cavern.

But, even as the people rose from their browsing and crowded through the cold, stale water behind her, Cilia-of-Gold's resolve wavered. The Seeker was a heavy presence inside her. She could *feel* its tendrils wrapped around her stomach, and—she knew—its probes must already have penetrated her brain, her mind, her *self*.

With a beat of her flukes, she thrust her body along the tunnel. She couldn't afford to show weakness. Not now.

"Cilia-of-Gold."

A broad body, warm through the turbulent water, came pushing out of the crowd to bump against hers: it was Strong-Flukes, one of Cilia-of-Gold's Three-mates. Strong-Flukes's presence was immediately comforting. "Cilia-of-Gold. I know something's wrong."

Cilia-of-Gold thought of denying it; but she turned away, her depression deepening. "I couldn't expect to keep secrets from you. Do you think the others are aware?"

The hairlike cilia lining Strong-Flukes's belly barely vibrated as she spoke. "Only Ice-Born suspects something is wrong. And if she didn't, we'd have to tell her." Ice-Born was the third of Cilia-of-Gold's mates.

"I can't afford to be weak, Strong-Flukes. Not now."

As they swam together, Strong-Flukes flipped onto her back. Tunnel water filtered between Strong-Flukes's carapace and her body; her cilia flickered as they plucked particles of food from the stream and popped them into the multiple mouths along her belly. "Cilia-of-Gold," she said. "I *know* what's wrong. You're carrying a Seeker, aren't you?"

". . . Yes. How could you tell?"

"I love you," Strong-Flukes said. "*That's* how I could tell."

The pain of Strong-Flukes's perception was as sharp, and unexpected, as the moment when Cilia-of-Gold had first detected the signs of the infestation in herself . . . and had realized, with horror, that her life must inevitably end in madness, in a purposeless scrabble into the Ice over the world. "It's still in its early stages, I think. It's like a huge heat, inside me. And I can feel it reaching into my mind. Oh, Strong-Flukes . . ."

"Fight it."

"I can't. I—"

"You can. You *must*."

The end of the tunnel was an encroaching disk of darkness; already Cilia-of-Gold felt the inviting warmth of the Chimney-heated water in the cavern beyond.

This should have been the climax, the supreme moment of Cilia-of-Gold's life.

The group's old Chimney, with its fount of warm, rich water, was failing; and so they had to flee, and fight for a place in a new cavern.

That, or die.

It was Cilia-of-Gold who had found the new Chimney, as she had explored the endless network of tunnels between the Chimney caverns. Thus, it was she who must lead this war—Seeker or no Seeker.

She gathered up the fragments of her melting courage.

"You're the best of us, Cilia-of-Gold," Strong-Flukes said, slowing. "Don't ever forget that."

Cilia-of-Gold pressed her carapace against Strong-Flukes's in silent gratitude.

Cilia-of-Gold turned and clacked her mandibles, signaling the rest of the people to halt. They did so, the adults sweeping the smaller children inside their strong carapaces.

Strong-Flukes lay flat against the floor and pushed a single eyestalk toward the mouth of the tunnel. Her caution was wise; there were species who could home in on even a single sound-pulse from an unwary eye.

After some moments of silent inspection, Strong-Flukes wriggled back along the Ice surface to Cilia-of-Gold.

She hesitated. "We've got problems, I think," she said at last.

The Seeker seemed to pulse inside Cilia-of-Gold, tightening around her gut. "What problems?"

"This Chimney's inhabited already. By *Heads*."

Kevan Scholes stopped the rover a hundred yards short of the wall-mountain's crest.

Irina Larionova, wrapped in a borrowed environment suit, could tell from the tilt of the cabin that the surface here was inclined upward at around forty degrees—shallower than a flight of stairs. This "mountain," heavily eroded, was really little more than a dust-clad hill, she thought.

"The wall of Chao Meng-Fu Crater," Scholes said briskly, his radio-distorted voice tinny. "Come on. We'll walk to the summit from here."

"Walk?" She studied him, irritated. "Scholes, I've had one hour's sleep in the last thirty-six; I've traveled across ninety million miles to get here, via tugs and wormhole transit links—and you're telling me I have to *walk* up this damn hill?"

Scholes grinned through his faceplate. He was AS-preserved at around physical-twenty-five, Larionova guessed, and he had a boyishness that grated on her. *Damn it*, she reminded herself, *this "boy" is probably older than me*.

"Trust me," he said. "You'll love the view. And we have to change transports anyway."

"Why?"

"You'll see."

He twisted gracefully to his feet. He reached out a gloved hand to help Larionova pull herself, awkwardly, out of her seat. When she stood on the cabin's tilted deck, her heavy boots hurt her ankles.

Scholes threw open the rover's lock. Residual air puffed out of the cabin, crystallizing. The glow from the cabin interior was dazzling; beyond the lock, Larionova saw only darkness.

Scholes climbed out of the lock and down to the planet's invisible surface. Larionova followed him awkwardly; it seemed a long way to the lock's single step.

Her boots settled to the surface, crunching softly. The lock was situated between the rover's rear wheels: the wheels were constructs of metal strips and webbing, wide and light, each wheel taller than she was.

Scholes pushed the lock closed, and Larionova was plunged into sudden darkness.

Scholes loomed before her. He was a shape cut out of blackness. "Are you okay? Your pulse is rapid."

She could hear the rattle of her own breath, loud and immediate. "Just a little disoriented."

"We've got all of a third of a gee down here, you know. You'll get used to it. Let your eyes dark-adapt. We don't have to hurry this."

She looked up.

In her peripheral vision, the stars were already coming out. She looked for a bright double star, blue and white. There it was: Earth, with Luna.

And now, with a slow grandeur, the landscape revealed itself to her adjusting eyes. The plain from which the rover had climbed spread out from the foot of the crater wall-mountain. It was a complex patchwork of crowding craters, ridges and scarps—some of which must have been miles high—all revealed as a glimmering tracery in the starlight. The face of the planet seemed *wrinkled*, she thought, as if shrunk with age.

"These wall-mountains are over a mile high," Scholes said. "Up here, the surface is firm enough to walk on; the regolith dust layer is only a couple of inches thick. But down on the plain the dust can be ten or fifteen yards deep. Hence the big wheels on the rover. I guess that's what five billion years of a thousand-degree temperature range does for a landscape. . . ."

Just twenty-four hours ago, she reflected, Larionova had been stuck in a boardroom in New York, buried in one of Superet's endless funding battles. And now this . . . wormhole travel was bewildering. "Lethe's waters," she said. "It's so—desolate."

Scholes gave an ironic bow. "Welcome to Mercury," he said.

Cilia-of-Gold and Strong-Flukes peered down into the Chimney cavern.

Cilia-of-Gold had chosen the cavern well. The Chimney here was a fine young vent, a glowing crater much wider than their old, dying home. The water above the Chimney was turbulent, and richly cloudy; the cavern itself was wide and smooth-walled. Cilia-plants grew in mats around the Chimney's base. Cutters browsed in turn on the cilia-plants, great chains of them, their tough little arms slicing steadily through the plants. Sliding through the plant mats Cilia-of-Gold could make out the supple form of a Crawler, its mindless, tube-like body wider than Cilia-of-Gold's and more than three times as long. . . .

And, stalking around their little forest, here came the Heads themselves, the rulers of the cavern. Cilia-of-Gold counted four, five, six of the Heads, and no doubt there were many more in the dark recesses of the cavern.

One Head—close to the tunnel mouth—swiveled its huge, swollen helmet-skull toward her.

She ducked back into the tunnel, aware that all her cilia were quivering.

Strong-Flukes drifted to the tunnel floor, landing in a little cloud of food particles. "*Heads,*" she said, her voice soft with despair. "We can't fight Heads."

The Heads' huge helmet-skulls were sensitive to heat—fantastically so, enabling the Heads to track and kill with almost perfect accuracy. Heads *were* deadly opponents, Cilia-of-Gold reflected. But the people had nowhere else to go.

"We've come a long way to reach this place, Strong-Flukes. If we had to undergo another journey—" *through more cold, stagnant tunnels* "—many of us couldn't survive. And those who did would be too weakened to fight.

"No. We have to stay here—to *fight* here."

Strong-Flukes groaned, wrapping her carapace close around her. "Then we'll all be killed."

Cilia-of-Gold tried to ignore the heavy presence of the Seeker within her—and its prompting, growing more insistent now, that she *get away* from all this, from the crowding presence of people—and she forced herself to *think*.

Larionova followed Kevan Scholes up the slope of the wall-mountain. Silicate surface dust compressed under her boots, like fine sand. The climbing was easy—it was no more than a steep walk, really—but she stumbled frequently, clumsy in this reduced gee.

They reached the crest of the mountain. It wasn't a sharp summit: more a wide, smooth platform, fractured to dust by Mercury's wild temperature range.

"Chao Meng-Fu Crater," Scholes said. "A hundred miles wide, stretching right across Mercury's South Pole."

The crater was so large that even from this height its full breadth was hidden by the tight curve of the planet.

The wall-mountain was one of a series that swept across the landscape from left to right, like a row of eroded teeth, separated by broad, rubble-strewn valleys. On the far side of the summit, the flanks of the wall-mountain swept down to the plain of the crater, a full mile below.

Mercury's angry sun was hidden beyond the curve of the world, but its corona extended delicate, structured tendrils above the far horizon.

The plain itself was immersed in darkness. But by the milky, diffuse light of the corona, Larionova could see a peak at the center of the plain, shouldering its way above the horizon. There was a spark of light at the base of the central peak, incongruously bright in the crater's shadows: that must be the Thoth team's camp.

"This reminds me of the Moon," she said.

Scholes considered this. "Forgive me, Dr. Larionova. Have you been down to Mercury before?"

"No," she said, his easy, informed arrogance grating on her. "I'm here to oversee the construction of Thoth, not to sightsee."

"Well, there's obviously a superficial similarity. After the formation of the main System objects five billion years ago, all the inner planets suffered bombardment by residual planetesimals. That's when Mercury took its biggest strike: the one which created the Caloris feature. But after that, Mercury was massive enough to retain a molten core—unlike the Moon. Later planetesimal strikes punched holes in the crust, so there were lava outflows that drowned some of the older cratering.

"Thus, on Mercury, you have a mixture of terrains. There's the most ancient landscape, heavily cratered, and the *planitia*: smooth lava plains, punctured by small, young craters.

"Later, as the core cooled, the surface actually shrunk inward. The planet lost a mile or so of radius."

Like a dried-out tomato. "So the surface *is* wrinkled."

"Yes. There are *rupes* and *dorsa:* ridges and lobate scarps, cliffs a couple of miles tall and extending for hundreds of miles. Great climbing country. And in some places there are gas vents, chimneys of residual thermal activity." He turned to her, corona light misty in his faceplate. "So Mercury isn't really so much like the Moon at all. . . . Look. You can see Thoth."

She looked up, following his pointing arm. There, just above the far horizon, was a small blue star.

She had her faceplate magnify the image. The star exploded into a compact sculpture of electric blue threads, surrounded by firefly lights: the Thoth construction site.

Thoth was a habitat to be placed in orbit close to Sol. Irina Larionova was the consulting engineer contracted by Superet to oversee the construction of the habitat.

Thoth's purpose was to find out what was wrong with the Sun.

Recently, anomalies had been recorded in the Sun's behavior; aspects of its interior seemed to be diverging, and widely, from the standard theoretical models. Superet was a loose coalition of interest groups on Earth and Mars, intent on studying problems likely to impact the long-term survival of the human species.

Problems in the interior of mankind's only star clearly came into the category of things of interest to Superet.

Irina Larionova wasn't much interested in any of Superet's semi-mystical philosophizing. It was the work that was important, for her: and the engineering problems posed by Thoth were fascinating.

At Thoth, a Solar-interior probe would be constructed. The probe would be one Interface of a wormhole terminal, loaded with sensors. The Interface would be dropped into the Sun. The other Interface would remain in orbit, at the center of the habitat.

The electric-blue bars she could see now were struts of exotic matter, which would eventually frame the wormhole termini. The sparks of light moving around the struts were GUTships and short-haul tugs. She stared at the image, wishing she could get back to some real work.

Irina Larionova had had no intention of visiting Mercury herself. Mercury was a detail, for Thoth. Why would *anyone* come to Mercury, unless they had to? Mercury was a piece of junk, a desolate ball of iron and rock too close to the Sun to be interesting, or remotely habitable. The two Thoth exploratory teams had come here only to exploit: to see if it was possible to dig raw materials out of Mercury's shallow—and close-at-hand—gravity well, for use in the construction of the habitat. The teams had landed at the South Pole, where traces of water-ice had been detected, and at the Caloris Basin, the huge equatorial crater where—it was hoped—that ancient impact might have brought iron-rich compounds to the surface.

The tugs from Thoth actually comprised the largest expedition ever to land on Mercury.

But, within days of landing, both investigative teams had reported anomalies.

Larionova tapped at her suit's sleeve-controls. After a couple of minutes an image of Dolores Wu appeared in one corner of Larionova's faceplate. *Hi, Irina*, she said, her voice buzzing like an insect in Larionova's helmet's enclosed space.

Dolores Wu was the leader of the Thoth exploratory team in Caloris. Wu was Mars-born, with small features and hair greyed despite AntiSenescence treatments. She looked weary.

"How's Caloris?" Larionova asked.

Well, we don't have much to report yet. We decided to start with a detailed gravimetric survey . . .

"And?"

We found the impact object. We think. It's as massive as we thought, but much—much—too small, Irina. It's barely a mile across, way too dense to be a planetesimal fragment.

"A black hole?"

No. Not dense enough for that.

"Then what?"

Wu looked exasperated. *We don't know yet, Irina. We don't have any answers. I'll keep you informed.*

Wu closed off the link.

Standing on the corona-lit wall of Chao Meng-Fu Crater, Larionova asked Kevan Scholes about Caloris.

"Caloris is *big*," he said. "Luna has no impact feature on the scale of Caloris. And Luna has nothing like the Weird Country in the other hemisphere . . ."

"The what?"

A huge planetesimal—or *something*—had struck the equator of Mercury, five billion years ago, Scholes said. The Caloris Basin—an immense, ridged crater system—formed around the primary impact site. Whatever caused the impact was still buried in the planet, somewhere under the crust, dense and massive; the object was a gravitational anomaly which had helped lock Mercury's rotation into synchronization with its orbit.

"Away from Caloris itself, shock waves spread around the planet's young crust," Scholes said. "The waves focused at Caloris' antipode—the point on the equator diametrically opposite Caloris itself. And the land there was shattered, into a jumble of bizarre hill and valley formations. *The Weird Country.* . . . Hey. Dr. Larionova."

She could *hear* that damnable grin of Schole's. "What now?" she snapped.

He walked across the summit toward her. "Look up," he said.

"Damn it, Scholes—"

There was a pattering against her faceplate.

She tilted up her head. Needle-shaped particles swirled over the wall-mountain from the planet's dark side and bounced off her faceplate, sparkling in corona light.

"What in Lethe is that?"

"Snow," he said.

Snow . . . On Mercury?

In the cool darkness of the tunnel, the people clambered over each other; they bumped against the Ice walls, and their muttering filled the water with crisscrossing voice-ripples. Cilia-of-Gold swam through and around the crowd, coaxing the people to follow her will.

She felt immensely weary. Her concentration and resolve threatened continually to shatter under the Seeker's assault. And the end of the tunnel, with the deadly Heads beyond, was a looming, threatening mouth, utterly intimidating.

At last the group was ready. She surveyed them. All of the people—except the very oldest and the very youngest—were arranged in an array which filled the tunnel from wall to wall; she could hear flukes and carapaces scraping softly against Ice.

The people looked weak, foolish, eager, she thought with dismay; now that she was actually implementing it her scheme seemed simpleminded. Was she about to lead them all to their deaths?

But it was too late for the luxury of doubt, she told herself. Now, there was no other option to follow.

She lifted herself to the axis of the tunnel, and clacked her mandibles sharply.

"Now," she said, "it is time. The most important moment of your lives. And you must *swim!* Swim as hard as you can; swim for your lives!"

And the people responded.

There was a surge of movement, of almost exhilarating *intent.* The people beat their flukes as one, and a jostling mass of flesh and carapaces scraped down the tunnel.

Cilia-of-Gold hurried ahead of them, leading the way

toward the tunnel mouth. As she swam she could feel the current the people were creating, the plug of cold tunnel water they pushed ahead of themselves.

Within moments the tunnel mouth was upon her.

She burst from the tunnel, shooting out into the open water of the cavern, her carapace clenched firm around her. She was plunged immediately into a clammy heat, so great was the temperature difference between tunnel and cavern.

Above her the Ice of the cavern roof arched over the warm Chimney mouth. And from all around the cavern, the helmet-skulls of Heads snapped around toward her.

Now the people erupted out of the tunnel, a shield of flesh and chitin behind her. The rush of tunnel water they pushed ahead of themselves washed over Cilia-of-Gold, chilling her anew.

She tried to imagine this from the Heads' point of view. This explosion of cold water into the cavern would bring about a much greater temperature difference than the Heads' heat-sensor skulls were accustomed to; the Heads would be *dazzled*, at least for a time: long enough—she hoped—to give her people a fighting chance against the more powerful Heads.

She swiveled in the water. She screamed at her people, so loud she could feel her cilia strain at the turbulent water. *"Now!* Hit them now!"

The people, with a roar, descended toward the Heads.

Kevan Scholes led Larionova down the wall-mountain slope into Chao Meng-Fu Crater.

After a hundred yards they came to another rover. This car was similar to the one they'd abandoned on the other side of the summit, but it had an additional fitting, obviously improvised: two wide, flat rails of metal, suspended between the wheels on hydraulic legs.

Scholes helped Larionova into the rover and pressurized it. Larionova removed her helmet with relief. The rover smelled, oppressively, of metal and plastic.

While Scholes settled behind his controls, Larionova checked the rover's data desk. An update from Dolores Wu was waiting for her. Wu wanted Larionova to come to Caloris, to see for herself what had been found there. Larionova sent a sharp message back, ordering Wu to summarize her findings and transmit them to the data desks at the Chao site.

Wu acknowledged immediately, but replied: *I'm going to find this hard to summarize, Irina.*

Larionova tapped out: *Why?*

We think we've found an artifact.

Larionova stared at the blunt words on the screen.

She massaged the bridge of her nose; she felt an ache spreading out from her temples and around her eye sockets. She wished she had time to sleep.

Scholes started the vehicle up. The rover bounced down the slope, descending into shadow. "It's genuine water-ice snow," Scholes said as he drove. "You know that a day on Mercury lasts a hundred and seventy-six Earth days. It's a combination of the eighty-eight-day year and the tidally locked rotation, which—"

"I know."

"During the day, the Sun drives water vapor out of the rocks and into the atmosphere."

"What atmosphere?"

"You really don't know much about Mercury, do you? It's mostly helium and hydrogen—only a billionth of Earth's sea-level pressure."

"How come those gases don't escape from the gravity well?"

"They do," Scholes said. "But the atmosphere is replenished by the solar wind. Particles from the Sun are trapped by Mercury's magnetosphere. Mercury has quite a respectable magnetic field: the planet has a solid iron core, which . . .''

She let Scholes' words run on through her head, unregistered. *Air from the solar wind, and snow at the South Pole* . . .

Maybe Mercury was a more interesting place than she'd imagined.

''Anyway,'' Scholes was saying, ''the water vapor disperses across the planet's sunlit hemisphere. But at the South Pole we have this crater: Chao Meng-Fu, straddling the Pole itself. Mercury has no axial tilt—there are no seasons here—and so Chao's floor is in permanent shadow.''

''And snow falls.''

''And snow falls.''

Scholes stopped the rover and tapped telltales on his control panel. There was a whir of hydraulics, and she heard a soft crunch, transmitted into the cabin through the rover's structure.

Then the rover lifted upward through a foot.

The rover lurched forward again. The motion was much smoother than before, and there was an easy, hissing sound.

''You've just lowered those rails,'' Larionova said. ''I knew it. This damn rover is a sled, isn't it?''

''It was easy enough to improvise,'' Scholes said, sounding smug. ''Just a couple of metal rails on hydraulics, and Vernier rockets from a cannibalized tug to give us some push. . . .''

''It's astonishing that there's enough ice here to sustain this.''

''Well, that snow may have seemed sparse, but it's been falling steadily—for five billion years . . . Dr. Larionova, there's a whole frozen ocean here, in Chao Meng-Fu Crater: enough ice to be detectable even from Earth.''

Larionova twisted to look out through a viewpoint at

the back of the cabin. The rover's rear lights picked out twin sled tracks, leading back to the summit of the wall-mountain; ice, exposed in the tracks, gleamed brightly in starlight.

Lethe, she thought. *Now I'm skiing. Skiing, on Mercury. What a day.*

The wall-mountain shallowed out, merging seamlessly with the crater plain. Scholes retracted the sled rails; on the flat, the regolith dust gave the ice sufficient traction for the rover's wide wheels. The rover made fast progress through the fifty miles to the heart of the plain.

Larionova drank coffee and watched the landscape through the viewports. The corona light was silvery and quite bright here, like moonlight. The central peak loomed up over the horizon, like some approaching ship on a sea of dust. The ice-surface of Chao's floor—though pocked with craters and covered with the ubiquitous regolith dust—was visibly smoother and more level than the plain outside the crater.

The rover drew to a halt on the outskirts of the Thoth team's sprawling camp, close to the foothills of the central peak. The dust here was churned up by rover tracks and tug exhaust splashes, and semi-transparent bubble-shelters were hemispheres of yellow, homely light, illuminating the darkened ice surface. There were drilling rigs, and several large pits dug into the ice.

Scholes helped Larionova out onto the surface. "I'll take you to a shelter," he said. "Or a tug. Maybe you want to freshen up before—"

"Where's Dixon?"

Scholes pointed to one of the rigs. "When I left, over there."

"Then that's where we're going. Come on."

Frank Dixon was the team leader. He met Larionova on the surface, and invited her into a small opaqued bubble-shelter nestling at the foot of the rig.

Scholes wandered off into the camp, in search of food.

The shelter contained a couple of chairs, a data desk, and a basic toilet. Dixon was a morose, burly American; when he took off his helmet there was a band of dirt at the base of his wide neck, and Larionova noticed a sharp, acrid stink from his suit. Dixon had evidently been out on the surface for long hours.

He pulled a hip flask from an environment suit pocket. "You want a drink?" he asked. "Scotch?"

"Sure."

Dixon poured a measure for Larionova into the flask's cap, and took a draught himself from the flask's small mouth.

Larionova drank; the liquor burned her mouth and throat, but it immediately took an edge off her tiredness. "It's good. But it needs ice."

He smiled. "Ice we got. Actually, we have tried it; Mercury ice is good, as clean as you like. We're not going to die of thirst out here, Irina."

"Tell me what you've found, Frank."

Dixon sat on the edge of the desk, his fat haunches bulging inside the leggings of his environment suit. "Trouble, Irina. We've found trouble."

"I know that much."

"I think we're going to have to get off the planet. The System authorities—and the scientists and conservation groups—are going to climb all over us, if we try to mine here. I wanted to tell you about it, before—"

Larionova struggled to contain her irritation and tiredness. "That's *not* a problem for Thoth," she said. "Therefore it's not a problem for me. We can tell Superet to bring in a water-ice asteroid from the Belt, for our supplies. You know that. Come on, Frank. Tell me why you're wasting my time down here."

Dixon took another long pull on his flask, and eyed her.

"There's *life* here, Irina," he said. "Life, inside this frozen ocean. Drink up; I'll show you."

The sample was in a case on the surface, beside a data desk.

The thing in the case looked like a strip of multicolored meat: perhaps three feet long, crushed and obviously dead; shards of some transparent shell material were embedded in flesh that sparkled with ice crystals.

"We found this inside a two-thousand-yard-deep core," Dixon said.

Larionova tried to imagine how this would have looked, intact and mobile. "This means nothing to me, Frank. I'm no biologist."

He grunted, self-deprecating: "Nor me. Nor any of us. Who expected to find life, on Mercury?" Dixon tapped at the data desk with gloved fingers. "We used our desks' medico-diagnostic facilities to come up with this reconstruction," he said. "We call it a *mercuric*, Irina."

A Virtual projected into space a foot above the desk's surface; the image rotated, sleek and menacing.

The body was a thin cone, tapering to a tail from a wide, flat head. Three parabolic cups—*eyes?*—were embedded in the smooth "face," symmetrically placed around a lipless mouth. . . . No, not eyes, Larionova corrected herself. Maybe some kind of sonar sensor? That would explain the parabolic profile.

Mandibles, like pincers, protruded from the mouth. From the tail, three fins were splayed out around what looked like an anus. A transparent carapace surrounded the main body, like a cylindrical cloak; inside the carapace, rows of small, hairlike cilia lined the body, supple and vibratile.

There were regular markings, faintly visible, in the surface of the carapace.

"Is this accurate?"

"Who knows? It's the best *we* can do. When we have your clearance, we can transmit our data to Earth, and let the experts get at it."

"Lethe, Frank," Larionova said. "This looks like a fish. It looks like it could *swim*. The streamlining, the tail—"

Dixon scratched the short hairs at the back of his neck and said nothing.

"But we're on Mercury, damn it, not in Hawaii," Larionova said.

Dixon pointed down, past the dusty floor. "Irina. It's not all frozen. There are *cavities* down there, inside the Chao ice-cap. According to our sonar probes—"

"Cavities?"

"Water. At the base of the crater, under a couple of miles of ice. Kept liquid by thermal vents, in crust-collapse scarps and ridges. Plenty of room for swimming. . . . We speculate that our friend here swims on his back—" he tapped the desk surface, and the image swiveled "—and the water passes down, between his body and this carapace, and he uses all those tiny hairs to filter out particles of food. The trunk seems to be lined with little mouths. See?" He flicked the image to another representation; the skin became transparent, and Larionova could see blocky reconstructions of internal organs. Dixon said, "There's no true stomach, but there is what looks like a continuous digestive tube passing down the axis of the body, to the anus at the tail."

Larionova noticed a thread-like structure wrapped around some of the organs, as well as around the axial digestive tract.

"Look," Dixon said, pointing to one area. "Look at

the surface structure of these lengths of tubing, here near the digestive tract.''

Larionova looked. The tubes, clustering around the digestive axis, had complex, rippled surfaces. ''So?''

''You don't get it, do you? It's *convoluted*—like the surface of a brain. Irina, we think that stuff must be some equivalent of nervous tissue.''

Larionova frowned. *Damn it, I wish I knew more biology.* ''What about this thread material, wrapped around the organs?''

Dixon sighed. ''We don't know, Irina. It doesn't seem to fit with the rest of the structure, does it?'' He pointed. ''Follow the threads back. There's a broader main body, just here. We think maybe this is some kind of parasite, which has infested the main organism. Like a tapeworm. It's as if the threads are extended, vestigial limbs. . . .''

Leaning closer, Larionova saw that tendrils from the worm-thing had even infiltrated the brain-tubes. She shuddered; if this was a parasite, it was a particularly vile infestation. Maybe the parasite even modified the mercuric's behavior, she wondered.

Dixon restored the solid-aspect Virtual.

Uneasily, Larionova pointed to the markings on the carapace. They were small triangles, clustered into elaborate patterns. ''And what's this stuff?''

Dixon hesitated. ''I was afraid you might ask that.''

''Well?''

''. . . We think the markings are artificial, Irina. A deliberate tattoo, carved into the carapace, probably with the mandibles. Writing, maybe: those look like symbolic markings, with information content.''

''Lethe,'' she said.

''I know. This fish was smart,'' Dixon said.

The people, victorious, clustered around the warmth of their new Chimney. Recovering from their journey and from their battle-wounds, they cruised easily over the gardens of cilia-plants, and browsed on floating fragments of food.

It had been a great triumph. The Heads were dead, or driven off into the labyrinth of tunnels through the Ice. Strong-Flukes had even found the Heads' principal nest here, under the silty floor of the cavern. With sharp stabs of her mandibles, Strong-Flukes had destroyed a dozen or more Head young.

Cilia-of-Gold took herself off, away from the Chimney. She prowled the edge of the Ice cavern, feeding fitfully.

She was a hero. But she couldn't bear the attention of others: their praise, the warmth of their bodies. All she seemed to desire now was the uncomplicated, silent coolness of Ice.

She brooded on the infestation that was spreading through her.

Seekers were a mystery. Nobody knew *why* Seekers compelled their hosts to isolate themselves, to bury themselves in the Ice. What was the point? When the hosts were destroyed, so were the Seekers.

Perhaps it wasn't the Ice itself the Seekers desired, she wondered. Perhaps they sought, in their blind way, something *beyond* the Ice. . . .

But there *was* nothing above the Ice. The caverns were hollows in an infinite, eternal Universe of Ice. Cilia-of-Gold, with a shudder, imagined herself burrowing, chewing her way into the endless Ice, upward without limit. . . . Was that, finally, how her life would end?

She hated the Seeker within her. She hated her body, for betraying her in this way; and she hated herself.

"Cilia-of-Gold."

She turned, startled, and closed her carapace around herself reflexively.

It was Strong-Flukes and Ice-Born, together.

Seeing their warm, familiar bodies, here in this desolate

corner of the cavern, Cilia-of-Gold's loneliness welled up inside her, like a Chimney of emotion.

But she swam away from her Three-mates, backward, her carapace scraping on the cavern's Ice wall.

Ice-Born came toward her, hesitantly. "We're concerned about you."

"Then don't be," she snapped. "Go back to the Chimney, and leave me here."

"No," Strong-Flukes said quietly.

Cilia-of-Gold felt desperate, angry, confined. "You know what's wrong with me, Strong-Flukes. I have a *Seeker*. It's going to kill me. And there's nothing any of us can do about it."

Their bodies pressed close around her now; she longed to open up her carapace to them and bury herself in their warmth.

"We know we're going to lose you, Cilia-of-Gold," Ice-Born said. It sounded as if she could barely speak. Ice-Born had always been the softest, the most loving, of the Three, Cilia-of-Gold thought, the warm heart of their relationship. "And—"

"Yes?"

Strong-Flukes opened her carapace wide. "We want to be Three again," she said.

Already, Cilia-of-Gold saw with a surge of love and excitement, Strong-Flukes's ovipositor was distended: swollen with one of the three isogametes which would fuse to form a new child, their fourth. . . .

A child Cilia-of-Gold could never see growing to consciousness.

"*No!*" Her cilia pulsed with the single, agonized word.

Suddenly the warmth of her Three-mates was confining, claustrophobic. She had to get away from this prison of flesh; her mind was filled with visions of the coolness and purity of *Ice*: of clean, high *Ice*.

"Cilia-of-Gold. Wait. Please—"

She flung herself away, along the wall. She came to a tunnel mouth, and she plunged into it, relishing the tunnel's cold, stagnant water.

"Cilia-of-Gold! *Cilia-of-Gold!*"

She hurled her body through the web of tunnels, carelessly colliding with walls of Ice so hard that she could feel her carapace splinter. On and on she swam, until the voices of her Three-mates were lost forever.

We've dug out a large part of the artifact, Irina, Dolores Wu reported. *It's a mash of what looks like hull material.*

"Did you get a sample?"

No. We don't have anything that could cut through material so dense. . . . Irina, we're looking at something beyond our understanding.

Larionova sighed. "Just tell me, Dolores," she told Wu's data desk image.

Irina, we think we're dealing with the Pauli Principle.

Pauli's Exclusion Principle stated that no two baryonic particles could exist in the same quantum state. Only a certain number of electrons, for example, could share a given energy level in an atom. Adding more electrons caused complex shells of charge to build up around the atom's nucleus. It was the electron shells—this consequence of Pauli—that gave the atom its chemical properties.

But the Pauli principle *didn't* apply to photons; it was possible for many photons to share the same quantum state. That was the essence of the laser: billions of photons, coherent, sharing the same quantum properties.

Irina, Wu said slowly, *what would happen if you could turn off the Exclusion Principle, for a piece of baryonic matter?*

"You can't," Larionova said immediately.

Of course not. Try to imagine anyway.

Larionova frowned. What if one could lase mass? "The

atomic electron shells would implode, of course.''

Yes.

''All electrons would fall into their ground state. Chemistry would be impossible.''

Yes. But you may not care . . .

''Molecules would collapse. Atoms would fall into each other, releasing immense quantities of binding energy.''

You'd end up with a superdense substance, wouldn't you? Completely non-reactive, chemically. And almost unbreachable, given the huge energies required to detach non-Pauli atoms.

Ideal hull material, Irina. . . .

''But it's all impossible,'' Larionova said weakly. ''You *can't* violate Pauli.''

Of course you can't, Dolores Wu replied.

Inside an opaqued bubble-shelter, Larionova, Dixon and Scholes sat on fold-out chairs, cradling coffees.

''If your mercuric was so smart,'' Larionova said to Dixon, ''how come he got himself stuck in the ice?''

Dixon shrugged. ''In fact it goes deeper than that. It looked to us as if the mercuric burrowed his way up into the ice, deliberately. What kind of evolutionary advantage could there be in behavior like that? The mercuric was certain to be killed.''

''Yes,'' Larionova said. She massaged her temples, thinking about the mercuric's infection. ''But maybe that thread-parasite had something to do with it. I mean, some parasites change the way their hosts behave.''

Scholes tapped at a data desk; text and images, reflected from the desk, flickered over his face. ''That's true. There are parasites which transfer themselves from one host to another—by forcing a primary host to get itself eaten by the second.''

Dixon's wide face crumpled. ''Lethe. That's disgusting.''

"The lancet fluke," Scholes read slowly, "is a parasite of some species of ant. The fluke can make its host climb to the top of a grass stem and then lock onto the stem with its mandibles—and wait until it's swallowed by a grazing sheep. Then the fluke can go on to infest the sheep in turn."

"Okay," Dixon said. "But why would a parasite force its mercuric host to burrow up into the ice of a frozen ocean? When the host dies, the parasite dies too. It doesn't make sense."

"There's a lot about this that doesn't make sense," Larionova said. "Like, the whole question of the existence of life in the cavities in the first place. There's no *light* down there. How do the mercurics survive, under two miles of ice?"

Scholes folded one leg on top of the other and scratched his ankle. "I've been going through the data desks." He grimaced, self-deprecating. "A crash course in exotic biology. You want my theory?"

"Go ahead."

"The thermal vents—which cause the cavities in the first place. The vents are the key. I think the bottom of the Chao ice-cap is like the mid-Atlantic ridge, back on Earth.

"The deep sea, a mile down, is a desert; by the time any particle of food has drifted down from the richer waters above it's passed through so many guts that its energy content is exhausted.

"But along the Ridge, where tectonic plates are colliding, you have hydrothermal vents—just as at the bottom of Chao. And the heat from the Atlantic vents supports life: in little colonies, strung out along the mid-Atlantic Ridge. The vents form superheated fountains, smoking with deep-crust minerals that life can exploit: sulphides of copper, zinc, lead, and iron, for instance. And there are very steep temperature differences, and so there are high energy gradients—another prerequisite for life.''

''Hmm.'' Larionova closed her eyes and tried to picture it. *Pockets of warm water, deep in the ice of Mercury; luxuriant mats of life surrounding mineral-rich hydrothermal vents, browsed by Dixon's mercuric animals . . .* Was it possible?

Dixon asked, ''How long do the vents persist?''

''On Earth, in the Ridge, a couple of decades. Here we don't know.''

''What happens when a vent dies?'' Larionova asked. ''That's the end of your pocket world, isn't it? The ice chamber would simply freeze up.''

''Maybe,'' Scholes said. ''But the vents would occur in rows, along the scarps. Maybe there are corridors of liquid water, within the ice, along which mercurics could migrate.''

Larionova thought about that for a while.

''I don't believe it,'' she said.

''Why not?''

''I don't see how it's possible for life to have *evolved* here in the first place.'' In the primeval oceans of Earth, there had been complex chemicals, and electrical storms, and . . .

''Oh, I don't think that's a problem,'' Scholes said.

She looked at him sharply. Maddeningly, he was grinning again. ''Well?'' she snapped.

''Look,'' Scholes said with grating patience, ''we've two anomalies on Mercury: the life forms here at the South Pole, and Dolores Wu's artifact under Caloris. The simplest assumption is that the two anomalies are connected. Let's put the pieces together,'' he said. ''Let's construct a hypothesis. . . .''

Her mandibles ached as she crushed the gritty Ice, carving out her tunnel upward. The rough walls of the tunnel scraped against her carapace, and she pushed Ice rubble down between her body and her carapace, sacrificing fragile cilia designed to extract soft food particles from warm streams.

The higher she climbed, the harder the Ice became. The Ice was now so cold she was beyond cold; she couldn't even feel the Ice fragments that scraped along her belly and flukes. And, she suspected, the tunnel behind her was no longer open but had refrozen, sealing her here, in this shifting cage, forever.

The world she had left—of caverns, and Chimneys, and children, and her Three-mates—were remote bubbles of warmth, a distant dream. The only reality was the hard Ice in her mandibles, and the Seeker heavy and questing inside her.

She could feel her strength seeping out with the last of her warmth into the Ice's infinite extent. And yet *still* the Seeker wasn't satisfied; still she had to climb, on and up, into the endless darkness of the Ice.

. . . But now—impossibly—there was something *above* her, breaking through the Ice. . . .

She cowered inside her Ice-prison.

Kevan Scholes said, "Five billion years ago—when the solar system was very young, and the crusts of Earth and other inner planets were still subject to bombardment from stray planetesimals—a ship came here. An interstellar craft, maybe with FTL technology."

"Why? Where from?" Larionova asked.

"I don't know. How could I know that? But the ship must have been massive—with the bulk of a planetesimal, or more. Certainly highly advanced, with a hull composed of Dolores's superdense Pauli construction material."

"Hmm. Go on."

"Then the ship hit trouble."

"What kind of trouble?"

"I don't *know*. Come on, Dr. Larionova. Maybe it got

hit by a planetesimal itself. Anyway, the ship crashed here, on Mercury—''

''Right.'' Dixon nodded, gazing at Scholes hungrily; the American reminded Larionova of a child enthralled by a story. ''It was a disastrous impact. It caused the Caloris feature. . . .''

''Oh, be serious,'' Larionova said.

Dixon looked at her. ''Caloris *was* a pretty unique impact, Irina. Extraordinarily violent, even by the standards of the system's early bombardment phase. . . . Caloris Basin is *eight hundred miles* across; on Earth, its walls would stretch from New York to Chicago.''

''So how did anything survive?''

Scholes shrugged. ''Maybe the starfarers had some kind of inertial shielding. How can we know? Anyway the ship was wrecked; and the density of the smashed-up hull material caused it to sink into the bulk of the planet, through the Caloris puncture.

''The crew were stranded. So they sought a place to survive. Here, on Mercury.''

''I get it,'' Dixon said. ''The only viable environment, long term, was the Chao Meng-Fu ice cap.''

Scholes spread his hands. ''Maybe the starfarers had to engineer descendants, quite unlike the original crew, to survive in such conditions. And perhaps they had to do a little planetary engineering too; they may have had to initiate some of the hydrothermal vents which created the enclosed liquid-water world down there. And so—''

''Yes?''

''And so the creature we've dug out of the ice is a degenerate descendant of those ancient star travelers, still swimming around the Chao sea.''

Scholes fell silent, his eyes on Larionova.

Larionova stared into her coffee. ''A 'degenerate descendant.' After *five billion years?* Look, Scholes, on Earth it's only three and a half billion years since the first prokaryotic cells. And on Earth, whole phyla—groups of species—have emerged or declined over periods less than a *tenth* of the time since the Caloris Basin event. Over time intervals like that, the morphology of species flows like hot plastic. So how is it possible for these mercurics to have persisted?''

Scholes looked uncertain. ''Maybe they've suffered massive evolutionary changes,'' he said. ''Changes we're just not seeing. For example, maybe the worm parasite is the malevolent descendant of some harmless creature the starfarers brought with them.''

Dixon scratched his neck, where the suit-collar ring of dirt was prominent. ''Anyway, we've still got the puzzle of the mercuric's burrowing into the ice.''

''Hmm.'' Scholes sipped his cooling coffee. ''I've got a theory about that, too.''

''I thought you might,'' Larionova said sourly.

Scholes said, ''I wonder if the impulse to climb up to the surface is some kind of residual yearning for the stars.''

''What?''

Scholes looked embarrassed, but he pressed on: ''A racial memory buried deep, prompting the mercurics to seek their lost home world. . . . Why not?''

Larionova snorted. ''You're a romantic, Kevan Scholes.''

A telltale flashed on the surface of the data desk. Dixon leaned over, tapped the telltale and took the call.

He looked up at Larionova, his moon-like face animated. ''Irina. They've found another mercuric,'' he said.

''Is it intact?''

''More than that.'' Dixon stood and reached for his helmet. ''This one isn't dead yet. . . .''

The mercuric lay on Chao's dust-coated ice. Humans stood around it, suited, their faceplates anonymously blank.

The mercuric, dying, was a cone of bruised-purple meat a yard long. Shards of shattered transparent carapace had been crushed into its crystallizing flesh. Some of the cilia, within the carapace, stretched and twitched. The cilia looked differently colored from Dixon's reconstruction, as far as Larionova could remember: these were yellowish threads, almost golden.

Dixon spoke quickly to his team, then joined Larionova and Scholes. "We couldn't have saved it. It was in distress as soon as our core broke through into its tunnel. I guess it couldn't take the pressure and temperature differentials. Its internal organs seem to be massively disrupted. . . ."

"Just think." Kevan Scholes stood beside Dixon, his hands clasped behind his back. "There must be millions of these animals in the ice under our feet, embedded in their pointless little chambers. Surely none of them could dig more than a hundred yards or so up from the liquid layer."

Larionova switched their voices out of her consciousness. She knelt down, on the ice; under her knees she could feel the crisscross heating elements in her suit's fabric.

She peered into the dulling sonar-eyes of the mercuric. The creature's mandibles—prominent and sharp—opened and closed, in vacuum silence.

She felt an impulse to reach out her gloved hand to the battered flank of the creature: to *touch* this animal, this person, whose species had, perhaps, traveled across light years—and five billion years—to reach her. . . .

But still, she had the nagging feeling that something was wrong with Scholes' neat hypothesis. The mercuric's physical design seemed crude. Could this really have been a starfaring species? The builders of the ship in Caloris must have had some form of major tool-wielding capability. And Dixon's earlier study had shown that the creature had no trace of any limbs, even vestigially. . . .

Vestigial limbs, she remembered. *Lethe*.

Abruptly her perception of this animal—and its host parasite—began to shift; she could feel a paradigm dissolving inside her, melting like a Mercury snowflake in the Sun.

"Dr. Larionova? Are you all right?"

Larionova looked up at Scholes. "Kevan, I called you a romantic. But I think you were almost correct, after all. *But not quite*. Remember we've suggested that the *parasite*—the infestation—changes the mercuric's behavior, causing it to make its climb."

"What are you saying?"

Suddenly, Larionova saw it all. "I don't believe this mercuric is descended from the starfarers—the builders of the ship in Caloris. I think the rise of the mercurics' intelligence was a *later* development; the mercurics grew to consciousness *here*, on Mercury. I *do* think the mercurics are descended from something that came to Mercury on that ship, though. A pet, or a food animal—Lethe, even some equivalent of a stomach bacteria. Five billion years is time enough for anything. And, given the competition for space near the short-lived vents, there's plenty of encouragement for the development of intelligence, down inside this frozen sea."

"And the starfarers themselves?" Scholes asked. "What became of them? Did they die?"

"No," she said. "No, I don't think so. But they, too, suffered huge evolutionary changes. I think they did devolve, Scholes; in fact, I think they lost their awareness.

"But one thing persisted within them, across all this desert of time. And that was the starfarers' vestigial will to *return*—to the surface, one day, and at last to the stars. . . ."

It was a will which had survived even the loss of consciousness itself, somewhere in the long, stranded aeons: a relic of awareness long since transmuted to a deeper biochemical urge—*a will to return home*, still embedded within a once-intelligent species reduced by time to a mere parasitic infection.

But it was a home which, surely, could no longer exist.

The mercuric's golden cilia twitched once more, in a great wave of motion which shuddered down its ice-flecked body.

Then it was still.

Larionova stood up; her knees and calves were stiff and cold, despite the suit's heater. "Come on," she said to Scholes and Dixon. "You'd better get your team off the ice as soon as possible; I'll bet the universities have their first exploratory teams down here half a day after we pass Earth the news."

Dixon nodded. "And Thoth?"

"Thoth? I'll call Superet. I guess I've an asteroid to order. . . ."

And then, she thought, *at last I can sleep. Sleep and get back to work.*

With Scholes and Dixon, she trudged across the dust-strewn ice to the bubble shelters.

She could feel the Ice under her belly . . . but above her *there was no Ice*, no water even, an infinite *nothing* into which the desperate pulses of her blinded eyes disappeared without echo.

Astonishingly—impossibly—she *was*, after all, above the Ice. How could this be? Was she in some immense upper cavern, its Ice roof too remote to see? Was this the nature of the Universe, a hierarchy of caverns within caverns?

She knew she would never understand. But it didn't seem to matter. And, as her awareness faded, she felt the Seeker inside her subside to peace.

A final warmth spread out within her. Consciousness splintered like melting ice, flowing away through the closing tunnels of her memory.

DAWN VENUS

G. David Nordley

"Dawn Venus" appeared in the August 1995 issue of Asimov's, *with a cover illustration by Chris Moore and an interior illustration by George H. Krauter. G. David Nordley is a retired Air Force officer and physicist who has become a frequent contributor to* Analog *in the last couple of years, winning that magazine's Analytical Laboratory readers poll in 1992 for his story "Poles Apart"; he later won the same award for his story "Into the Miranda Rift." Although he's become a mainstay of our sister publication,* Analog, *he has also sold a fair number of stories to* Asimov's *over the last few years, including the hair-raising thriller that follows, which takes us to a terraformed Venus, for a frantic land-rush unlike any seen before in human history . . . one with stakes so high that almost any risk is acceptable, even ones that seem almost certainly fatal—like jumping out of an orbiting space station.*

Nordley lives in Sunnyvale, California.

August 1995

The road to Venus apparently led through people, Bik Wu thought as he struggled sideways against the crush of the crowd and vertically against the crush of gravity while strange odors, colorful costumes, and not-quite-lost languages assaulted his other senses. People. Kai was gone now—another man was her widower. But for Bik there had been no one else.

This must be the Earth immigrants lounge, he realized; the soft chairs promised to Mercury immigrants were nowhere to be seen. Nor was there any help; personal comm circuits were saturated. His bones ached with over twice his usual weight. Once on the elevator, he told himself, there would be a soft, form-fitting, reclining chair for the three-hundred-kilometer ride down to the surface. Until then, he just had to endure.

The Venus maglev interplanet port was swamped with late arrivals. Some media types were saying that the opening of the Devana Archipelago south of Beta Regio was the largest new land rush in the history of the human race. Judged by the average standards of big project management, Bik figured that it was probably a textbook success. But from his worm's eye viewpoint in the middle of this mob, it looked like a fiasco. Nevertheless, after six decades of living in domes with permafrost below and vacuum above, Bik was going to find some elbow room down there.

Maybe enough to show the custody board that he cared enough to have Junior.

Gravity or no, he was a bigger and stronger man than average, so he bulled his way, with apologies left and right, to the elevator booking counter and slapped his palm on the reader.

"Mercury, Idaho?" The transport receptionist smiled when her local cybe displayed his ID. A big woman with a trace of east Asian heritage in her face, or her smile, she was full of a cheerfulness that didn't match his mood. Where were the robots when you *wanted* one? But around here it seemed that any job that could be done by a human was being done by a human. Service was in style. He shook his head. So, apparently, were madhouses.

"No, no," he groaned. "That's a Mercury *eye dee* number. Mercury the planet. Chao Meng-Fu Dome."

She raised an eyebrow. "You're in the wrong lounge."

"I've figured that out," he said with forced evenness, "but this is where they sent me. I'd like a reservation to the surface, surface transportation to Port Tannhauser and a room when I get there."

Only eighteen hundred kilometers to go! Port Venus was on the Circumplanetary Maglev Railroad, a planet-girding ring of frictionless magnetic levitation railways held above the atmosphere by a dozen trains of mass circulating at greater than orbital velocity. Built to remove the ancient carbon dioxide atmosphere and increase the spin of the planet, the CMR was one of the wonders of the solar system—but it was also a transportation bottleneck.

The receptionist stared at the screen, looked at seating charts, and grinned. "I'm surprised you're still standing. In fact, I'm surprised to see *any* immigrants from Mercury. Worked out a bit?"

"Yes." He shrugged, not wanting to admit his misery. "Some. I would have had more time on the regular transport, but I got pulled back for some unnecessary work at New Loki. I got a friend to get me on the express, so here I am. Their centrifuge time was limited, but I'm in reasonable shape."

Reasonable? He was maybe ten kilos over his theoretical optimum, and it showed more here than on Mercury. Four days in a centrifuge hadn't done much more than retrain his reflexes from Mercury's gravity. On the plus side, he told himself, his strength was okay, his bone mass was fine and thirty laps a day in the dome pool gave him an underlying endurance on which he could draw. "I can do this."

The receptionist shook her head, her long jet-black hair lending a semblance of femininity to a well-muscled, almost masculine, figure. Bik wondered if she might be a swimmer or maybe a climber.

"Grab," she said, "that there's going to be a lot of standing around. There are only so many elevators, we have to be fair, and there are—" She got the distant look that people get when they link with the cybersystem for some detail they don't have immediately. Born with a radio interface gene mod, probably. He shuddered—what if she ever *wanted* to be out of touch? "—uh, twelve thousand six hundred and fifty-seven would-be homesteaders in port as we speak."

Bik rolled his eyes up.

She grinned. "Including sixteen from the planet Mercury! So you're not the only one."

"Fine," Bik sighed. "Now, when can I get on an elevator car down?"

Once down he would have to catch an air shuttle fifteen hundred kilometers northeast to Port Tannhauser, where the land rush was being staged. Once there, he could reserve a parcel. Then all he would have to do was to get there within twenty-four hours, universal time—by the local dawn of Venus's leisurely day. The planet, of course, was spinning like a top compared to what it used to be— once about every fifty days, retrograde, making for thirty days from sun to sun when you included its orbital motion. Before the CMR, it had taken 243 days for Venus to turn under the stars.

Bik kept going through new world things in his mind; so much history, so much background, so many different ways of doing things, so many hoops to jump through, so little time to jump. The way things were going, every boat and aircraft for a thousand kilometers around would be taken by the time he arrived. Then he'd have to try to pick something within walking distance, which, for his already-aching Mercurian feet, wasn't very far.

Thousands of kilometers. Chao Meng-Fu was hardly 150 kilometers across, and *it* looked huge.

"The elevators are pretty crowded," the attendant reminded him. "It should ease up in a couple of hours."

"Land parcel registration is first-come, first-serve. I just want to have a fair chance." He sighed. "I did everything I was supposed to do. Isn't there any faster way down?"

She pursed her lips and grinned mischievously. "Do you like to walk the edge? Take risks?"

"Citizen, I spent half a decade supervising the Chao Meng-Fu construction job, outside. Something goes wrong outside on Mercury's south pole and you can freeze your feet and boil your head. Simultaneously." Bik grinned. He exaggerated a little, but he thought it would impress her.

Impress her? His therapist might consider that progress, Bik thought. It had been a while since he cared about what any woman except Kai had thought of him.

The receptionist smiled. Damn if she hadn't gotten his mind off his aching feet. "The name's Suwon and *you* can take a flying leap."

Another tease, of course. When would he learn? "Sorry, I didn't mean to bother you."

She laughed at his devastated expression. "No, I meant literally. Grab this; a personal evac unit from this far up has enough cross range, in theory, to get you to Port Tannhauser if you jump down line a ways. They have recreational versions, and I've used them a couple of times with a boyfriend from farther down the line. The cybes don't like it, but screw them. It's my life. I'll show you the ropes—if you've got the nerves."

He shook his head. He'd been had; he couldn't read people and had misread her playfulness for something more serious. She'd worked the boyfriend in smoothly, too—a nice warn off.

A neat woman, he had to admit, and she probably meant to help, but jumping off a three-hundred-kilometer high railroad wasn't in his plans. "That's a last resort. Let's try to get me on the tube first."

She nodded and looked off in space for a moment again. "I can get you on the ten-hundred with an earlier standby on the oh-three, standing room only."

His bones, muscles, ligaments, and cartilage screamed at him, but he grimaced and said, "I'll take it. Look, if there's any way you can move me up, it's important."

She looked a question at him.

His first thought was that his problems were none of her business, but his aching body had put him in need of some sympathy, so he decided to chance telling her.

"It's about my kid. His mother just died, and I'm in a custody fight with her second husband. If I can get a small island, or a cut of a large one, that'll help me in my custody case. I've got a board to impress and I think they'll think this would be a good place to raise a kid, understand?"

The grin faded and she pursed her lips. "I'll do what I can. Meanwhile, I've cleared your prints for the lounge for low-gravity-world immigrants. They have plenty of recliners. Down the corridor to your left, door RS-3."

He might get to like the woman, he decided, as he waved a goodbye and headed for relief.

The waiting list for the oh-three hundred elevator turned out to have more names on it than the elevator cab had seats. He checked registration statistics. There were some ten thousand people down at Port Tannhauser already and only about fifteen thousand parcels, distributed among the several hundred islands. Pickings were getting thin.

The place was beautiful. The archipelago just south of the city was a drowned mountain range less than a century old. Its shorelines still expanded with every wave striking higher or lower as the gentle solar tide completed its monthly cycle. Its vids sparkled with dark green sensuous surf-flecked beaches and shiny green palms punctuated with bright birds and flowers.

Kai would have loved it, if she'd only stuck with him long enough to see it, Bik thought. See, Kai, I *do* have some romance in my soul.

Staring at the brightly colored wall above the other low-gee couch sitters, Bik's memory went back to their wedding under the stars at Mercury's south pole. Then fast-forward to the birth of their son, to weekend visits during the months of separation on the New Loki project, to when Kai told him she'd fallen in love with a starship officer from Ceres named Thor Wendt, was going off with him and was taking Bikki with her.

What had he done wrong? What could he have done differently? As always there were no answers.

Hurt as he had been, he'd never stopped loving Kai— she had just been too beautiful, too bright and vivacious for him to keep up with. He still thought himself fortunate to have had those few years with her. He had to admit he'd been a practical, safe, duty-bound drag on her free spirit.

She'd told Bik that she and Thor wanted Bikki to bond with his new father, and so didn't want any real time interaction between Bik and the kid for now. Bik had joint custody, and could have tried to enjoin her from doing that, or sued, for custody himself. But Mercurian courts generally favored two-parent families in such cases. The lawyer he consulted said it would have been a waste of time.

He sent presents and letters out to the belt for birthdays and New Year's and got receipts, but lightspeed delays made two-way contact difficult, and having to talk to Kai in the process made it even more so. There had never been any acknowledgment. Once he'd gotten a fax of a crayon Father's Day card from the school, but that had been all in five years. He didn't hold it against Junior; kids his age didn't understand that kind of thing. Anyway, his work on New Loki's three-million-person dome at the Mercurian north pole had made the years go by quickly.

Bik remembered the call. It came from Ceres a year ago. Some suicidal Nihilists had wanted to make a statement about robotics, technology, and what they felt was the general meaningless direction of civilization. That was fine with Bik as long as they wrote their propaganda in their own blood; but their tactics had gotten twisted somehow into rationalizing general mayhem—and Kai had been in the wrong place at the wrong time.

A quiet, sincere gentleman had called to tell him that Thor and "Ted Wendt" had survived a bomb at Ceres Starport, but his ex-wife had not. Until then he had hoped that, somehow, Wendt would go and they would be together again. Hope died with Kai.

Bik had hesitated in filing for custody. Thor Wendt considered the boy his own now; he had raised Junior for five of the boy's eight years, and felt that Kalinda station in the Kruger 60 system would be a safer place for him. But finally Bik had called legal services. Junior was his flesh and blood, and a living memory of Kai and those few glorious years that he'd shared with her.

It turned out that Thor was well connected in the shady cash world, and had gotten an effective advocate. What it was now down to was that Thor's starship would leave in three months, and Bik's government-supplied lawyer had been blunt. Wendt was vulnerable, but just what did Bik have to offer a child beyond a genetic relationship? A sterile apartment and day care while Bik was away being a superfluous supervisor of construction robots smarter than he was?

A tone brought him out of his musings; the oh-three-hundred elevator had departed without taking any stand-

bys. A glance at the overhead showed him the
oh-four-hundred didn't look much better. Standby hope-
fuls were to check in with the attendants.

The original receptionist had said a personal evac unit
might reach Port Tannhauser directly from up here. Not
making any internal commitment just yet, Bik decided to
investigate how a person would get one. Did people really
do that for sport? He pulled out his intellicard and asked
it to get central data.

Bik pursed his lips and stared at the single glass eye in
the wall behind the sport jumping concession counter.
"Lessons?" He hadn't anticipated that kind of delay.

"The sport units are made for manual operation; that's
the sport of it!" the cyberservant answered in clear standard English as its Waldos handed Bik a heavy bag of
gear. "But it is highly advisable that you go through a
virtual simulation and pass the evaluation."

"Highly advisable?"

"You won't be allowed outside the airlock otherwise,
I'm afraid. Now let's go over the equipment inventory.
Aerobrake sled?"

Bik opened the duffelbag and shook his head, "I
don't—"

"It's the heavy transparent pouch," a new, but somehow familiar, voice informed him. He spun around and
saw the elevator attendant. Out of the uniform and in a
skin-tight vacuum suit with bright diagonal slashes, she
looked—not beautiful, he decided, but, well, formidable.
"You strap it on your front side and inflate it on the way
down. You steer by shifting your body. When you get
subsonic, you can pop the tross wing—that's for albatross—and glide forever."

"Uh, thanks. . . ."

She laughed. "Suwon. From the elevator. Look, I said
I'd do what I could. I figured I'd find you here; you

looked like a guy on a mission. Let's go through the rest of this stuff."

It took them the better part of an hour. In addition to the tross wing for long-range gliding, there was an emergency parasail that weighed less than a hundred grams, fluorescent dyes and beacon, a harness that could really chafe if you didn't put it on just right, and various techniques for putting everything on and then getting at all of it.

Then there was the simulator, a virtual reality shell with a harness suspended inside. Despite Suwon talking him through it, he burnt up the first time down, stalled to subsonic way too early the second time, and didn't get the range the third time. On the fourth run he had a survivable burn-through and hit it more or less right on his fifth run.

It was oh eight hundred, and he had to register by sixteen hundred.

"Well, thanks," he told her. "I'm going to give it a try."

"You're going to kill yourself—if not by burning up, by dropping in the ocean so far from anywhere that you'll drown before anything can get to you."

She didn't understand.

"Suwon, I want you to understand, uh, 'grab onto' this. There's a great big hole inside me where there used to be a wife and a son. If there's a chance to get some of that back, I'll take it. And if not, well, a simple clean death would be a welcome end to all of this."

"Crap. I'm coming with you."

"Huh?" Bik stared at her. Why was she trying to become part of his life? Painful memories extinguished a flicker of biological excitement; the last thing he wanted now was another woman in his life. But he couldn't just tell her to get lost, not after all the help she'd given him and not when time was running out. "This is my problem," he said, finally. "I just met you; why should you care?"

She stared back at him and pursed her lips again, as if she were determined not to let another word out until she'd thought it carefully through. "A fair question. You're on a mission, doing something other than just trying to amuse yourself. That's the most excitement I've run across in years. I guess I find that attractive. There's something else. Venus Surface Commission workers aren't eligible for the land rush. The way around that is to team up with someone who is—easier said than done."

"Team up?"

"Eligible partners can transfer a portion of their share to others after fifty years, or enter a joint tenancy arrangement. . . ."

Bik held up his hand. "Okay. Thirty percent of the land if you get me there."

Suwon smiled and shook her head. "Fifty."

Damn, she was easy to look at, once you got used to muscles on a woman. Especially when she smiled. Bik finally nodded to her; he was low on options. "Okay, 50 percent." Bik wasn't a haggler—he'd let Kai have all his Chao property just to avoid fighting her for it. "Let's go, then. What about your boyfriend?"

"He got careless on a jump about a month ago. Burned in. Five hundred and twenty years old and he burned in on a jump." Suwon shrugged her shoulders, but it was clear that she had been hurt.

Maybe she did understand. Bik thought about sympathy, rebound logic, unknown backgrounds, and all the rest of the dangerous stuff and cast it aside mentally. This acquaintance, relationship, whatever it became, would be a calculated risk, one that he was walking into with his eyes open.

"Sorry to hear that." He put his hand on hers, and found it was a muscular, callused, well-used hand that went with the rest of its owner's body. He gave it a firm squeeze and let go.

She gave him a lopsided smile. Clearly, Suwon's approach to a setback was to challenge her fears and throw herself right back at it, immediately, passionately. Without another word, she checked out a personal evacuation unit and inspected it. Then they were ready.

They emerged from the elevator terminal onto a maintenance balcony with a waffle grid floor and a severe functional guardrail. The view stunned Bik. The CMR was a fairyland forest of open trusses made of gray composite beams that somehow became shiny as they seemed to merge into a single ribbon toward the distant horizon. Occasionally a car on one of the upper tracks would silently flash by, pressed upward to the overhead rails by the centrifugal force from its higher-than-orbital velocity. Every so often a track would lift out like a stray fiber in a paintbrush, straightening to a zero gravity trajectory and ending abruptly to wait for an outbound maglev spacecraft.

There were still enough traces of atmosphere here to make the noses of the escaping cars glow as they left these tracks on trajectories leading to the rest of the solar system.

The wide gray band of the CMR railbed dwarfed the elevator tower that helped tether it to the planet. The tower quickly shrank to a barely discernible thread under their perch that connected to a small island that was just barely visible in a vast blue-black sea. There was a trace of a blue-green land mass on the edge of their northern horizon, and a scattering of islands, but these were minor details of a vast cloud-flecked ocean, that, through some trick of perspective, seemed like a concave bowl.

"Chao looks like that, from the dome top, except the water/land ratio is reversed. The dome top's only fifty kilometers up, but you can't tell the scale."

"Surprised you didn't get a piece of that."

"I did. I let her have it, hoping that maybe she'd change her mind. I let her have everything."

"Too proud to fight, huh?" Suwon turned her gold-plated helmet face toward him, and he saw himself against the rising filtered sun, in miniature.

"Something like that." The sun had just risen below them and would take two weeks to reach local noon. Pride? Bik smiled; once Venus had taken the better part of a year to turn on its axis, but a millennium of launching out carbon dioxide frozen from the atmosphere, and volcanic sediment scraped from the low basaltic plains, and two centuries of bringing water in had given it a rotational period of about an Earth month. Human beings and their machines had done that, and Bik couldn't help feeling a little pride. The crust was still adjusting through an abundance of volcanoes and quakes that would be part of Venusian life for something like ten million years, according to most projections. Below, they built for it.

The sun was tiny by Bik's Mercurian standards, and seemed to sparkle inside a broad, off-center ring of diffuse light. This, he realized, was the twenty-four-million-meter sunshield. His engineering imagination saw the vast structure balance gravity with constantly adjusted photon pressure the Lagrange point between Venus and the sun. A sun-sieve now, it let half the light get through to Venus and converted the other half to energy for starship ports and antimatter factories. His eyes saw a ghostly, sparkling disk, visibly larger and nearer than the sun, with edges that caught and reflected light in a grazing incidence that created the effect of the bright ring.

"Finished sightseeing?" Suwon asked, gently.

"I can see why you like living up here."

She laughed. "You should see a gigaton water freighter match cradle vee on the landing track; that's the dark band in the middle. It lets you grab just how astro this operation is. Magnificent! Nothing due in today, though. Let's check the equipment one more time.''

Bik did, then checked Suwon's gear as she checked his.

"Ready. Now, Bik," she continued in a low, stagily seductive voice, "do you ever have fantasies of sacrificing yourself? Being a human bomb for some cause? Letting a lover kill you? Falling on your sword? Taking Joan of Arc's place at the stake?"

Bik couldn't see her eyes, but he imagined that they glowed. Yes, of course he had, but he couldn't bring himself to say so; it wasn't the sort of thing one shared in Mercurian society. On an airless planet, suicides sometimes took others with them, and even to fantasize about it where people could hear got a lot more attention than one wanted. Bik shivered.

"Can't admit it, can you? Well, they're normal. Everyone has them, and some day, when I've had enough of this immortal body that our genetic engineers have given me, I think I'm going to do this dive without any equipment. Oh, maybe a pressure suit so I can experience a little more of it—the burning part for instance—but nothing else. I'll just run out and throw myself off and let nature take its course. End my life as a shooting star!"

She straddled the rail, reached and grabbed his hand and laughed demonically. "Like I said, we all have these fantasies . . . and the time to indulge them is now! Come on!"

Almost in a trance, he swung one leg over the rail and then the other and stood on his toes hanging onto the rail, three hundred kilometers above the sea.

Suwon's chest rose and fell with each excited breath. "Now," she shouted, "push off and *die!*" Then she did it, with a bloodcurdling yell, falling rapidly away below him.

Bik craned his neck to see her, and in doing so started to slip. What the hell? Go, something inside said, *do it!*

He pushed hard and was in free fall; the CMR dwindled to a dark ribbon far above him, the Devana Sea waited below. Soon he seemed to stop moving; there was nothing still near enough by which to judge his falling. Suwon's manic laughter filled his helmet. Finally she stopped.

"One hundred fifty kilometers, buddy. Time to get serious."

Below him, a crystalline lady slipper bloomed, tumbling and glinting in the sun. Bik remembered the sled cord and found it. There *was* a temptation not to pull it, to delay a little, to enjoy zero gravity and flirt with that ecstasy of self destruction. He was beginning to get warm.

"Pull the red ring, Bik!" Suwon shouted. He jerked it open automatically, and quickly found himself surrounded by a huge, triangular, transparent pillow. It pressed against him gently in the tenuous slipstream, turning and righting itself so that he lay prone. It began to vibrate slightly as the pressure gradually began to increase, and he could hear a low, eerie moan.

"I'm over here," Suwon called. "Shift your weight left."

He leaned left, and the transparent lifting body began a long, steady curve in that direction. "I'm going to wiggle a little," Suwon said. "Do you see me?"

Bik scanned ahead, right and left, and saw nothing.

"You're below me a bit, but right behind me now. Shift your weight right a bit, then steady."

He did it. "Okay."

"Now look up."

Far, far ahead of him in the vast black distance above the thin glowing band of atmosphere, he caught a sparkle. He stared at it for several seconds, then began to pick out the transparent envelope and the tiny white figure inside. The front of the envelope had begun to glow.

"I found you."

"Good. Now we're going to have to do things together

as much as possible. We're building up a fair amount of northward velocity, but we need more, so I'm going to dive a bit. Follow me by shifting your weight forward, but be ready to shift back when I do. We don't want to get too hot.''

"Okay."

She started to pull ahead, and he pulled himself forward on the handholds. He shot forward, passing her underneath. In a near panic, he pushed himself back again.

"Whoa. Hold it right there. I'll catch up," she said, and scooted smoothly back into view above and in front of him. "Now edge forward just a bit. There. Hold that."

He was back at full weight again and there was a definite, diffuse glow in front of him.

"Your boyfriend. Are you sure it was an accident?"

Silence.

He waited.

Finally she answered, in measured tones. "No. But I think so; I mean there was no note to grab or anything. That's a pretty drastic way of breaking up and I don't think I'm that scary. But you can never be sure with people. Let's change the subject, huh?"

It really wasn't any of his business. "This must be spectacular at night," he finally remarked.

"Yeah. When I go, it'll be at night. I'll become a comet, a Valkyrie pyre in the sky. It'll burn the guilt right out of me."

"You sound like you're looking forward to it."

"I am . . ." She laughed ". . . in a thousand years or so. The anticipation will keep me going. Right now, we're down to thirty kilometers and it's time to back off a bit. Edge back just a little, bring your nose up. We've got another thousand klicks to go. Okay. Now a little more. Okay."

"Optimum glide path?" he asked. He knew she was linked to the terminal computer and had everything calculated to the nth degree, but he wanted the reassurance. The ocean was very big and blue below him.

"Feels right," she responded. "I think we hit it pretty good."

"What's the range projection?" he inquired.

"Range projection?" She laughed. "We just go as far as we can. Never tried to make Beta Regio from the elevator head before."

He began to have a sinking feeling. "What do the cybes say?"

"Cybes? Grab this, Bik. We're out of contact—on our own. These radios are only good for a few kilometers unless we're talking to a big directional antenna. Frequency management. This is strictly by feel from here on; that's the fun of it. Besides, the last few hundred kilometers all depend on air currents, and that's weather. No telling. Hold on there, you're shifting your weight. Shift forward again, just a little and catch up. You really have to watch body position."

Bik got Suwon in sight again and kept her there. Silently. Any fantasies about casting himself into oblivion were long ago and far away. Now, he was very, very scared. And excited—he understood why people did this—to challenge real danger, with their own muscles, reflexes, and brains, without relying on some cybernetic safety net. It would be a great feeling, if you survived. And maybe, even, in the last moments, if you didn't.

"Bik, do you know an asshole by the name of Deccar Brunt?"

A chill colder than anything his suit could fix went through Bik. "Too well. He's a lawyer working for the space jock that took Kai—my ex. Brunt is hellishly well connected and thinks that I'm some kind of monster. He's determined to keep Junior away from me. How'd you run into him?"

"He came asking questions after I put you in the computer for an elevator cab reservation. I'd say he didn't want you to get down to the surface—thought I was working too hard on your behalf. You say you had problems getting on the transport here in the first place?''

Of course, Bik thought. "Yes. What did he offer?''

"He hinted that he could do things for me if I didn't help you. Not clearly enough for me to hand him to the cybes, but clearly enough. Look, is there money involved in this?'' Her voice showed she shared his contempt for the stuff, Bik thought. With robot factories all through the solar system, manufactured things were either free or not allowed. Scarce necessities, such as habitable land or electromagnetic frequencies, were allocated fairly by need or lot. Money, he felt, was a game for people who wanted things they'd be better off without, but for which they were willing to trade.

"Kai liked having the stuff. She'd trade, uh, favors, for it. It was a game to her—but I think that's how she met Thor.'' It was appropriate, in a way—as legend went, the underground "economy'' had started within months of the official elimination of money when some enterprising prostitute had started issuing promissory notes. Since money proved impossible to repress and didn't threaten anyone's welfare, the governments, cybes, and Bik generally ignored it. When he could.

Bik's sled started to vibrate and hum with ever-increasing loudness, matching his mood. Why, Kai? "Why?''

"Going transsonic. Just stay centered and ride through; you're inherently stable. Bik, you put up with all that?'' She meant Kai's adventures, he realized—smiling at the metaphorical coincidence.

"I didn't own her, I was away a lot, and up until she left, things were fine, uh, more than fine.''

"Sounds like a good actress. So she had money, and your rights in that dome on Mercury, and Bikki. Now this

Thor has it all and wants to keep it all. Some big male thing with him, I bet. But how the hell can he threaten me?''

Bik felt miserable. ''He's got an ethics problem, I think. Smart, competent, used to having his own way. Big stud, except he's never been given a repro permit. As for threats, all it takes is having someone on a board or having some authority that wants something money can buy. Maybe one of your bosses.''

''Crap.'' The bitterness in Suwon's voice was understandable; real jobs were scarce and hers was in jeopardy. ''Well, I didn't listen to it. Just made me want to help you. Hey, grab on, we're subsonic, down to thirty kilometers, beginning to lose lift. Time to pop the wings. Orange ring, on three. Ready?''

''Ready.''

''One . . . two . . . Now.''

He pulled and his translucent white wings, astoundingly long and thin, rolled out of his backpack to the sides and a long, stiff tube with a triangular duct canard shot out in front of him, bent alarmingly, and began to vibrate like a bassoon reed.

''What—'' He was really shaking. The sims hadn't been like this.

''Bistable polymorphon. Sometimes takes a second to lock into its deployed shape. Don't worry, you look good.''

As if at Suwon's command, the loud hum quickly softened to a gentle whoosh as he accelerated upward with breathtaking force. He remembered to shift forward to lower his angle of attack before he lost too much air speed, and saw the canard structure bend down slightly as he did it; its smart materials almost anticipated what he wanted to do. When he got himself straightened out, he searched for Suwon.

''I'm pretty far ahead and above you,'' she called out,

as if reading his mind. "Deflate your lifting body now. It will remember its folds and repack itself. That will cut your drag."

"How?" he asked.

"Green ring on your chest; Venturi suction tube. Keep pulling until it's in."

He did so, and felt his airspeed increase as the transparent envelope collapsed into a stiff aerodynamic sled. When he caught up to Suwon, she did the same and made an S-turn to take station off his right wing.

"We're a couple of kilometers lower than I'd like to be for the range we need, but with some luck on the air currents, we'll make it. Just now, you need to practice gliding. We're heading for the shadow line."

By fifteen hundred, they'd passed into night. Earth and its L1 sunshield lit the sky like a close pair of distant arc lights, glinting off waves that were getting entirely too close. But they had reached the archipelago; here and there a single light or campfire showed where people had already spread to the islands.

Suwon caught an updraft on the windward side of a ghostly volcanic island and slipped off to the east to avoid the trailing downdraft. The couple of kilometers they gained helped them almost reach the next island, but that was all. It was a long, faint green wall on the horizon, with what looked to be a geodesic dome glowing from inside lights on the east end.

"We're going in," Suwon said. "Reinflate your entry sled."

"Huh?"

"Now. It'll float. Your wings are buoyant, too, and will help keep you upright. Watch me." She shot ahead of him in a shallow dive, squandering her remaining energy.

"I flare—" She seemed to hang in the air over the dark sparkling waves like some ghostly albatross. "—inflate and drop in. Now you do it. Use the red ring."

He'd gotten used to following her instructions and did it, but it was easier watched than done. Bik stalled before he got the sled inflated again, dropped through the waves and popped up again with water spilling from the top of the sled. It was embarrassing, but since he was still in his vacuum suit, he didn't get wet. The water was quite warm.

"You all right?" Suwon called. Her voice seemed tinny and distant, and it took him a couple of seconds to realize that he was hearing her acoustically, instead of on radio. He looked around and found her helmet flashing about thirty meters to his left; their wingtip beacons were almost touching.

He opened his faceplate and took a deep breath of sea air. Childhood memories. He'd been five when his father had taken him on a walk by the sea near their home in Victoria, B.C., and told him that, sometimes, people can't live together anymore, and that he would be going away. Did Bik know the way home? Bik had nodded yes. His father had nodded gravely, turned, and walked away. Forever.

"Bik?"

"All right physically. Feeling a little silly and disappointed. I suppose it was worth the shot. Great fun, anyway. Haven't smelled the sea since I was a kid."

"You've still got a couple of hours to register."

"But we've got to be a couple of hundred kilometers short of Port Tannhauser."

"There's a homesite on this island in front of us."

"The dome?"

"You grabbed it. That's Mabel Beautaux's place; Mabel and I go way back."

"I thought this wasn't open to settlement yet."

"It's an old terraforming station; she's been squatting since oxygen hit 15 percent. She probably got to be first in line to register it when they opened up."

"Does she have transportation?"

"Float plane—she'll be out to pick us up in a bit."

"Huh?"

Suwon pointed to her head and smiled. "My brain is part radio, remember? We're in range."

"You knew all along; you were just letting me suffer!"

Suwon laughed and Bik reached down to try to splash her, but he almost fell out of his makeshift raft and found himself teetering on his stomach, getting his face wet with every wave. The situation was so ridiculous that when he finally wriggled himself back to safety, he had to laugh, too.

They were both laughing when the graceful W-shaped aircraft settled into the waves beside them.

Mabel Beautaux turned out to be a tiny, almost elfin, woman with a discernible African heritage and soft bird-like voice. She seemed to have stopped growing in her early teens, but her archaic name made Bik think she might go back to the early days of the terraforming project.

He was not, however, quite prepared for how *far* back she went. As they tied the lines of the aircraft to a simple wooden dock, he asked when she was born.

"In 1993. I was 135 when the geriatric retrovirus came along; there are only a couple of dozen others that are older. Most of my life, I've been a farmer; in Alabama the first century or so, Peary dome on Luna after I got my treatment and degree, then I came here and helped manage the bioforming project, from right after they let the sun back through, 'bout two hundred years ago.

"What a ride that was! Storms and quakes! Populations of this, that, and the other critter breeding out of control! I worked on fertility retroviruses, and we had a devil of a time playing God, I tell you." She grinned and shrugged her shoulders. "Now everything's so settled down they can start giving the land away to whoever comes along. But that's why we did it, isn't it? So there!" She hitched the plane's nose line to a dock cleat. "You're dealing with a living fossil in her third millennium!"

"A very beautiful one," Bik gushed, clumsy with awe.

"Oh? Well, now, gravity is good for the bones, and I do a fair amount of physical work around here." She waved a hand at a tidy wood building next to the geodesic dome station building and a clear field surrounded by palms and eucalyptus. There were three—cows. Not obviously penned, just standing there munching grass. One of them looked at him suspiciously just as Mabel asked "Got any idea of where you two want to settle?"

"We're not . . ." Bik stammered. Would a cow charge, like in a bullfight? Was there something he should do, or shouldn't? He wasn't wearing red. "I mean we just met today. Business arrangement."

"Oh? Well, let's see what's available for you to claim. I'll slice some chicken squash, and if you'll grab a few of those tomatoes, Suwon, we can have some sandwiches while we figure it out. We can wash that down with some of my peach wine and then I'll fly you over to Port Tannhauser to register."

Suwon gave Mabel a hug and went to work. Bik, who'd never seen a meal prepared, let alone by human hands, stood around helpless and fascinated. After a feast that somehow tasted better than any home appliance or restaurant had ever given him, Mabel's computer started to print the latest claim maps. With the maps, however, came a news item that gave Mabel a hard frown.

"You didn't tell me they fired you, Suwon."

"What!" Suwon was clearly shocked.

"Says here that the settlement board is taking under advisement the status of people who get transportation outside normal channels and those who aid them. Mentions you in particular, Bik—and cites you for showing unprofessional favoritism, Suwon."

"But that's nonsense," Suwon protested. "And anyone

with guts enough can dive from the CMR! Nothing wrong with that. What do the cybes say?''

Mabel held up her hand for a moment and concentrated. ''They say no settlement rules were broken, but fairness issues are a human judgment call.'' Her brow wrinkled. ''By the time they get a committee to debate that, it will be too late even if you win! I'd say someone clever is out to get you, Bik. But why you, Suwon?''

''I was warned.'' Suwon shook her head, more angry than afraid. ''By a lawyer working for someone trying to keep Bik from getting his kid back. *He* tried to bribe *me!* Mabel, this is outrageous.''

Mabel was muttering under her breath.

No, Bik realized, she was subvocalizing to another built-in radio link.

She smiled at Bik's stare. ''This old body's been through so many updates, what was one more? When Suwon showed me her radio a few years back, well, I had to have one, too. Comes in handy when your hands are busy milking cows!'' She didn't quite giggle, but she was clearly amused by her joke. ''Now, I've been around a while and I know a few people too. I've got them injuncted by the cybes from doing anything worse until after the rush. Anything legal, that is. Let's look at the map. You get three choices. Let's see what you want.''

The intelliprint was linked and the colors on the map of the archipelago changed as they watched, white areas growing pink as they filled with tiny red rectangles. The red signified a claimed parcel.

''Everything near Port Tannhauser has been grabbed,'' Suwon observed.

''Then we'd best get over there.'' Mabel raised an eyebrow. ''But first, let's look at this area.''

She put her finger on the east end of the archipelago and the map expanded in scale to reveal a dozen tiny islands, all white. ''Here's where we are now.'' Mabel's island was the first offshore peak of the range running south from Port Tannhauser, separated from the mainland of Beta Regio by a narrow strait. She moved her finger west toward Asteria Regio. "A polar current comes down this way and wells up between Beta and Asteria." She grinned at them. "Some of it gets over to us, bringing some fog. But the effects are much more pronounced over there. There'll be good fishing and lots of moisture near the coast with a north wind, but clear and sunny when it comes the other way." She pointed to a small group of numbered islands. "Any of these 12-300's should do."

Bik looked at his "partner" and Suwon nodded.

"Let's go, then," he said.

Port Tannhauser was a controlled riot, its sleepy streets filled with people. They had to anchor Mabel's seaplane well out in the harbor and raft in. Fortunately, once the cybes confirmed that they were physically present, they were eligible to register their choices at a public terminal.

Just in time, it turned out. There were still a couple of hours to go for registration, but when they unfolded the map, the entire area was red with claimants except for a pink fringe that included the western islands.

"We'll see the sights, have dinner at the Crab House and fly back to spend the night at my place, and fly out there early next morning."

"Uh," Bik asked, "why not just go there directly? Your place is in the opposite direction. All I have to do is touch down and leave an occupancy marker. Then you could leave me at the air terminal on the way back. I wouldn't have to impose."

Suwon looked at the ground, her lips tight. Did she, Bik wondered, have something else in mind for the night? Did she think he was out of line for suggesting something other than what Mabel had suggested? Was she just momentarily tired? Damn his inability to read people—the

cybes should outlaw nonverbal communication. But, he
thought ruefully, any experienced cybe could probably do
better than he did. Kai had complained, gently at first,
then with increasing sarcasm and severity, about his lack
of sensitivity to her needs. She'd had a point—something
always seemed to be going on among other people, some
form of communication, that excluded him. But he
couldn't help it; all he had to go on, really, was what
people's words meant; the rest was just too uncertain.

"I have to get back too," Mabel declared, and smiled
at him. "Don't forget, I have to claim my place as well.
I was allowed to preregister the claim, but that's all."

"Oh," Bik responded, relieved to have some clear priority, "in that case, I look forward to it."

Suwon looked up and smiled at him. He returned an
embarrassed grin, still uncertain.

On the way back from registration, they visited a small
museum in the northern section of Port Tannhauser, an
easy hike up from the harbor on the randomly corrugated
fused sand walkway. The buildings along the way were
preciously eclectic, many showing an old German influence to be sure, but really products of their owners' fantasies. The exterior of the museum itself was carefully
authentic, and wouldn't have been out of place in six-
teenth century Heidelberg.

Inside, Bik, Suwon, and Mabel browsed through holographic dioramas of Port Tannhauser during the various
stages of the terraforming project. The first showed the
hellish original surface, and almost glowed. Then came a
dark fairyland of carbon dioxide snow. This was followed
by a glacier being eaten away by massive excavators on
the edge of a starlit liquid nitrogen sea with the arc of the
CMR on the horizon. Then came a dramatic stormswept
boiling-nitrogen seascape lit by the first rays of the sun
allowed through the sunshield. The sight made him shiver.
It was followed by a dry desert overlooking a deep empty

basin speckled with mining robots. There was another, gentler, storm scene from early in the forty years of rain, showing the half-filled basins and massive waterfalls. Then finally a fuzzy, meadow-like shore covered with the first bioforming grasses.

There were artifacts as well, ranging from a broken pair of recreational skis used by scientists monitoring the carbon dioxide snowfall eight hundred years ago, to a comet shepherd child's duck. That had somehow survived the entry and breakup of a water shipment to be discovered floating on the Port Tannhauser beach. It sat on the museum shelf with a picture of its former owner, now living on a ring colony in the Kuiper belt of the Kruger 60 system.

Bik, who had only been looking for a home to share with his son, left with a sense of his chance to become part of the history of a new world. To look back over the past twelve hundred years let him see the next twelve hundred, or twelve thousand, more clearly. He could be in at the beginning and contribute his name to legend. It was a chance that few understood, an opportunity that fewer grabbed. Thinking like Suwon, now, he thought wryly. How could someone so completely overwhelm him in less than a day? Yet it was the second time. A second chance.

Only an hour remained of the registration period when they returned to the seaside and ordered dinner. The light-ringed harbor, except for Mabel's plane, was deserted; everyone had headed out to their claims to be there at the start of the homesteading window.

They were well into some fairly tasty hand-made *Crabe Asteria* when they heard what sounded like a muffled thunderclap. They looked out the restaurant window to the harbor, now lit by a bright orange flame climbing up from its center.

"My plane!" Mabel cried.

Bik was on his feet and out the door, meaning to grab a fire extinguisher and swim for it. But the local anti-fire utility had what remained of the plane covered in foam by the time he got to the water's edge. Mabel and Suwon were right behind him.

Mabel looked grim. "Repro and shipment say it will take three days to replace the plane; too much in the queue just now with all the new settlers. I'm . . . This is outrageous!"

"Maybe we can borrow a maintenance vehicle?" Bik hazarded.

Suwon concentrated, then shook her head. "Everything that can be borrowed has been borrowed. They've only got the minimum needed for emergencies. Like that." She gestured to the flames.

They stood silently for a minute trying to absorb the disaster. To have come so far, Bik thought, and then this. He was sure the lawyers had something to do with it— what could they do with money, he wondered, that made it worth doing this to someone to get it?

"I'm sorry, Mabel," he choked out. "Your homestead . . . If it hadn't been for me they wouldn't have done this. And Bikki . . . I feel like. . . ."

"They aren't going to get away with it," she declared, her voice a calm, cheerful bell against the gloom. "I've already filed a protest saying who I think did it and why. I'll get my land, and you'll get yours." Mabel pursed her lips. "But not before Wendt has your kid on the way to Kalinda station! You think a nice home environment with plenty of elbow room will make that much difference to a custody board?"

"There's no telling what a human board will do, but I'm told it will help a lot."

"Well, then," Mabel said, "we have a long hike ahead of us."

Bik's Mercury conditioned feet and muscles suddenly remembered where they were. "Hike?"

"First to the land registration office. It's open for another fifteen minutes."

There was a human clerk there, a very tall, dark-skinned woman in a simple blue robe with a bemused smile on her face. She clearly knew Mabel, but simply took Mabel's hand by way of greeting; the difference in their heights would have made an embrace embarrassing for both of them.

"Hi Mabel! Good to see you, but I don't think I can help anyone. Everything's gone and there's no transportation anyway. People have to be on the property when the sun rises here, in about twenty-five hours."

"Kris. I know. I want to open my island up to registration. Abandon my priority."

Suwon sucked in a breath and Kris' eyes went wide.

"But . . . whatever you say. It's going to come out as two parcels."

"Right. Register me for the one with the old station, and Bik Wu, here, for the rest of it. See if you can wriggle the dividing line down to the north beach."

Kris concentrated a moment. "You've got it." She handed an intelliprint to Mabel that showed the division. "But how are you going to get there?"

"Dawn on Venus," Mabel declared, "is low tide. The strait narrows down to a shallow only a couple of kilometers across. We're going to hike a dozen kilometers over the hills to South Point, and then swim."

Bik's mouth dropped, and he might have collapsed if Suwon hadn't put her arm around him.

The ground trail was easy, the gravity was not. Bik pushed himself until his legs gave out about five kilometers from the coast and he could not stand up. Suwon and Mabel cut down a couple of small trees with the emergency knife in Suwon's jump belt. Then they made a travois hammock from their clothes. Bik's jump tights formed the makeshift harness for Suwon and Mabel to use to put the weight of the travois on their shoulders. Mabel donated her green jumpsuit to tie the bottoms of the poles so that they wouldn't spread apart more than the path width.

Bik was intrigued to find the women were wearing simple, functional white support halters under their shifts. In Mercury's lower gravity, most women didn't bother with support garments, and instead used their bodies to display all kinds of rings, tattoos, and other decorations. But the Venusian women's bodies were completely bare of any decoration, and Suwon seemed to find Bik's own utilitarian nipple rings an item of amusement. His intellicard hung from one and a holo of Junior on his second birthday from the other. But he was much too exhausted to care about differing aesthetics as he dragged himself onto the rig.

They pulled him for two kilometers to the crest of the trail before he told them to stop.

"It's downhill now. Let me try walking again," he suggested. "I can use the poles as walking sticks. They can support my arms and let me use my arm muscles to help support the rest of me. You can have your clothes back. It's getting cold." With a light western breeze, it was getting about as chilly as it got in the Venusian tropical lowlands.

"That's because you've been lying on your back for an hour!" Suwon objected. "I'm sweating."

"I'll take mine, thank you," Mabel said. "I'm a lot smaller and lose heat faster."

Bik grabbed a branch hanging over the path and carefully stood up again. His knees burned and feet ached, but otherwise he simply felt tired.

They disassembled the travois and cut a meter from its

poles. Bik took one in each hand and started out again, half hanging on, half pushing with the poles, while Mabel shrugged into her jumpsuit. Suwon tied the other two jumpsuits together and draped them over her neck. The women quickly caught up to him, but walked behind, letting him set the pace.

Bik's calves ached on the verge of cramping with each step, but he forced himself to a slow, regular pace, somewhat like a cross-country skier in slow motion. Very slow. Less, he thought, than half a kilometer an hour. Would it be enough? The exertion made him sweat profusely and the waistband of his shorts was beginning to chafe. He was miserable, but he had to continue. Everything was at stake.

After an eternity of pain, they reached the shoreline and he sprawled in the cool sand. They had a clear view of the western horizon, and it was already a brilliant orange: only Earth and Mercury were still visible in the brightening sky.

Suwon came over to him, stripped for the swim. She laughed, a bit self-consciously. "Curious?"

"Oh. Uh, didn't mean to stare. The fashion on Mercury is to have all sorts of things—" He self-consciously unclipped his intellicard from its ring. "—dyed or clipped on your body. There's nothing there but, well, you. You're very—bare."

"I like it that way, at least for swimming. Come on, give me your stuff. I'll stash it under a rock and we'll pick it up later. If you think those shorts were chafing on the hike, wait until you see what a couple of hours in salt water do."

After all this, could he swim for two hours? He was mentally exhausted from fighting unaccustomed aches and pains, but his wind was holding up well and now that he was off his feet, he seemed to be reviving. In the water, gravity wouldn't matter. Anyway, he had no choice. He

removed what remained of his clothes and gave them to
Suwon, who bundled them up with hers and Mabel's and
put them under a big rock in from the shoreline.

Mabel, looking more like some ethereal bronzed nymph
than a grown woman, took one side of him and Suwon
the other as they waded into the gentle surf. It was cold
to start with, but getting rid of his weight seemed to restore his energy. He established a smooth crawl at about
two seconds a stroke, breathing on every other left arm,
a pace which felt well within his capabilities.

The women easily matched him.

A hundred meters later he tired and switched to a back
stroke.

Mabel glided by him effortlessly, leaving no wake that
Bik could see.

Suwon pulled up to him with an easy side stroke. "I
know that feels like a rest, but you should get back to
your crawl as soon as you can. It's a much more efficient
distance-eater. Vary your pace, if you have to, but keep
going."

Bik nodded and resumed, one hand over another,
breathing every time now. It went on and on. The shore
behind them receded but the island shore seemed to get
no closer. Stroke, breathe, stroke.

A few minutes or an eternity later he faltered to a breast
stroke, just enough to keep his feet up.

"Look," Suwon called. "The sunshield rim!"

On the crest of the next wave, Bik saw it: a tiny golden
arc over the wavetops.

"Then we've lost," he croaked. It was all for nothing.
Mabel would lose her homestead, he would lose his son,
Suwon would lose her chance for land on which to settle
down.

"Come on!" Mabel shouted from ahead, her musical
voice carrying clearly over the waves. Then she added in
short phrases between breaths: "We're on the west side

of the time zone. And we're seeing it early. It's really below the horizon. Because of refraction. Venus only rotates at about, uh, four-tenths of a degree an hour. Astronomical sunrise isn't for another hour yet. We can still make it. Come on, keep stroking.''

With renewed desperation, Bik plunged ahead. His arms, he told himself, weren't nearly as tired as the rest of him. Ahead, Suwon was fighting her own battle, silently maintaining the pace she had started, not looking anywhere but ahead at the still-distant dark shore of the island.

Bik heard the buzz of a fan skimmer, but he didn't see where. Then, so quickly he had no time to think, it was coming right at him, out of the gloom of the island shore, skimming the wave tops. Instinctively he ducked underwater as it roared over him.

That was it, he thought as he surfaced. If they were going to do that to him, he was done. He had no strength left. No energy. There was maybe one thing he could do, though.

''Mabel!'' He shouted, took a stroke, and caught a breath. ''They want me. Go on. Get your land. I'll keep them busy. They can't stop all of us.''

He saw the skimmer this time—a blur to his wet, unfocused eyes—as it looped around to come at him again. With a supreme effort, he waved a fist at them and resumed his crawl. He looked left and right and couldn't see the women—underwater, he hoped. Okay, bastards, he thought as the fan skimmer grew in front of him. Do your worst. I'm not stopping. I'm not ducking. Too damn tired.

Off to his right, something came up out of the waves, high up. He couldn't see it clearly; a head on two necks? It bent back, whipped forward and its ''head'' flew off toward him. Then his vision cleared some and in this instant he saw it was a large rock, and standing on the water was . . . but the skimmer was on him and despite himself he ducked deep and heard a solid tick as the rock bounced off the skimmer and slammed into the water somewhere behind him.

What he thought he had seen was a woman standing high on the waves silhouetted against the rising sun, proud and triumphant like the goddess Venus herself.

He surfaced, exhausted, barely able to float, and glanced behind him as he gasped for air. The fan skimmer, its hum wavering now, was heading away, not coming back.

"Bik!" Suwon called. "Put your legs down! We're here!"

He rolled, put his feet down, and looked toward her voice, toward the sun. To his surprise there was sand barely a meter under him. Suwon was standing on the sea off to his right, about ankle deep. She was, his numb mind finally realized, on a higher part of the sand bar.

"Grab this! I hit them!" she shouted, gleeful. "I threw a big rock behind you with both hands. When you ducked, they nosed down right into it!"

Bik looked toward the island, dazed. It was there. Close by. He couldn't remember it getting so close. He caught his breath in great gasps. It was all he could do to stand on the shallow bar, even with the fortunately calm water helping, but if he didn't try to move, he was okay. The sun was clearly up now, huge on the horizon, shining through the sunshield with its rim just touching the lower rim of the sunshield, and both just touching the horizon.

"We made it," Mabel called from the beach. "I've reported us in, and they'll give you credit for getting on the bar. Less legal mess that way. You've got land."

Suwon splashed down the slope of the bar to him, and with her help Bik found the strength to wade ashore. Then he collapsed on the cool sand of the beach.

"Do you think it will be enough?" Mabel asked as he caught his breath.

Bik managed a weak shrug. "I hope so."

It took him a dozen seconds to say anything else. "At least Junior will know I tried." Breathe. "That might be important to him someday. I did everything I could."

"What about getting a wife?" The gleam in Mabel's eyes belied the innocent tone of her voice.

"Mabel! I found him first!" Suwon protested, then stared open-mouthed.

"That's quite all right, dear. I have a half-dozen perfectly good relationships going."

"Why you old—matchmaker. You tricked me!"

Mabel laughed and turned to Bik with a sly grin. "Well, what about it, Bik? Take a chance on her? I've known her for thirty years, which isn't much these days, but that's all she's got. You couldn't do any better."

Bik shook his head and stared at the sea. She was too much like Kai, he told himself: too wild and spontaneous. She was someone who jumped off three-hundred-kilometer bridges for fun: someone who probably had a wrong take on him, because, once, scared to death and for something that mattered more to him than his own life, he had jumped with her. She was someone who was willing to risk a putative eternity with someone she knew less than twenty-four hours just to accomplish a goal, to complete a mission. No way, except . . . except that, with the board, it might work. And if he were really committed, he'd do everything.

"How about an engagement?" he asked. "Give us six months to get to know each other?"

"That sounds very reasonable." Mabel shook her head. "But I'm sure Mr. Wendt's lawyers will point out that if you call it off, it will be too late to give Bik, junior, back to the starship captain. I'd say they'll want to see at least a twenty-year contract. Suwon, dear, are you really sure?"

"Hell, no. If I were, it wouldn't be so exciting. Grab this, Mabel, Bik. Nothing's certain. It all depends on initial conditions, chance, and how you play it—like a jump. But I like the weather."

"Well," Mabel added, "in the old days, a lot of good marriages started when the parents matched you with someone you'd never seen before. Other people dated for a decade, lived together, got married and still broke up. Only question is if you're committed to it long enough to raise Bikki. There are some things, Suwon, that people have to *make* certain."

Suwon sat beside him, her bare arm and thigh burning against his. "You can count on me, Bik."

He could almost feel her purr. Talk about leaping into space!

In his mind, Bik could hear Kai laughing at her. You'll never get to first base with that wimp, his ex would have said to Suwon. For the first time, Bik found himself a little angry with his mental image of Kai, and it dawned on him that Kai perhaps had not really been such an exemplar of womanhood, that their split had not necessarily been all his fault, and that what she would have said about Suwon shouldn't really be his measure of things.

Bik set his jaw and reached for Suwon's firm, callused, hand. She was not Kai. Her whole body, her attitude, was different from Kai's, and maybe better. She did wild things, and thought wild thoughts, true, but, unlike Kai, there was nothing flaky about how she did them. Suwon seemed competent and responsible. And she dared to take responsibility.

His thoughts were interrupted as she wrapped her arms around him and kissed him on the lips, and seemed to melt into him. He kissed back, tentatively at first, then with increasing warmth. Despite his tiredness, his body started to respond.

Mabel cleared her throat, Bik released Suwon, and they

all laughed. But strangely, he felt no real embarrassment, nor urgency either. Everything felt very easy and natural. It would be like that with Suwon, he realized—just fun. With Kai there had always been tension, a performance, an evaluation, something to live up to.

Bik shook his head, sighed, and looked at Mabel. "Can we just register the contract?" he asked. "At least that's how we did it on Mercury."

Mabel nodded. "I'll send it in and witness it. There, I've bent-piped my audio to the registrar; it hears what I hear. Do you two want a twenty-year marriage contract? Bik?"

He took a breath and let go for the second time today. "Yes."

"Suwon?"

"Yes."

"Congratulations! May I kiss the groom?"

"Wait until I'm done," Suwon objected, and launched another round of physical affection, including Mabel this time. Bik felt embarrassed at first, but that passed into simple goodness.

The next morning, universal time, Bik sat in Mabel's dome wearing a beach towel as a sort of ersatz sarong, looking at the iron-gray crew cut and steel cold blue eyes of lawyer Deccar Brunt. "We did not anticipate such resolve on your part, Mr. Wu. As your lawyers, and the cybernetic advisors have undoubtedly told you by now, you are in a commanding position from a legal standpoint."

Bik wondered if Brunt had bribed someone to monitor his calls. It didn't matter. The cybes had traced the attack and Mabel's friends had turned a few screws of their own. Bik simply nodded. Yes, his being married now, and having a rich, open environment in which to raise Junior was one plus. But the opposition's tactics, starting from witholding his messages and presents, and running right through the attempts to interfere with his getting the homestead were now all faithfully recorded and arrayed against them. It would be, everyone conceded, an open and shut custody board decision.

"However," the attorney continued, no trace of caring in his voice, "Captain Wendt would like to plead to you in the child's interest."

"He's here?"

The attorney nodded. "Your bimbo almost killed him with a rock while he was driving, perfectly legally, well over your head, after his inspection of this jungle to which you want to take Ted."

It made sense—Wendt was too smart to risk a conspiracy; he'd do his own dirty work. Bik squirmed momentarily at the mention of the name Wendt had given Junior. Suwon, who had managed to fit tightly into a loose shift of Mabel's, put a hand on Bik's shoulder. There was no point in working themselves up by arguing with a professional liar.

But Suwon tensed suddenly. "Then Bikki's here too! Wendt wouldn't have dared to leave Bikki two months away in the asteroid belt if he expected to win a custody battle!"

"Yes, *Ted* is here," Brunt said, his voice grating at the interruption. "Perhaps you should first listen to what he has to say."

A young male child's image appeared in the holo stage. A legend assured them it was a faithful recording of a board interview with "Ted Wendt." The boy seemed relaxed and polite, gave his name as Ted Wendt, and declared that he did not want to go to live with "Mr. Wu."

That image was replaced by a picture of a genial, fit man in a starship captain's coveralls.

"Well, Mr. Wu, we appear to have had some misunderstandings—"

Bik dismissed this with a gesture.

"I really don't mean you or your new wife any harm, however, if you really care for this young man—" the field expanded to include Junior, sitting quietly in a comfortable chair behind Wendt, staring at the floor "—you need to consider his view of this. I recognize that you might feel that what we did in restricting communications to keep his identity straight was a little unfair to you, but that's all by the by. *Fait accompli*. You have to deal with the situation as it is, however unfair.

"You could win this legally with the cybe's evidence. I'll concede that. But that would devastate my son. The fact is that I'm the only father he's known; Ted was only three when your marriage ended and you left his life. It's the reality he knows that counts. Please consider his interests. If you really want a child, have another one."

Bik shifted uncomfortably. However unfair the situation, the argument made too much sense.

"He's never been on a high-gravity planet," Wendt continued. "He wants to go out on starships with me and see the rest of the universe, not be stuck on some artificial hot-house garden world. It's not fair to take him from the only father he's ever known, especially in view of his mother's recent death. I suppose this doesn't mean anything to you, but I loved Kai, and he's all I have left of her."

Suwon touched Bik's arm and looked wide-eyed at him. "No, no, it's not," she whispered. then turned to Mabel. Something went between them.

Mabel concentrated, then her eyes went wide. "The inheritance. Kai left it all to Bikki!"

Bik took a breath. Had there been some good in Kai after all, something that had been worth his love? Some mothering instinct that had put her son ahead of her selfishness? But that tainted money didn't matter now, nor did the property rights. All that mattered was—damn, what did matter?

Wendt appeared not to hear anything and made a helpless, open-handed gesture. "I don't have a legal leg to stand on, I know it. So I'm pleading with you. Don't ruin two lives, Ted's and mine, just to get back at Kai for going off with me. She's dead now. Gone. Please just let us be."

Bik stared at the floor. If . . . if they'd made their appeal that way in the first place.

"I," he began, then hesitated. "I don't want to hurt anyone. . . ."

Suwon's hand clamped on Bik's shoulder like a vice. "Don't you dare give in," she whispered. "I grab that recording's a morph, at least the audio, fake as hell. Otherwise we would have got it realtime." Then she said, loud, "Can he see us, Wendt? Can he hear us?"

Bik looked up. Wendt made a nervous gesture to someone offstage and moved his lips. The sound didn't come through. The boy nodded slightly and stared at the floor again.

"Wu," Wendt pleaded, "you heard the recording; he doesn't want to go. I'm sure he remembers what to say. Why put him through that?"

"I'll bet Brunt gets to manage the estate while they're gone," Mabel whispered. "Bik, it stinks."

"I know," he whispered back. "But does that justify hurting my kid?"

"Bik, he'll understand," Suwon pleaded. "Trust me."

Another leap, Bik told himself, and you're still alive after the first two. If Junior didn't remember, it was all over, he'd look ridiculous and prove Wendt was right; that his custody fight would just be ruining lives for his own self-gratification. But no one who had pulled the crap Wendt had pulled could be that good a father, and some memories go way back. At the very least Bikki needed to know he hadn't been abandoned; to know that Bik cared and always had cared. Bik decided to take the leap.

"Bikki," Bik said.

The boy looked up, through the holoviewer, at Bik, and expressions of recognition, confusion, and wonder crossed his young face.

"Daddy?"

In that one word, Bik saw a future unfold before him. A wife, a son to raise, and maybe a daughter. A huge rambling house with lanais all around and a pool leading right to the ocean. Friends. But space to be alone, too. Fishing trips. Bik, junior, would grow up here, maybe go to the stars and come back with kids of his own in a century or two. And he and Suwon would be here. Forever? It seemed possible. Anything seemed possible, if he could just reach out. Now.

Bik stood up, grabbed Suwon's hand and stared the tight-lipped spaceman in the eyes. "Wendt, get out of there and let me talk to my son."

TOUCHDOWN

Nancy Kress

"Touchdown" appeared in the October 1990 issue of Isaac Asimov's Science Fiction *magazine, with an illustration by Janet Aulisio. It was one of a long sequence of elegant and incisive stories by Kress that have appeared in* Asimov's *under four different editors over the last twenty years, since her first* Asimov's *sale to George Scithers in 1979—stories that have made her one of the most popular of all the magazine's writers. Her books include the novels* The Prince of Morning Bells, The Golden Grove, The White Pipes, An Alien Light, *and* Brain Rose. *She won both the Hugo and the Nebula Award in 1992 for her novella, "Beggars in Spain," an* Asimov's *story; the novel version,* Beggars in Spain, *appeared the following year, and was followed by a sequel,* Beggars and Choosers. *Her short work has been collected in* Trinity and Other Stories *and the recent* The Aliens of Earth. *Her most recent books are the thriller* Oaths & Miracles *and a new SF novel,* Maximum Light. *She has also won a Nebula Award for her story "Out of All Them Bright Stars." Born in Buffalo, New York, Nancy Kress now lives in Silver Spring, Maryland, with her husband, SF writer Charles Sheffield.*

Here she takes us to the mysterious third planet

*from the sun, and gives us a suspenseful look at a
very unusual (and very dangerous) high-tech competition, played out across the gameboard of a deserted and devastated Earth—and in the process
gives us some clues as to how it got that way in the
first place . . .*

Maria told me that Team B had found Troy. It took me
a moment to find the right answer (all we had found was
Tokyo), and in that moment there was no way to tell how
unprotected my expression had been. But I did find the
answer. "That's impossible. Troy was *early*."

"Nonetheless, Team B found it. Excavated ruins."

"It wouldn't be big enough to carry any points!"

"It's on the exception list."

"I don't believe it."

Maria shrugged, watching (what had my face shown?)
"So access the channel."

"But there wasn't anything *there*."

"There were enough exposed excavations or whatever
to be on the list. Three hundred points. Leader just made
the official acceptance." She smiled at me sweetly. "He
said he was pleased."

Bitch. She knew I didn't access the open channel as
often as she did; I work best with uninterrupted team-
channel access. She also knew that Team B Leader had
been my second husband. Her background psych research
was always thorough. I toggled my 'plant to "record"
and made a note to bid for her next season.

Tokyo was worth only forty-five points. *Anybody* can
identify Tokyo, even starting from a fucking Pacific Island.

My Team Leader's voice buzzed in my 'plant. "Time's
up, Cazie. Come on in."

"We have another four hours!"

"Touchdown city by Team A. Quarter's over."

Maria smirked; she was on Team A. Her 'plant had of course already told her about the touchdown. No appeal; someone on Team A had actually done it, gone out and touched an artifact from one of their cities. I turned away from her and pretended to study my console, my face under careful control. *She'll say it*, my 'plant said, programmed for this. The programming had been expensive, but worth it: no point in giving away rage if you can be warned those few seconds in advance that let you get your reactions under control. A few times the 'plant had even been wrong, audio context analysis being as uncertain as it is. A few times no one had even said it.

Maria said it.

"Don't be too upset. After all, Cazie—it's just a game."

Flying back is the part I hate the worst. Going out for the first quarter, of course, you can't see anything. The portholes are opaqued; even a loose chair strap could disqualify you in case it might let you glimpse something. During actual play, you're concentrating on the console readings, the team chatter as it comes over your 'plant, the hunches about where to search next, the feints to keep your flyer-mate off-balance. Especially the feints. You hardly notice the actual planet at all, even when you play in what passes for daylight.

But flying back to base, the quarter's over, the tension's broken, and there's nothing much going on over the 'plant to distract you from the place. And God, it was depressing. Even Maria felt it, she of the alloy sensitivity. We had been playing a day game in Tokyo; the computer flew us west, into the dying light. Ocean choked with slime or else just degree after degree of gray water, followed by great barren dusty plains howled over by winds of unbreathable air. Continents' worth of bare plains. Nothing hard, nothing bright or shiny, nothing cozy and compact.

Just the bare huge emptiness. And overhead, the constant thick clouds that make it impossible to even guess where the sun is.

Once I told Ari—now Team Leader B—I wasn't sure the game was worth the aftermath, it was so depressing. He stared at me a long time and then asked, in that sweet voice that meant attack, whether the openness frightened me? And we were still married at the time. I said of course it didn't frighten me, what was there about such a dead world that was frightening? I kept my voice bored and disdainful. But he went on watching me anyway. And that was when we were even still *married*.

"Nothing," Maria said. She stood deliberately staring out the porthole as we whizzed over some dead plain. Showing off. Thinking she was out-psyching me. She even made a little song of it: "No-thing, no-thing, no-thing."

I didn't look at her. Maria smiled.

At the base we all gathered in the dome while the computer reffed the first quarter. The four members of Team A had found Sydney, Newcastle, Wollangong, Capetown, Oudtshoorn, Port Elizabeth, Shanghai, Beijing, and Hong Kong. The touchdown was for Sydney, but it was only a piece of bent metal, not a whole artifact, so it wasn't worth a lot of points. They had a lot of cities but the team had concentrated on coastal cities, which aren't worth as much overall because they're easier to find and to identify (although they did get extra points for Hong Kong, because it had sunk so deep).

Team B found Troy, Istanbul, Thessaloniki, New York, Yonkers, Greenwich, Stamford, Norwalk, Edmonton, Calgary, and Chikon: high initial points but a big loss after reffing because the North American cities were so close together and because they had misidentified Chikon—*twice*. I watched while the computer announced the adjusted score, but Maria went on smiling and her face gave away nothing. Neither did Ari's, damn him.

Team C found Rio de Janeiro, Santos, Campinas, Ouriphos—the actual Ouriphos, or what had been left of it after the earthquake—Bujumbura, Kigall, Dallas, Fort Worth, Waco, Austin, Leningrad, Tallinn, and Helsinki. An impressive score—and for nine of the cities they had been playing in the dark. The floating cameras zoomed in for close-ups of their smiles.

Team D found Tokyo, Jakarta, Bandung, Herat, Ferah, and (at the last minute, thanks to Nikos), Wichita. But we were saved from last place by Team E, who had found only *two* cities, Saskatoon and Kifta, and had misidentified Kifta. They couldn't hide their embarrassment, not even the Team Leader, not even when the cameras targeted him. The glances that went around the dome were almost compensation for our losing the quarter. Team Leader E stared straight ahead, mottled color rising on the back of his neck; unless he made a fast recovery in the next quarter, he'd be fucking his hand for *months*. And the fan reaction and betting back home on his orbital didn't even bear thinking about—let alone the sponsor's reaction. The team ended with only twenty-eight points adjusted.

Team C won the quarter, of course, 480 adjusted. Team Leader instructed me through my 'plant to try to find out their I.D. tactics in the coffee hour.

Larissa always does that to me. As if I were some kind of tactical genius, just because once I'd been quarterback for the team that racked up the record, 996 points in a single quarter. We'd found Pax. But you can't find Pax every quarter—after all this time, the accursed place is still floating around the Pacific—and underneath I'm always afraid some flyer-mate will psych out how bad I really am at team tactical programs.

What had Maria seen on my face?

I didn't find out. I didn't find out Team C's I.D. tactics either, because the coffee hour is only fifty-six minutes by strict rule before the blackout period, and Team B Leader had taken the risk of doping all of his people on Impenetrables set to kick in right after the ref announcements. God, he was self-confident. I looked at him sideways, when I was sure Maria or the cameras weren't watching. He hadn't changed much in the two years since our divorce. Short, muscled, smiling. Ari.

Then the coffee hour was over and the Leaders took the dome field down and Maria and I went back to the flyer and shot each other with the time-release knock-out drugs. The camera hovered close as we laid the strips on each other's necks, and stayed close afterward. There's a hazy period while the stuff takes effect. Players are vulnerable: it's a warm sweet letting go, sometimes of words as well as consciousness. But I was pretty sure I didn't give anything away. Maria finally stopped talking to me and rolled over in her bunk, and I smiled to myself in the darkness.

Preparation for second quarter.

When I woke, Maria was blinking sleepily. The camera was already on. I felt rested, but of course that was no clue to how much time had elapsed—the drug made me feel rested. Had we been out two hours or twenty? However long it had been, the computer had moved all the flyers for the second round. I knew the latitude and longitude of where we had been, but now we could be literally anywhere in the world. Again.

Adrenaline surged, and my stomach tightened with pleasure.

We strapped ourselves into the kick-off chairs. The portholes were shallow opaque caves. "Tallyho," Maria said. I ignored her. The computer kept us waiting for ten minutes. When the seat straps finally unlocked, Maria

tried a direct run for her console (she's strong), but I was
ready for her and made a flying tackle. She went down.
I scrambled over her, reached my console, and activated
it. The first half-hour control of the flyer was mine.

Maria got up slowly. She wasn't hurt, of course, but
she made a show of rubbing her shoulder for the camera.
She's a high-ranked player on a number of orbitals. Very
dramatic.

The portholes de-opaqued. Daylight. More barren plain,
more dust blown by unbreathable air, some scraggly plant
stuff in dull olive. Not much rock. No coast. No snow or
frost, but of course with the greenhouse effect worsening
every year that ruled out less than fifteen degrees of latitude. We could still be anywhere. You always hope the
random patterns generated by the computer will set you
down right at the edge of a qualifiable city, but that has
only happened to me once. And it was Moscow, only
ninety points unreffed.

I lifted the flyer for an aerial view, taking it up as high
as the rules allowed. Maria and I both peered through
every single porthole. Nothing but plain. Then I saw it, a
quick flash of silver on the right horizon. Water. I headed
right.

"Water over there!" I said excitedly, jazzing it up for
the camera. It was watching Maria for the reaction shot,
of course, but she just looked thoughtful: the serious
young player concentrating for the fans back home.

A small river meandered across the dust. Along its
banks, plants were a little greener, a little fuller. They
disgusted me; pitiful things, trying to actually grow in this
place. God knew what chemicals were in the river.

I followed it at top speed, needing to reach a city before
my half-hour was up. With speed limited during play to
sixty-five miles per hour, every minute counted. I didn't
want to arrive at a city just as Maria's console cut in and
mine shut down.

We flew for twenty minutes. Ruins appeared below us, some broken concrete and the mound pattern that means structures under the dust. But visual was enough to tell me that the place was too small to qualify as a city. Some stupid little town, not even enough left of it to get a fix on the architecture and make a guess what continent we were on.

Then the alarm bells went off.

"Lift! For God's sake lift the fucking flyer!" Maria screamed. I thought she was over-reacting for the camera until I saw her face. She was terrified.

Maria was—or rather, somewhere along the line had become—toxiphobic.

The computer had removed the aerial ceiling the second the radiation detectors had registered the toxic dump. I took the flyer up to forty thousand feet. It was the one time the rules allowed a major overview during a quarter, but Maria didn't even glance at a porthole. She stood breathing hard, eyes on the deck, pale as dust. By the time she had control of herself again, we had shot forward and I was dropping back to legal height.

Maria was toxiphobic.

And she hadn't even seen the ruins over the horizon at 342 degrees.

I used the five minutes I had left to take us as far in the other direction as I could. Five minutes would never be enough time to fly there and do an I.D. My best bet was to hope she didn't fly that way during her half-hour.

She didn't. She veered off at twenty-eight degrees, and I kept careful track on my compass of everything she did after that. We came across three more polluter towns, but nothing big enough to qualify for points. When my console came back on, I headed straight back to my ruins, flying with that cocky grin that alerts fans that something is going to happen. Maria watched me sourly, at least when the camera was off her. "Know where we're going, do we?" I didn't answer. I didn't have to.

The city ruins were extensive, with roads leading in from all directions and a downtown section of fallen concrete and steel poking above the blowing dust. There were no clues, however, in the architecture, or at least none that I could identify. Ari had been the architectural whiz.

I started the chatter on the 'plant. "Cazie on. I've found one. Daylight, doesn't seem to be waxing or waning. No architectural clues to describe. Central downtown core, roads leading in from all directions, collapsed overpasses, plain with a 1.62 degree incline, small river flowing outside the city but not through it, no other still-existing visible waterways."

"Team Leader on. What's the diameter?"

"Crossing it now . . . I estimate three miles metropolitan . . . hard to be sure."

"Regular perimeter?"

"Circling now . . ." The detector shrilled.

I started to take the flyer up and to the right, but after a minute the alarm shut down.

"Cazie on. There's a toxic dump, but it's small—a few seconds moved me out of range."

"Did you see anything significant while you were lifting?"

"No. I'll circle in the other direction, try to get a shape for the perimeter."

By now the fans would be glued to their sets. They, of course, already knew what city we had. The name would be shimmering across their screens. The question now was, how would we players identify it? And who would get the points? I had 14.3 minutes left. Maria stood at her console, jaw clenched so tight her lips flared out slightly, like a flower.

"Cazie on. The shape is pretty regular. No, wait, it flattens out into a sort of corridor of ruins extending out

at 260 degrees. There's a *river* here. Another one. A big
one, but really muddy, clogged, and sluggish. . . .'' Not
for the first time, I wished that soil analysis from inside
the flyer was legal. Although then where would the challenge be?

"Jack on," he said through the 'plant. "Do the city
ruins go right to the edge of the river or was there a
park?"

"Cazie on. Seems to be extensive flat area between
even the smallest ruins and the river."

"Team leader on. Vestigial vegetation?"

"None. The . . ." The alarm shrilled again.

This time the computer let me take the flyer all the way
up. Maria started to tremble, clutching the edge of her
console with both hands. Even over the alarms I could
hear her: "Near cities. In their water, by their parks, goddamn fucking polluters, toxic dumps all over the place
they *deserved* to all die . . ." But I didn't have time to
gloat over her loss of control. Over twenty thousand feet
the high-altitude equipment kicked in, all per game rules,
and I got it all: aerial photos before we broke the cloud
cover, sonar dimensions, sun position above the clouds,
steel density patterns. Of course we couldn't access the
computer banks, but we didn't have to. We had Jack, who
had been a first-draft pick for his phenomenal memory. I
passed him the figures right off the console, such a sweet
clean information pass it almost brought tears to my eyes,
and in less than a minute Jack said, "Syracuse, United
States, North America!" Team Leader filed it, the computer confirmed, and the news went out over 'plants and
cameras. The first score of the quarter. 185 points, plus
points for initial continent identification, and no fouls for
holding too long in toxic range. Mine.

I took the flyer down and grinned at Maria.

•　　•　　•

Once we knew where we were, the plays became a cinch. Chatter flew heavy over team channels: if you're in waning light and Cazie is in full light at 76 20' W 43 07' N, where might I be in what seems to be dawn? I pictured fans flipping channels, listening, arguing, the serious betters plotting flyer trails on map screens.

Maria found Rochester, United States. Her time ran out and I got Buffalo, United States and Niagara Falls, Canada, which barely qualified for size and wasn't very many points, given that the falls are still there, torrents of water over eroded rock. Ari once told me that those falls are one of the few places on earth with relatively clean water because water going that fast through rapids cleanses itself every hundred yards. He was probably teasing.

Time was called a few hours after we reached dusk. Maria looked tired and angry, the anger probably because she'd given away so much. She was behind in points, behind in psych-out, undoubtedly down in the betting back home.

I whistled some Mozart.

Maria stared at me coldly. "Did you know they buried him in an open grave for outcasts? With lime over him so the body wouldn't smell? Just threw him in like garbage?"

I shrugged. I couldn't see that it mattered. His music is glorious, but he was probably just as morally guilty as all the rest of them. Polluters do not deserve to live. That's the first thing children are taught: do not foul the life systems. I had a sudden flash of memory: myself at four or five, marching around kindergarten, singing the orbital anthem and fingering the red stitching on my uniform: MY BODY, MY ORBITAL.

I said maliciously, "At least limestone isn't toxic." But she didn't even react. She really was depressed.

The screen in the corner suddenly flashed to life: Team Leader A. It startled both of us so much we turned in unison, like mechanical dolls. Only Team Leader A can use the screen to contact everyone during a game, and then only for game called, for an emergency, or for important news from home. He's the only one allowed direct orbital contact. My stomach tightened.

"Team Leader A. News flash. Don't panic, anyone, it's *not* an orbital. Repeat, no orbital is in danger. But something has happened: they've opened warfare on the moon."

Maria and I looked at each other. She was breathing hard. Not that she knew anybody on the moon, of course; it's been two generations since anybody but diplomats have made contact with those maniacs. Generations before that their ancestors chose their way off planet, ours chose ours. To qualify for an orbital, you had to be a certain kind of person: non-violent, non-polluting, no criminal record of any kind, clearly self-supporting (you had to have money, of course, but money alone wouldn't do it), intelligent, and *fair*. You had to be able to respect rules.

Nobody else got in, not even relatives of qualifiers. Our founders knew they were choosing the future of the human race.

Everybody else with enough money but not enough decency tried to get to a moon colony.

"As far as orbital diplomats can tell, the war started when one underground moon colony mined another and detonated by remote. We don't yet know how many colonies are involved. But the orbitals agree that there is no danger to us. This war, if it is a war, is confined to themselves."

Team Leader A looked at us a minute longer. I couldn't read his expression. Then the screen went blank.

"Oh, God," Maria said. "All those people."

I looked at her curiously. "What do you care? There's no threat to any orbital."

"I *know* that. But even so, Cazie . . . that's not a game.

It's real. Dying trapped underground while everything explodes around you. . . ."

I got out the third set of black-out strips. To tell you the absolute truth, I find attitudes like Maria's tiresome. She can't really care about moonies; how could she? They're no different from the maniacs who ruined Earth in the first place. She was just pretending because it made her look sensitive, cosmopolitan . . . to me it looked flabby. Moonies weren't like us. They didn't understand moral obligations. They didn't follow the rules. If they all blew each other up, it would just make space that much safer for the orbitals.

And her depression was ruining my triumph in the game.

That was when I realized that she must be doing it deliberately. And pretty neat it was. I had almost lost my edge for the game, thinking about moonies trapped underground . . . there's nothing so terrible about being underground anyway. It probably wasn't that much different from the coziness of an orbital. It was wide, open, unprotected spaces that were scary.

Unless you were scoping them from thirty thousand feet, making a high, clean information pass, the first one of the quarter and a total of two hundred points. . . .

I opened her black-out drug, grinning.

In the third quarter the computer set us down in darkness, on sand. Blowing sand as far as the high beams could see at maximum altitude. Miles and miles of blowing sand. Over my 'plant Nikos, our broad-base geography offense, ran me through the most likely deserts. Maria used a sweet triple-feint to get to her console first, and she called the first play.

We didn't find *anything* for hours. Team C reported Glasgow just as our sky began to pale in the east, and that gave us an approximate longitude. Jack found Colombo. Team A reported Managua and Baghdad. Then, slowly, mountains began to rise on our horizon. I calculated how far away they must be; they were *huge*.

"Nikos on," he said. "All right, I have to make this quick, Cazie, my play starts in forty-five seconds and we're coming into something. The mountains are part of the Rockies, and you're between them and the Mississippi River in the Great Central Desert of North America. Fly close enough to describe specific mountain profiles with degree separations to Jack and he'll take it from there. Jack, can you take it now?"

"Jack on. Got it. Cazie, go."

I described for three minutes and he suggested where I should look. I did, but not quick enough. Maria got La Junta, United States, North America. I got Pueblo, just barely. Then we hit a toxic dump and an announcement from Team Leader A simultaneously.

"Team Leader A. News flash. Orbital diplomats in three moon colonies have ceased communicating: Faldean, Troika, and Alpha. The assumption is that all three colonies are destroyed and our . . . our diplomats are dead."

His image stared straight ahead. After a minute he added, "I'll let you all know if they call the game."

Call the game.

"They won't do that, will they, do you think?" I said to Maria.

She said, "I don't know."

I found Colorado Springs.

But how many fans were even watching?

They didn't call the game. We finished the day almost dead even. Right after we took the black-out drug, Maria crawled into my bunk. I was surprised—flabbergasted. But it turned out she didn't even want to fuck, just to be held. I held her, wondering what the hell was going on, if she thought I'd fall for some kind of sexual psych-out. The idea was almost insulting; I'd been a pro for nearly eight years. But she just lay there quietly, not talking, and when black-out was over she again seemed focused and tough, ready for the last quarter.

"Tallyho."

I never did learn what that meant. But I wasn't about to ask. I knew Maria had finished most of the two-year Yale software, and I've never even accessed a college program.

We de-opaqued in rocky hills, in daylight. Twenty minutes later we found a saltwater coast. After that it was almost too easy: Algiers. Bejaia. Skikda. Bizerte. Tunis. Not even any toxic dumps to speak of.

Too easy. And Maria and I were almost even in pre-reffed points.

"My play!"

"Take it, asshole. You won't reach Kalrouan or Monastir by the time the quarter ends."

"The hell I won't."

Of course I didn't. It was too far. But I reached something else.

The light had begun to fail. I gambled on sticking to the coast rather than flying inland towards Kalrouan. Out of the gathering darkness loomed red cliffs. Piles of rubble clung to their sides, banked on terraces and ledges that had been folded by earthquakes and eroded by wind. From the sides of the cliffs twisted steel beams bristled like matted hair. "Cazie on. There's a city—maybe not a city—just below me. We're twenty-two minutes out of Tunis following the coast. Jack?"

"Jack on. Too small to qualify."

"Team Leader on. Sorry, Cazie. Come on in."

"It doesn't look too small!"

"It's too small."

"Maybe it's in the supplementary d-base." Nobody

memorizes the supplementary database; it's all those cities and towns that don't qualify for points. Unless, of course, there's a tie, or a field goal at endgame. . . .

Seventeen minutes left.

"Team Leader on. We don't have any reason to think we're that close to a tie, Cazie. And if you earn a penalty by calling it wrong—"

Nobody can call in advance how the computer will ref points. Base points are of course known, but there are too many variables altering base points. If there's a flash of sunshine that the flyer registers as strong enough to count as a latitude clue, you lose points, even if you didn't notice that the fucking clouds parted. There are penalties assessed against other teams that you don't hear about until the quarter's over. There are points added for plays in darkness, subtracted for nuclear-radiation clues above certain level, multiplied by a fractional constant for the number of cities already found during the quarter, factored for dozens of other things. But against all that, I *knew*. I did. We were close to a tie. You don't play this game for eight years without developing a sixth sense, a feeling. A hunch.

Sixteen minutes.

"Cazie on. I got a hunch. I just do. Let me try for a touchdown."

"Team Leader on. Cazie, last time you . . ."

"Larissa—*please*."

She didn't say anything. Neither did Jack or Nikos. Last time I tried for an endgame touchdown I froze. Just froze, out there alone in the howling unbreathable desert with no walls, no life support, unprotected under that naked angry sky. . . . We were disqualified. Disgraced. Odds on us lengthened to the moon, all four of us slept alone for a month. It took three flyers to get me in.

"Please. I have the hunch."

"Team Leader on. Go."

Fifteen minutes.

I slammed my fist onto the console code and struggled into my suit. The camera floated in for close-ups. Maria watched me through narrowed eyes. My 'plant said, *She's going to say it.*

"Cazie, it's only a game. It's not worth risking your life for a game."

I sealed the suit.

"You'll be exposed right at the edge of the ocean. God knows what toxins you'll be exposed to, even through the suit. You know that. We went right over that dump down the coast, and that ocean looks terrible. When your field's off, you'll be completely exposed."

I reached for my helmet. She was talking her fears, not mine.

"*And* you'll be right there in the *open*. God, all that open space around you, desolate, winds blowing—completely *exposed*. Unprotected. The winds could blow you off the—"

I sealed my helmet, shutting out her words.

The airlock took one minute to empty and open. Eleven minutes. The second the door opened, I was out.

The winds hit me so hard I cried out and fell against the flyer. The camera, buffeted by winds, was right behind me. I straightened and started away from the flyer. Almost immediately the fear was there, clawing at me from inside. *Open. Unprotected. Poisoned. Life systems fouled, death in the air and soil and water.* . . . Twenty-eight years of conditioning. And the fact that my conscious mind knew it was conditioning didn't help at all. Dead, foul, exposed, dead, dead, unprotected. . . .

I made myself keep walking. Nine minutes.

The city—town, village—had been built down the cliff and, probably, along a coastal strip that was now all underwater. When they had built like that, often "richer" people lived higher up, in sturdier structures. Ahead of

me the cliff turned in on itself a little, giving more shelter
to whatever structures had been there. I made for the bend,
running as fast as I could, the wind at my back, fighting
the desire to scream. To fall. To freeze.

Around the curve of rock were twisted steel beams,
welded together and extending back inside the rock. I
wrenched at them, which was stupid; they were huge, and
nothing was going to break off a piece that could be carried into a flyer. There were chunks of concrete all around,
but concrete doesn't count. Below me, the poisoned ocean
howled and thrashed.

I worked my way between the steel beams. Whatever
walls had been here had long since fallen down, the rubble
blown away or washed away or just disintegrated. Dust
blew all over everything; the steel and concrete were pit-
ted by grit. It was the ugliest place I had ever seen. And
it could shift under my feet any second. But between the
steel beams a kind of cave, still roughly rectangular, led
back into the cliff. The polluters had built into the earth
before they destroyed it.

Three minutes.

I climbed over fallen rocks and rubble to get deeper
into the cave house. For a moment I remembered the underground war on the moon and my breath stopped, but
at the same moment I passed some kind of threshold and
the sound from the horrible winds diminished abruptly. I
kept on going.

Two minutes.

At the very back of the house I found it.

There was a loose fall of rock from the ceiling in the
most protected corner; smashed wood stuck out from under it. Some piece of furniture. I tugged at the rocks; when
they wouldn't move, I scrabbled with my hands behind
them. Oh God don't tear the suit, don't let the ground
shift or more rocks fall from the ceiling, don't . . . my fingers closed on something smooth and hard.

And whole.

It was a keyboard, wedged between two rocks, slimy with some kind of mold but in one piece. I wiggled it free and started to run. For the first time in many minutes I became aware of the camera, floating along behind me. Not slowing, I held the keyboard in front of it, screaming words it couldn't hear and I couldn't remember. The winds hit me like a blow, but if I was clear enough of the cave for wind, I was clear enough for transmission.

"Cazie on! Larissa? Fuck it—*Larissa!*"

"Go!"

"I got it! A touchdown! A whole! A touchdown!"

"Touchdown by Team D!" Larissa screamed, on what I assumed to be all channels. "Touchdown!"

Thirty seconds.

The earth moved under me.

I screamed. I was going to die. The game was over but I was going to die, exposed unprotected poisoned dead on the fucking earth. . . .

The quake was small. I wasn't going to die. I swayed, sobbed, and began to fight my way back against the wind. Darkness was falling fast. But I could see the flyer, I was almost there, I had the whole, I was not going to freeze, and the treacherous earth was not going to take its revenge on me. On someone, almost certainly, eventually, but not on me. Touchdown.

We won.

The reffed score among three teams—not just two, but *three*—was close enough to make the endgame play legal. We got 865 points adjusted, and beat the closest team, C, by 53 points. My keyboard gave us Sidi Bou Said, Tunisia, North Africa, from the supplementary database—a town no one had scored before.

The party at the base was wild, with fans at home flashing messages on the screen so fast you could barely read them. Drink flowed. I got pounded on the back so often I was sore. I had five whispered bids for the traditional post-game activity, *three* of them from Team Leaders. High on victory, I chose Ari. He had always been the best lover I had, and we even, in drunken pleasure, talked about getting together again back home. It was an astonishing party. Fans will talk about it for years.

Team Leader A says they'll put the keyboard in a museum in one of the orbitals, after the thing is cleaned up and detoxed. I don't care what they do with it. It served its purpose.

The moon war apparently was brief and deadly. No transmissions from any colony. They're assumed all dead. But while I was downing my third victory drink and Larissa and I were laughing it up for the cameras, I got a great idea. All the moon colonies were underground, so it won't take long for the surface marks to disappear: collapse the energy domes and in a few years meteors will make the surface look pretty much like the rest of the moon. But the colonies will still be there underground, or their ruins will, detectable to sonar or maybe new heatseekers. As long as the heat lasts, anyway. Looking for them will be a tremendous challenge, a new kind of challenge, with new plays and feints and tactics and brand new rules.

I can hardly wait.

THE DIFFICULTIES INVOLVED IN PHOTOGRAPHING NIX OLYMPICA

Brian W. Aldiss

"The Difficulty Involved in Photographing Nix Olympica" appeared in the May 1986 issue of Isaac Asimov's Science Fiction *magazine, with an illustration by George Thompson. Aldiss doesn't appear in the magazine nearly as often as we'd like, but each appearance has been memorable. In the subtle and quietly profound story that follows, he takes us along to a military base on the Red Planet, Mars, fourth from the sun and long the most popular destination of all for science fiction writers and other visionary dreamers, and shows us that what's most important is not so much what you see, as how you see it.*

One of the true giants of the field, Brian W. Aldiss has been publishing science fiction for more than a quarter of a century, and has more than two dozen books to his credit. His classic novel The Long Afternoon of Earth *won a Hugo Award in*

1962. His novella, "The Saliva Tree," won a Nebula Award in 1965, and his novel Starship *won the Prix Jules Verne in 1977. He took another Hugo Award in 1987 for his critical study of science fiction,* Trillion Year Spree, *written with David Wingrove. His other books include the acclaimed* Helliconia trilogy—Helliconia Spring, Helliconia Summer, Helliconia Winter—The Malacia Tapestry, An Island Called Moreau, Frankenstein Unbound, *and* Cryptozoic. *His latest books include the collection* Seasons in Flight, *the novels* Dracula Unbound *and* Remembrance Day, *and a collection of poems,* Home Life with Cats. *He lives in Oxford, England.*

It was unprecedented for anyone stationed on Mars to refuse home leave. Ozzy Brooks refused. He secretly wanted to photograph Olympus Mons.

For his whole two-year tour of duty, Sgt. Brooks had saved money and hoarded material. Had made friends with the transport section. Had ingratiated himself with the officer in charge of rations. Had gone out of his way to be nice to practically everyone in Atmosphere Control. Had wooed the guys in the geological section. Had made himself indispensible in Engineering.

Almost everyone in Fort Arcadia knew and, within their lights, liked little Sgt. Brooks.

Brooks was small, dark-skinned, lightly built, neat-boned—ideal fodder for Mars. He had nondescript sandy hair which grew like lichen over his skull, with eyes to match. He had what are often referred to as ageless looks, and the rather blank stare that goes with those looks.

Behind that blank and inoffensive gaze lay ambition. Brooks was an intellectual. Brooks never got drunk. He rarely watched TV screenings from Earth. Instead, he could be seen reading old books. He went to bed early. He never complained or scratched his armpits. And he seemed to know everything. It was amazing that the other troops stationed in Fort Arcadia liked him nevertheless: but Brooks had another qualification.

Ozzy Brooks was Fort Arcadia's Martian *t'ai chi* master. He taught two classes of *mar t'ai chi*, as he himself called it: an elementary class from eight to ten in the morning and an advanced class from eight to eleven in the evening. Even men for whom *mar t'ai chi* was not compulsory joined Brooks's classes, for they agreed that Brooks was a brilliant teacher; all "felt better" when each session was finished. Brooks's teaching was an antidote to the monotony of Mars.

After dismissing one of his morning classes, Brooks slipped out of his costume, put on denims, and strolled across the dome to Engineering, to work on the larger format camera he was building.

"What do you need a camera for on Mars?" Sgt. Al Shapiro asked.

"I want to photograph Olympus Mons from the ground," Brooks said.

Shapiro laughed, with contempt in the sound.

Brooks's secret in life was that he did not hate anything. He hated no man. He did not hate the Army, he did not hate Mars. All the rest of the men, his friends, spent long hours trying to decide whether they hated the Army or Mars most. Sometimes Mars won, sometimes the Army.

"It's the boredom. The monotony," they said. Referring to both or either.

Brooks was never bored. In consequence, he did not find life monotonous. He did not dislike Army discipline, since he had always strictly disciplined himself. Certainly he missed women; but he consoled himself by saying that instead he had this unique opportunity to know the Red Planet.

He loved Mars. Mars was the ideal place on which to do *t'ai chi*. Despite his ordinary name, Brooks was an exotic. While his grandmother, a refugee from Vietnam, had had the fortune to marry a seventh-generation American, his great-grandparents were Chinese from Szechwan Province. A *t'ai chi* tradition had been passed down in the family from generation to generation. Ozzy Brooks hugged this knowledge to himself: Mars, with its lighter gravity, was the perfect planet on which to develop his art. Some wise Chinese ancestor, many generations ago, had invented the postures of the White Crane *with Mars in mind*.

Under Brooks's American-ness ran a strong delight in his oriental heritage. He believed that it was a Chinese who had discovered the perfect way to live on another planet, in harmony with its elements, using those elements to become more perfect in oneself. Mars—he had realized this almost as soon as he had disembarked from the military spaceship—was the most Chinese of planets, even down to the *sang-de-boeuf* tint of its soil, the color of ancient Chinese gateways and porcelains.

In Brooks's mind, Mars became an extension of China, the China of long ago, crammed with warriors, maidens as fair as white willows, and tombs loaded high with carvings and treasure. Beyond the dome of Arcadia, he thought he saw Cathay.

It was some while before he realized he had a friend in Sgt. Al Shapiro.

He was working in the engineering laboratories, inserting the shutter mechanism in the 8 × 10 camera now rapidly nearing completion, when Shapiro strolled up. Shapiro was small, light on his feet, and darker in complexion than Brooks. He smiled at Brooks through a hank of black hair which hung across his face.

"What are you really going to use that camera for, Ozzy?"

"Pictures—like I told you. What else?"

"You're not going to be able to take it back to Earth in your kit. It's too heavy."

"What a nuisance," said Brooks, blandly.

Shapiro hesitated, then said, "You should photograph Mars with it, same as you said. Maybe I could help."

The remark took Brooks aback. He regarded Al Shapiro as a wooden man, cut off from his fellows, often to be seen reading the Army manuals other guys shunned. Al didn't even do *t'ai chi*. Could there be a vein of imagination under that stolid surface?

Mistaking his surprise, Shapiro lowered his voice and said, "Most guys see nothing in Mars, nothing at all. Except the officers. Do you notice when we're out doing maneuvers, Colonel Wolfe always says, 'Mars is fine fighting country'? That's how a professional soldier sees it, I guess. What do the men say about it? 'The dust-bowl'—that's what they call Mars, the squaddies. They can't see it except as a torn-off chunk of America's Badlands. They've got no imagination. Me—I've had a think about it . . ."

"How do you see Mars, Al?" Brooks asked, very calm and in control again.

Shapiro gave his flitting smile.

"How do I see it? Why, when I take a look out there, I see it as a fantastic piece of natural engineering. Uncluttered by trees and all the vegetation that hides Earth. Mars is honest, a great series of cantilevers and buttresses and platforms. God's naked handiwork. I'm the only guy I know who'd like to get out there among it all."

"Some of the men like to go out for the pigeon shoots," Brooks said.

There were Mars jeeps which toured nearby gulleys firing off clay pigeons in all directions. These shoots formed one of the few outdoor recreations available. But no one ever ventured more than a mile from the fort.

Shapiro shrugged. "Kid stuff . . . I'd just like to figure

on doing something memorable with my time on Mars. I've only got a month before they ship me back to Chicago.''

Brooks put out his hand.

''That's the way I think too. I wish to do something memorable.''

And so they came to draw up plans to photograph Olympus Mons from the ground.

Al Shapiro was as resourceful as Ozzy Brooks in getting what he wanted. He actually enjoyed the Army, and knew how to exploit all the weaknesses of that organisation. They indented for a week's base leave, they set about bribing Captain Jeschke in Transport to secure the unauthorised loan of a Mars jeep, they bartered services in return for supplies.

''I should be a general—I could run Mars single-handed!'' Shapiro said, laughing.

And all the while, he went ahead with his work in Engineering, and Brooks taught *mar t'ai chi*, instructing his squads how to love Mars as the ally of all their muscular exertions—thus, in his quiet way, subverting the army's purpose, which was to make the men hate the planet and anything on it which moved and was not capitalist.

Occasionally, maneuvers were undertaken in conjunction with the EEC dome in Eridania. The men had to fire missiles on the arctic ranges, or crawl around, cursing, in the red dust. Brooks saw then that his subversion had not had much effect. Everyone wanted to go back to Earth. They had no vision. He longed to give them one.

''Before we leave here, we must make a model of Nix Olympica, and study it from all angles, so that we decide the ideal position to which to drive.'' Brooks nodded sagely as he spoke and looked sideways at Shapiro.

''Cartography,'' said Shapiro. ''Lou Wright owes me a favor. Let's try Cartography.''

They obtained more than maps and photographs. As the most prominent physical feature on Mars, the extinct volcano had warranted a plastic model, constructed by a bygone officer in the Army Geological survey. Brooks inspected it with interest before rejecting it.

"It's too small. We can make a much better one between us," he said.

What he felt was that this army model of Olympus was contaminated by its source; it had no poetry. Whoever had ordered it had probably been concerned with how the sides of the crater could be scaled, or how the cordera itself might provide a base for ground-to-space missiles.

Brooks molded his model of the gigantic volcano in plastic, coloring it with acrylics. Shapiro occasionally came over to admire his work.

"You see, the formation is about the size of the state of Missouri. It rises to all of fifteen miles high," Brooks said. "The best idea is to approach it from the east. The lighting will be best from the east."

"What's your lens?"

"I'm taking a selection. The point about an 8×10 camera is that it will give terrific definition—through it feeds on sheet film, and I'll need a tripod to keep it steady."

"I can make you a tripod."

They surveyed the model of Olympus critically when it was finished. Brooks shook his head.

"It's a good model," Shapiro said. "Photograph it here against a black background and we can save ourselves a trip."

Although Brooks rarely laughed, he laughed now. Laughed and said nothing.

He was serenely happy drawing up his own map, entering the sparse names of features in fine calligraphic style, precision-drawing contour lines. The most dangerous aspect of the trip was its distance. They were contemplating a drive of almost seven hundred and ninety miles, with no filling stations on the way, and then the journey back. They would be unlikely to see anyone the whole trip, except possibly a patrol moving between the Arcadia base and the hemisphere of the planet held by the enemy.

No possible danger could deter Brooks. His mind was filled with his delight in having found a friend and in the prospects ahead. Ever since Mariner 9 had executed its fly-over back in 1971, Olympus Mons, the largest volcano in the solar system, had frequently been photographed, by both satellites and rockets. But never from the ground. Never as *he* would photograph it, with all the skill of an Ansel Adams.

He could visualize the prints now. They would be majestic, expressing both the violence and the deadness of the Martian landscape; he would create a serenity out of the conflicting tensions. He would create such an image that it would remain definitive: through the elusive art of photography, he would create a monument not only to the sublimity of the universe, but also to the greatness and the insignificance of mankind in the scheme of things.

With such exalted thoughts in his mind, Brooks had no room for fear.

The two men left Arcadia early one morning. Clad in suits, they slipped through one of the personnel locks in the main dome and made their way over to the transport hangar. There a stretched Mars jeep was waiting, loaded with fuel and supplies. As it rolled into the dim dawn light, the half-tracked vehicle resembled a cumbrous beetle.

There was little room to move in the cab. When they slept, their hammocks would be strung overhead. The ironically named Fort Arcadia was situated close to fifty degrees North, in the veined recesses of the Arcadia Planita. It was summer in the northern hemisphere of Mars, and they had a straightforward drive southwards to the giant volcano, according to the maps.

They reckoned on traveling for fourteen hours a day, and averaging something close to twenty-seven miles per hour, the best they could hope for over trackless terrain. They nodded with pleasure as the shabby collection of prefabricated buildings disappeared behind them, and they were alone with Mars. Shapiro was driving.

A chill, shrunken sun had pierced through the mists of the eastern horizon, where layers of salmon pink dissolved into the sky. The shadow of their vehicle spread across a terrain which resembled Earth's Gobi Desert. Dust lay in sculptured terraces, punctuated here and there by rocks of pumice. In the far distance to their right, a series of flat-topped escarpments suggested a kind of order completely lacking nearer at hand; they made their way through a geological rubbish dump.

This formless landscape was familiar to them from their military exercises. They had crawled through it, dressed in camouflaging sand-robes. Nothing moved but dusts and rusts; the rest—unlike Earth's restless territories—had endured without change for billions of years. It had no more life to offer than the Geological Survey map of the route pinned to the dash.

There was no cratering here, as in the southern hemisphere, to lend interest. Their one concern was to steer south, avoiding rocks and dust drifts. After the first hour of travel, with Al Shapiro at the wheel, Brooks began to want to talk.

Shapiro, however, had gone silent. As the sun climbed in the pinkish sky, he became more silent. He offered the information that his family came from the Cicero area of Chicago, and then gave up entirely. Brooks, tired of trying to make conversation, resorted to whistling.

The sun arched overhead. The two sergeants took the wheel by turns, driving till the sun sloped to the west, to sink behind a low dust cloud. They had covered three hundred and seventy miles, and were pleased with their good progress. With nightfall, Shapiro found his voice again and was more cheerful; they ate a companionable supper from their rations before climbing into their hammocks and sleeping.

Once in the night, Brooks woke and peered out of the window. The stars and the Milky Way were there in glory, remote yet curiously intimate, as if they shone only for him, like a hope at the back of his mind. He was caught between the tensions of awe and enjoyment, like a troglodyte before its god, unable to tear his gaze away from the glitter until an hour had passed. He climbed back into his hammock, smiling into the fuggy darkness, and slept.

Next dawn revealed no sign of the dust storm glimpsed at sunset—to Brooks's secret relief. Joy came to him. He sang. Shapiro looked doleful.

"Are you okay?" Brooks asked.

"I'm fine, sure."

"Anything worrying you? You wanted to get out among it all, and here we are."

"I'm fine."

"The Tharsis Bulge should be in view in an hour or two. Tomorrow we'll be within sight of Nix Olympica."

"Its name's Olympus," Shapiro said, sourly.

"I like to call it by the old name, Al. Nix Olympica . . . That was the name bestowed on it before anyone had ever set foot on the planet, or even left Earth. Nix Olympica is the old name, the name of mystery, of remoteness. I like it best. I'm going to photograph Nix Olympica and give a new image to Earth, before they come and build a missile site in the crater. Let's hope the atmosphere stays clear of dust."

Shapiro shrugged and brushed his hair from his eyes. He said nothing.

They were rolling by six-thirty. By eight, the terrain was changing. Petrified lavas created a series of steps over the ancient sand-rocks. Their gravimeter began to show fluctuations in the gravity field.

Brooks pointed ahead.

"There's the Tharsis Bulge," he said. "From here it stretches to south of the equator."

"I can see it," Shapiro said, without answering Brooks's excitement.

They began to steer southeast until the low wizened lips of Alba Patera lay distantly to their left. The view ahead became increasingly formidable.

The Tharsis Bulge distorted half a hemisphere. Earth held no feature as majestic. At its northwestern bastion stood the grim sentinel shape of Olympus, its cone rising a sheer fifteen and a half miles above the surrounding plain. As yet, they were too distant to see more than a pimpled shoulder of the Bulge looming above the ancient lands like a great bruise. Black clouds of dust rolled above the bruise. From the clouds, lightning showered, flickered like burning magnesium wire, died, flickered elsewhere. High above both Bulge and dust clouds, wispy white clouds formed a halo in the dark sky.

They climbed. The engine throbbed. The hours passed, the landscape took on power. It was as though the ancient rock breathed upwards. Despite the jeep, Brooks could feel the strength of the great igneous upthrust through the soles of his feet—the "Bubbling Well," as *t'ai chi* had it.

He breathed air deep into his *hora* center. But Shapiro sank back in his seat.

"You are suffering agoraphobia, Al," Brooks said. "Don't worry. Now we have something marvelous to distract your mind."

Brooks's intention was to drive some way up into the Bulge until Nix Olympica lay to the west; from there, he estimated he could photograph the formation at its most dramatic, with falling ground behind it.

The terrain which had been merely rutted now became much more difficult to drive. Long parallel fractures, remarkably uniform in spacing and orientation, ran downhill in their path. There was no way of avoiding the fracturing; as the map indicated, the faults extended for at least a hundred miles on either side of their course. Each fracture had straight, almost vertical, cliffs and reasonably flat bottoms. They found a point where a landslide had destroyed a cliff. By working their tracks on alternate sides, they contrived to slip down a small landslide to the bottom of the fracture, after which it was simple to drive along it. It was the width of an eight-lane highway.

Cliffs boxed them in on either side. The sky above was leaden, relieved by a strip of white cloud low ahead. It was just a matter of proceeding straight. No canyon on Earth was ever like this one.

Brooks pointed into the shadowed side of the fracture at the foot of the cliff. A trace of white lay across small boulders.

"It's a mixture of frost and snow, by the look of it," he said.

The sight delighted him. At least there was one natural process still functioning on the dead surface of the planet.

"How're we going to get out of this fault?" Shapiro asked.

"We're in a crack at least two and a half billion years old," Brooks said, more or less to himself. Even Cathay was not that ancient.

"And the satellites can't pick us up while we're down here," Shapiro said.

But Brooks would have nothing of misgivings. They would emerge somehow. He had never enjoyed himself so much.

"Just imagine it—once a great torrent rushed along here, Al. We're on an old river bed."

"No, this wasn't formed by water," Shapiro said expertly. "It's the result of stresses in the Martian lithosphere. You'll be looking out for fish-bones next."

Although Brooks was silenced by this rejoinder, he spent the next hour alert for signs of departed life. What a triumph to see a fossil in the fracture walls! Once he cried out and stopped the jeep, to peer more closely at the cliff; there was nothing to be seen but a pattern of splintering in the rock.

"Nothing living has ever lived here—not ever," Shapiro said, and began to shiver.

It was impossible to say anything sympathetic, but Brooks understood how Shapiro felt. These unknown spaces chilled Shapiro as much as they excited Brooks; it was what came of being born in a crowded Chicago slum. Besides, he understood intellectually how absurd it was to be experiencing such intense pleasure in such a forbidding place. The mountains of Western Szechwan Province, from which his Chinese ancestors had come, might be almost as unwelcoming as this.

It turned out that Brook's light-heartedness was not misplaced. The fracture cut into another at an oblique angle. Vast ramps, as smooth as if designed by a mortal architect, led up to the general level of the Bulge. The jeep climbed with ease, and they emerged onto the rainless elevations of the Tharsis Bulge. They were 1.3 miles above the datum, Mars's equivalent of sea level. The readout also showed a free-air gravity anomaly of 229 mgals. The wall of yellowish black dust had disappeared. Visibility was good in the thin atmosphere. The sun shone as if encased in lucite. There was a glazed aspect, too, to the great smooth features of the inclined plain about them, where strange bumps and undulations suggested bones under the basaltic skin.

"Wonderful!" Brooks said. He began to tease himself. "All we need now is for a devil to emerge and dance before us. A devil with a red and white face."

"For god's sake..." Shapiro protested. "Take your photographs and let's get home."

But Brooks wanted to climb out and dance. He was sick of being cooped in the cab of the vehicle, sick of the perpetual noise of the engine and air-purifier. It would be a time for the *t'ai chi* solo dance, even with the space suit on. He would celebrate Mars as no one else had done.

He controlled himself. A few more hours driving and they would see Nix Olympica itself. The sun was already descending. They had to make as much distance as they could before dark.

With nightfall, an electrical storm swept down from the heights. They stopped the jeep beside a corroded boulder. Flicking light surrounded them. Shapiro spent an hour checking through all the equipment, climbing restlessly about, and muttering to himself.

"One failure and we're dead," he said, catching Brooks's eye. "No one could get to us in time if anything went wrong. We embarked on this caper far too thoughtlessly. We should have planned it like a military operation."

"We shall see Nix Olympica tomorrow. Don't worry. Besides, imagine—wouldn't this spot really make a dramatic tomb?"

Shapiro was apologetic next morning. He did not realize that the desolate spaces of Mars would have such a bad effect on him. He knew he was acting foolishly. It was his determination to take a grip on himself. He was looking forward to seeing Olympus, and would be fine, he felt sure, on the way home. There was just—well, the realization that their lives balanced on a knife-edge.

Clapping him affectionately on the shoulder, Brooks said, "Life is always lived on a knife-edge. Don't worry."

By ten that morning, when the sun was shining through its blue glaze, they caught sight of a dark crust beyond the curve of the horizon. It was the volcano.

Both men cheered.

The volcano grew throughout the day, arising from behind the humps of the Bulge. Hour by hour, they gained a clearer impression of its size. It was a vast tomb of igneous rock which would have dominated any continent on Earth. It would have stretched from Shapiro's Chicago to Buffalo, obliterating Lake Erie. It would have stretched from Switzerland to London, obliterating Paris and most of Belgium. It would have stretched from Lhasa in Tibet to Calcutta, obliterating Mount Everest like a molehill on its way.

Above its shoulders, where the sky was indigo, little demons of lightning danced, corkscrewing their way down into its scarred crust.

It could not be imagined or described. Only photographed.

Brooks brought his films from the refrigerator. He had three SLR cameras besides his homemade "tank." He went to work with cameras, lenses, and filters when they were still over four hundred miles from the giant caldera of Olympus. In the thin air, it appeared deceptively close.

Talking excitedly as he worked, Brooks tried to explain what he felt to Shapiro, who drove with his gaze on the ridged ground ahead.

"Back in the eighteenth century, painters discriminated between the beautiful, the picturesque, and the sublime. You'd need to dream up another category for most of Mars, particularly the dull bits round Arcadia. You wouldn't find much that would square with definitions of 'beautiful' or 'picturesque,' but here we have the sublime and then some . . . This monster has all the elements of awfulness and grandeur which the sublime requires. I wonder what the great painters would have made of Nix Olympica. . . ."

The sun climbed to zenith, and then began to slope away down the western sky.

"Turn direct south, Al. Speed it up, if you can. I want to catch the sunset behind Nix. It should be wonderful."

Shapiro managed a laugh. "I'm doing my best, Ozzy. Don't want to shake the buggy to pieces."

Brooks began loading low-grain fast film into his cameras.

They were traveling over ground composed of flow after flow of lava, one wave upon another, slags, powders, and ejecta cast upon the previous outpourings in grotesque patterns, as if the almost indestructible material had been bent on destroying itself, to the depth of hundreds of fathoms.

Whatever ferment had taken place over eons of time, those eons were themselves now eons past; since then, only silence covered the forbidding highlands—silence without motion, without so much as a wisp of steam from a solitary fumarole.

"Stop here!" Brooks exclaimed suddenly. "Where's that tripod? Oh, god . . . I must get on top of the jeep and film from there."

Grunting, Shapiro did as he was told. Brooks screwed his helmet on, draped his cameras and telescopic lenses over one shoulder, and climbed to the ground. He stood for a while, staring at the ground sloping towards the distant formation, and the sky, in which thin cloud curled like feather some five miles overhead. He took several shots at various shutter speeds almost without thought.

Looking back on his modest life, without distinction of any kind, he could hardly believe his luck. Night was descending on Mars, and he was here to photograph it. Even if Earth soon blew itself up, still he was here, and could record the moment.

His luck was crowned as he started to photograph from the top of the vehicle, using the 8×10 tank, steadying it with the tripod.

Phobos, the innermost moon, appeared to rise from the west—its orbital period being less than Mars's rotation period.

It glittered above the barricades of Nix Olympica. An ice cloud trailed like a pennant above the great volcano. The setting sun emerged from under a band of mist, spilling its light like broken egg along the horizon. The volcano was black in silhouette against the sky. The tank's shutter clicked, as moment by moment the light enriched itself.

Totally engrossed, Brooks slotted a polarizing filter over the lens. Click. Wonderful. Click. Click.

The universe closed down like an oyster on the strip of brightness. The sun seemed to flare and was gone, leaving Nix Olympica to prop up its sky. Brooks opened up his aperture and kept shooting. He knew he would never witness anything like this again. Tomorrow night, they would be on their way home, racing the sinking gauge on the oxygen cylinders. Then it would be up to him to try and recreate this moment in his darkroom, where the hard work would be done.

Next morning, both sergeants were stirring before dawn.

"I've got to capture the first ray of light to touch those crater walls," Brooks said. "Let's try to get fifty miles nearer."

"How about something to eat first, Ozzy?"

"We can eat for the rest of our lives. You drive, okay?"

Shapiro drove while Brooks fussed over his equipment. He threw the vehicle recklessly forward, caught by Brooks's excitement.

He laughed.

"This'll be something to tell people about."

"No mistake there," Brooks said. "Maybe I'll publish an album of the best shots. Hey, Al, maybe we should climb the crater while we're here!"

"Forget it. Fifteen miles up in a space suit, with no climbing gear! I'm not mad even if you are."

They were racing across the bulbous incline. A worn stump of rock loomed ahead.

"Stop and I'll climb that," Brooks said.

When they got to it, the rock proved to be a small cone, a hundred yards across and several feet high. Unmoved by Shapiro's protests, Brooks unclasped the portable ladder from the jeep and climbed to the top. The crater was plugged with ancient magma and covered with dust. He got the tripod and the cameras in place just as the sun rose from behind a shoulder of Tharsis.

Click. This time, the fortress of Olympus was bright against a dark sky. For a moment, the outline of Tharsis was printed in shadow on its eastern flank. Click. Then like an iceberg of untold mass, it was floating on a sea of shadow. Click. The shadow withdrew across the plain towards the men. Mists rose. Click. For no more than five minutes, the great mesa was softened by evaporating carbon dioxide fumes. Click.

"Wonderful, wonderful!" said Brooks. He found that Shapiro had followed him up the ladder. Rapture was on both their faces. They hugged each other and laughed. They took shots of each other standing by the volcanic cone.

They forgot to eat and, throughout the morning, drove as fast as they could towards the volcano. It was a magnet, bathed in light.

At midday, they stopped to drink ham and green pea soup.

They were still over one hundred and fifty miles from Olympus. It spread grandly before them: its great shield, its summit caldera—not a vent as in Earth's familiar stratovolcanoes but a relapse of the summit region—its flanking escarpments, its pattern of frozen lava runs, which from this distance resembled tresses of hair. From above, as Brooks knew, Nix Olympica resembled the nipple of a Martian Juno.

They gazed out at this brilliant formation as they slurped down their soup. It occupied one hundred and twelve degrees of their vision, although it was still so distant.

Shapiro turned from the sight and checked their instruments.

"We're doing okay, but getting near the safety margin on both fuel and oxygen. Are you almost ready to turn homewards, Ozzy?"

Brooks hesitated, then spoke in a nonchalant manner. "I'm almost ready. There's just one thing left to do. We've got some fine photographs in the bag, and by the time I bring the negatives up, there just could be a masterpiece or two among them. The only problem is the question of scale. Since there's no means of comparison in any of the pictures, you can't get an idea of the magnitude of Nix."

They looked at each other. Shapiro said, "You want me to leave you here and then drive the jeep nearer, so that you can have it in the foreground?"

"I don't want the truck in. Besides, I need to be mobile myself. I want you in it, Al—the human figure. I want to put you forward in the landscape. Then I move around taking shots."

Shapiro became rigid.

"I won't do that, Ozzy."

"Why not?"

"I won't do it."

"Tell me why."

"Because I just won't."

"Look, Al, we'll never be out of sight of each other. We'll be in radio contact. You'll be able to see the jeep all the while. All you have to do is stand where I put you. It'll take an hour, no more."

"No, I said. I'm not standing out in that landscape alone. That's flat, okay?"

They glowered at each other.

"You go out there. I'll take the damned pictures."

"I'm not afraid to go out there. Come on, Al, we've come all this way. There's nothing to be scared of, for Christ's sake. One hour, that's all I ask."

Shapiro dropped his gaze, clenching his fists together.

"You can't make me do it."

"I'm not making you. What's so difficult? You just do it."

"Suppose something happens?"

"Nothing has happened here for century after century. Not a thing."

Shapiro expelled a sigh. His face showed the tension inside him. His skin gleamed in the flat light.

"Okay. I'll do it, I guess."

"Okay." Brooks hesitated then said, "I appreciate it, Al. The medics haven't yet got round to naming a fear of wide open alien spaces, but they will. I know it must take some fighting."

"I'll conquer it. Just don't talk about it," said Al, his teeth chattering, as Brooks helped him secure the helmet of his suit.

"Sometimes there's need for talk. Remember, same demons and spirits haunt wide open spaces of Mars as those of Earth. No difference really, since all apparitions are in the mind. If we import demons, then we can conquer them, because they must obey our laws."

"I'll try and bear that in mind," said Shapiro, forcing his teeth to stop chattering. "Now let me out before I think better of it."

• • •

All the while Brooks drove back and forth about that portion of the Bulge, taking his historic shots of Nix Olympica, he was aware of what the distant white figure was
undergoing as it stood alone in the grotesque landscape.
He proceeded without haste, but he worked as fast as possible, concentrating now on his wide-angle lenses:

The end result of the men's endeavor was the series of
photographs which became historic records of mankind's
expansion through the solar system. They rank as works
of art. As for Brooks, despite a period of fame, he eventually died in penury. General Shapiro ended up as Officer
Commanding Mars Base; his memoirs, in four volumes,
contain an account of his first reconnaissance of Olympus—which differs considerably from the facts as set
down here.

THE VERY PULSE OF THE MACHINE

Michael Swanwick

"The Very Pulse of the Machine" appeared in the February 1998 issue of Asimov's, *with an interior illustration by Alan Giana.*

Michael Swanwick made his debut in 1980, and in the nineteen years that have followed has established himself as one of SF's most prolific and consistently excellent writers at short lengths, as well as one of the premier novelists of his generation. Swanwick has published a long string of stories in Asimov's, *under two different editors, and has always been one of our most popular writers—being, for instance, the only writer ever to have two different novels serialized in our pages. He has several times been a finalist for the Nebula Award, as well as for the World Fantasy Award and for the John W. Campbell Award, and has won the Theodore Sturgeon Award and the* Asimov's *Readers' Award poll. In 1991, his novel* Stations of the Tide *won him a Nebula Award as well, and in 1995 he won the World Fantasy Award for his story "Radio Waves." His other books include his first novel,* In the Drift, *which was published in 1985, the novella*

Griffin's Egg, *1987's popular novel* Vacuum Flow-ers, *and a critically acclaimed fantasy novel* The Iron Dragon's Daughter, *which was a finalist for the World Fantasy Award and the Arthur C. Clarke Award (a rare distinction!). His most recent novel,* Jack Faust, *a sly reworking of the Faust legend that explores the unexpected impact of technology on society, has garnered rave reviews from nearly every source from the* Washington Post *to* Inter-zone. *His short fiction has been assembled in* Grav-ity's Angels *and in a collection of his collaborative short work with other writers,* Slow Dancing Through Time. *His most recent books are a collec-tion of critical essays,* The Postmodern Archipel-ago, *and a new collection,* A Geography of Unknown Lands, *and he's currently at work on a new novel. Swanwick lives in Philadelphia with his wife Marianne Porter, and their son Sean.*

Here he takes us on a visit to the Jupiter system, a place almost complex enough to be a miniature solar system on its own, where many moons and moonlets orbit the immense banded gas-giant, and then down to one of the strangest locations known to human science, to the tortured, molten, ever-changing surface of Jupiter's strangest moon, Io, for a close encounter of a unique and surprising kind . . .

Click.

The radio came on.

"Hell."

Martha kept her eyes forward, concentrated on walking. Jupiter to one shoulder, Daedalus's plume to the other. Nothing to it. Just trudge, drag, trudge, drag. Piece of cake.

"Oh."

She chinned the radio off.

Click.

"Hell. Oh. Kiv. El. Sen."

"Shut up, shut up, shut up!" Martha gave the rope an angry jerk, making the sledge carrying Burton's body jump and bounce on the sulfur hardpan. "You're dead, Burton, I've checked, there's a hole in your face-plate big enough to stick a fist through, and I really don't want to crack up. I'm in kind of a tight spot here and I can't afford it, okay? So be nice and just shut the fuck up."

"Not. Bur. Ton."

"Do it anyway."

She chinned the radio off again.

Jupiter loomed low on the western horizon, big and bright and beautiful and, after two weeks on Io, easy to ignore. To her left, Daedalus was spewing sulfur and sulfur dioxide in a fan two hundred kilometers high. The plume caught the chill light from an unseen sun and her visor rendered it a pale and lovely blue. Most spectacular view in the universe, and she was in no mood to enjoy it.

Click.

Before the voice could speak again, Martha said, "I am not going crazy, you're just the voice of my subconscious, I don't have the time to waste trying to figure out what unresolved psychological conflicts gave rise to all this, and I am *not* going to listen to anything you have to say."

Silence.

The moonrover had flipped over at least five times before crashing sideways against a boulder the size of the Sydney Opera House. Martha Kivelsen, timid groundling that she was, was strapped into her seat so tightly that when the universe stopped tumbling, she'd had a hard time unlatching the restraints. Juliet Burton, tall and athletic, so sure of her own luck and agility that she hadn't bothered, had been thrown into a strut.

The vent-blizzard of sulfur dioxide snow was blinding, though. It was only when Martha had finally crawled out from under its raging whiteness that she was able to look at the suited body she'd dragged free of the wreckage.

She immediately turned away.

Whatever knob or flange had punched the hole in Burton's helmet had been equally ruthless with her head.

Where a fraction of the vent-blizzard—"lateral plumes" the planetary geologists called them—had been deflected by the boulder, a bank of sulfur dioxide snow had built up. Automatically, without thinking, Martha scooped up double-handfuls and packed them into the helmet. Really, it was a nonsensical thing to do; in a vacuum, the body wasn't about to rot. On the other hand, it hid that face.

Then Martha did some serious thinking.

For all the fury of the blizzard, there was no turbulence. Because there was no atmosphere to have turbulence *in*. The sulfur dioxide gushed out straight from the sudden crack that had opened in the rock, falling to the surface miles away in strict obedience to the laws of ballistics. Most of what struck the boulder they'd crashed against would simply stick to it, and the rest would be bounced down to the ground at its feet. So that—this was how she'd gotten out in the first place—it was possible to crawl *under* the near-horizontal spray and back to the ruins of the moonrover. If she went slowly, the helmet light and her sense of feel ought to be sufficient for a little judicious salvage.

Martha got down on her hands and knees. And as she did, just as quickly as the blizzard had begun—it stopped.

She stood, feeling strangely foolish.

Still, she couldn't rely on the blizzard staying quiescent. Better hurry, she admonished herself. It might be an intermittent.

Quickly, almost fearfully, picking through the rich litter of wreckage, Martha discovered that the mother tank they used to replenish their airpacks had ruptured. Terrific.

That left her own pack, which was one-third empty, two
fully charged backup packs, and Burton's, also one-third
empty. It was a ghoulish thing to strip Burton's suit of
her airpack, but it had to be done. Sorry, Julie. That gave
her enough oxygen to last, let's see, almost forty hours.

Then she took a curved section of what had been the
moonrover's hull and a coil of nylon rope, and with two
pieces of scrap for makeshift hammer and punch, fashioned a sledge for Burton's body.

She'd be damned if she was going to leave it behind.

Click.

"This is. Better."

"Says you."

Ahead of her stretched the hard, cold sulfur plain.
Smooth as glass. Brittle as frozen toffee. Cold as hell. She
called up a visor-map and checked her progress. Only
forty-five miles of mixed terrain to cross and she'd reach
the lander. Then she'd be home free. No sweat, she
thought. Io was in tidal lock with Jupiter. So the Father
of Planets would stay glued to one fixed spot in the sky.
That was as good as a navigation beacon. Just keep Jupiter
to your right shoulder, and Daedalus to your left. You'll
come out fine.

"Sulfur is. Triboelectric."

"Don't hold it in. What are you really trying to say?"

"And now I see. With eye serene. The very. Pulse. Of
the machine." A pause. "Wordsworth."

Which, except for the halting delivery, was so much
like Burton, with her classical education and love of classical poets like Spenser and Ginsberg and Plath, that for
a second Martha was taken aback. Burton was a terrible
poetry bore, but her enthusiasm had been genuine, and
now Martha was sorry for every time she'd met those
quotations with rolled eyes or a flip remark. But there'd

be time enough for grieving later. Right now she had to concentrate on the task at hand.

The colors of the plain were dim and brownish. With a few quick chin-taps, she cranked up their intensity. Her vision filled with yellows, oranges, reds—intense wax crayon colors. Martha decided she liked them best that way.

For all its Crayola vividness, this was the most desolate landscape in the universe. She was on her own here, small and weak in a harsh and unforgiving world. Burton was dead. There was nobody else on all of Io. Nobody to rely on but herself. Nobody to blame if she fucked up. Out of nowhere, she was filled with an elation as cold and bleak as the distant mountains. It was shameful how happy she felt.

After a minute, she said, "Know any songs?"

Oh the bear went over the mountain. The bear went over the mountain. The bear went over the mountain. To see what he could see.

"Wake. Up. Wake. Up."

To see what he could—

"Wake. Up. Wake. Up. Wake."

"Hah? What?"

"Crystal sulfur is orthorhombic."

She was in a field of sulfur flowers. They stretched as far as the eye could see, crystalline formations the size of her hand. Like the poppies of Flanders field. Or the ones in *The Wizard of Oz*. Behind her was a trail of broken flowers, some crushed by her feet or under the weight of the sledge, others simply exploded by exposure to her suit's waste heat. It was far from being a straight path. She had been walking on autopilot, and stumbled and turned and wandered upon striking the crystals.

Martha remembered how excited she and Burton had been when they first saw the fields of crystals. They had piled out of the moonrover with laughter and bounding leaps, and Burton had seized her by the waist and waltzed her around in a dance of jubilation. This was the big one, they'd thought, their chance at the history books. And even when they'd radioed Hols back in the orbiter and were somewhat condescendingly informed that there was no chance of this being a new life-form, but only sulfide formations such as could be found in any mineralogy text . . . even that had not killed their joy. It was still their first big discovery. They'd looked forward to many more.

Now, though, all she could think of was the fact that such crystal fields occurred in regions associated with sulfur geysers, lateral plumes, and volcanic hot spots.

Something funny was happening to the far edge of the field, though. She cranked up her helmet to extreme magnification and watched as the trail slowly erased itself. New flowers were rising up in place of those she had smashed, small but perfect and whole. And growing. She could not imagine by what process this could be happening. Electrodeposition? Molecular sulfur being drawn up from the soil in some kind of pseudocapillary action? Were the flowers somehow plucking sulfur ions from Io's almost nonexistent atmosphere?

Yesterday, the questions would have excited her. Now, her capacity for wonder was nonexistent. Moreover, her instruments were back in the moonrover. Save for the suit's limited electronics, she had nothing to take measurements with. She had only herself, the sledge, the spare airpacks, and the corpse.

"Damn, damn, damn," she muttered. On the one hand, this was a dangerous place to stay in. On the other, she'd been awake almost twenty hours now and she was dead on her feet. Exhausted. So very, very tired.

"O sleep! It is a gentle thing. Beloved from pole to pole. Coleridge."

Which, God knows, was tempting. But the numbers

were clear: no sleep. With several deft chin-taps, Martha overrode her suit's safeties and accessed its medical kit. At her command, it sent a hit of methamphetamine rushing down the drug/vitamin catheter.

There was a sudden explosion of clarity in her skull and her heart began pounding like a jackhammer. Yeah. That did it. She was full of energy now. Deep breath. Long stride. Let's go.

No rest for the wicked. She had things to do. She left the flowers rapidly behind. Good-bye, Oz.

Fade out. Fade in. Hours had glided by. She was walking through a shadowy sculpture garden. Volcanic pillars (these were their second great discovery; they had no exact parallel on Earth) were scattered across the pyroclastic plain like so many isolated Lipschitz statues. They were all rounded and heaped, very much in the style of rapidly cooled magma. Martha remembered that Burton was dead, and cried quietly to herself for a few minutes.

Weeping, she passed through the eerie stone forms. The speed made them shift and move in her vision. As if they were dancing. They looked like women to her, tragic figures out of *The Bacchae* or, no, wait, *The Trojan Women* was the play she was thinking of. Desolate. Filled with anguish. Lonely as Lot's wife.

There was a light scattering of sulfur dioxide snow on the ground here. It sublimed at the touch of her boots, turning to white mist and scattering wildly, the steam disappearing with each stride and then being renewed with the next footfall. Which only made the experience all that much creepier.

Click.

"Io has a metallic core predominantly of iron and iron sulfide, overlain by a mantle of partially molten rock and crust."

"Are you still here?"

"Am trying. To communicate."

"Shut up."

She topped the ridge. The plains ahead were smooth and undulating. They reminded her of the Moon, in the transitional region between Mare Serenitatis and the foothills of the Caucasus Mountains, where she had undergone her surface training. Only without the impact craters. No impact craters on Io. Least cratered solid body in the solar system. All that volcanic activity deposited a new surface one meter thick every millennium or so. The whole damned moon was being constantly repaved.

Her mind was rambling. She checked her gauges, and muttered, "Let's get this show on the road."

There was no reply.

Dawn would come—when? Let's work this out. Io's "year," the time it took to revolve about Jupiter, was roughly forty-two hours fifteen minutes. She'd been walking seven hours. During which Io would've moved roughly sixty degrees through its orbit. So it would be dawn soon. That would make Daedalus's plume less obvious, but with her helmet graphics that wouldn't be a worry. Martha swiveled her neck, making sure that Daedalus and Jupiter were where they ought to be, and kept on walking.

Trudge, trudge, trudge. Try not to throw the map up on the visor every five minutes. Hold off as long as you can, just one more hour, okay, that's good, and another two miles. Not too shabby.

The sun was getting high. It would be noon in another hour and a half. Which meant—well, it really didn't mean much of anything.

Rock up ahead. Probably a silicate. It was a solitary six meters high brought here by who knew what forces and waiting who knew how many thousands of years just for her to come along and need a place to rest. She found a flat spot where she could lean against it, and, breathing heavily, sat down to rest. And think. And check the airpack. Four hours until she had to change it again. Bringing her down to two airpacks. She had slightly under twenty-four hours now. Thirty-five miles to go. That was less than two miles an hour. A snap. Might run a little tight on oxygen there toward the end, though. She'd have to take care she didn't fall asleep.

Oh, how her body ached.

It ached almost as much as it had in the '48 Olympics, when she'd taken the bronze in the women's marathon. Or that time in the internationals in Kenya when she'd come up from behind to tie for second. Story of her life. Always in third place, fighting for second. Always flight crew and sometimes, maybe, landing crew, but never the commander. Never class president. Never king of the hill. Just once—once!—she wanted to be Neil Armstrong.

Click.

"The marble index of a mind forever. Voyaging through strange seas of thought, alone. Wordsworth."

"What?"

"Jupiter's magnetosphere is the largest thing in the solar system. If the human eye could see it, it would appear two and a half times wider in the sky than the sun does."

"I knew that," she said, irrationally annoyed.

"Quotation is. Easy. Speech is. Not."

"Don't speak, then."

"Trying. To communicate!"

She shrugged. "So go ahead—communicate."

Silence. Then, "What does. This. Sound like?"

"What does what sound like?"

"Io is a sulfur-rich, iron-cored moon in a circular orbit around Jupiter. What does this. Sound like? Tidal forces from Jupiter and Ganymede pull and squeeze Io sufficiently to melt Tartarus, its sub-surface sulfur ocean. Tartarus vents its excess energy with sulfur and sulfur dioxide volcanoes. What does. This sound like? Io's metallic core generates a magnetic field that punches a hole in Jupiter's magnetosphere, and also creates a high-energy ion flux tube connecting its own poles with the north and south poles of Jupiter. What. Does this sound like? Io sweeps up and absorbs all the electrons in the million-volt range. Its volcanoes pump out sulfur dioxide; its magnetic field breaks down a percentage of that into sulfur and oxygen ions; and these ions are pumped into the hole punched in the magnetosphere, creating a rotating field commonly called the Io torus. What does this sound like? Torus. Flux tube. Magnetosphere. Volcanoes. Sulfur ions. Molten ocean. Tidal heating. Circular orbit. What does this sound like?''

Against her will, Martha had found herself first listening, then intrigued, and finally involved. It was like a riddle or a word-puzzle. There was a right answer to the question. Burton or Hols would have gotten it immediately. Martha had to think it through.

There was the faint hum of the radio's carrier beam. A patient, waiting noise.

At last, she cautiously said, ''It sounds like a machine.''

''Yes. Yes. Yes. Machine. Yes. Am machine. Am machine. Am machine. Yes. Yes. Machine. Yes.''

''Wait. You're saying that Io is a machine? That you're a machine? That you're *Io*?''

''Sulfur is triboelectric. Sledge picks up charges. Burton's brain is intact. Language is data. Radio is medium. Am machine.''

''I don't believe you.''

Trudge, drag, trudge, drag. The world doesn't stop for strangeness. Just because she'd gone loopy enough to think that Io was alive and a machine and talking to her, didn't mean that Martha could stop walking. She had promises to keep, and miles to go before she slept. And

speaking of sleep, it was time for another fast refresher—
just a quarter-hit—of speed.

Wow. Let's go!

As she walked, she continued to carry on a dialogue
with her hallucination or delusion or whatever it was. It
was too boring otherwise.

Boring, and a tiny bit terrifying.

So she asked, "If you're a machine, then what is your
function? Why were you made?"

"To know you. To love you. And to serve you."

Martha blinked. Then, remembering Burton's long rem-
iniscences on her Catholic girlhood, she laughed. That
was a paraphrase of the answer to the first question in the
old Baltimore Catechism: *Why did God make man?* "If I
keep on listening to you, I'm going to come down with
delusions of grandeur."

"You are. Creator. Of machine."

"Not me."

She walked on without saying anything for a time.
Then, because the silence was beginning to get to her
again, "When was it I supposedly created you?"

"So many a million of ages have gone. To the making
of man. Alfred, Lord Tennyson."

"That wasn't me, then. I'm only twenty-seven. You're
obviously thinking of somebody else."

"It was. Mobile. Intelligent. Organic. Life. You are.
Mobile. Intelligent. Organic. Life."

Something moved in the distance. Martha looked up,
astounded. A horse. Pallid and ghostly white, it galloped
soundlessly across the plains, tail and mane flying.

She squeezed her eyes tight and shook her head. When
she opened her eyes again, the horse was gone. A hallucination. Like the voice of Burton/Io. She'd been thinking
of ordering up another refresher of the meth, but now it
seemed best to put it off as long as possible.

This was sad, though. Inflating Burton's memories until

they were as large as Io. Freud would have a few things to say about *that*. He'd say she was magnifying her friend to a godlike status in order to justify the fact that she'd never been able to compete one-on-one with Burton and win. He'd say she couldn't deal with the fact that some people were simply better at things than she was.

Trudge, drag, trudge, drag.

So, okay, yes, she had an ego problem. She was an overambitious, self-centered bitch. So what? It had gotten her this far, where a more reasonable attitude would have left her back in the slums of greater Levittown. Making do with an eight-by-ten room with bathroom rights and a job as a dental assistant. Kelp and talapia every night, and rabbit on Sunday. The hell with that. She was alive and Burton wasn't—by any rational standard that made her the winner.

"Are you. Listening?"

"Not really, no."

She topped yet another rise. And stopped dead. Down below was a dark expanse of molten sulfur. It stretched, wide and black, across the streaked orange plains. A lake. Her helmet readouts ran a thermal topography from the negative 230°F at her feet of 65°F at the edge of the lava flow. Nice and balmy. The molten sulfur itself, of course, existed at higher ambient temperatures.

It lay dead in her way.

They'd named it Lake Styx.

Martha spent half an hour muttering over her topo maps, trying to figure out how she'd gone so far astray. Not that it wasn't obvious. All that stumbling around. Little errors that she'd made, adding up. A tendency to favor one leg over the other. It had been an iffy thing from the beginning, trying to navigate by dead reckoning.

Finally, though, it was obvious. Here she was. On the

shores of Lake Styx. Not all that far off course after all. Three miles, maybe, tops.

Despair filled her.

They'd named the lake during their first loop through the Galilean system, what the engineers had called the "mapping run." It was one of the largest features they'd seen that wasn't already on the maps from satellite probes or Earth-based reconnaissance. Hols had thought it might be a new phenomenon—a lake that had achieved its current size within the past ten years or so. Burton had thought it would be fun to check it out. And Martha hadn't cared, so long as she wasn't left behind. So they'd added the lake to their itinerary.

She had been so transparently eager to be in on the first landing, so afraid that she'd be left behind, that when she suggested they match fingers, odd man out, for who stayed, both Burton and Hols had laughed. "I'll play mother," Hols had said magnanimously, "for the first landing. Burton for Ganymede and then you for Europa. Fair enough?" And ruffled her hair.

She'd been so relieved, and so grateful, and so humiliated too. It was ironic. Now it looked like Hols—who would *never* have gotten so far off course as to go down the wrong side of the Styx—wasn't going to get to touch rock at all. Not this expedition.

"Stupid, stupid, stupid," Martha muttered, though she didn't know if she were condemning Hols or Burton or herself. Lake Styx was horse-shoe-shaped and twelve miles long. And she was standing right at the inner toe of the horseshoe.

There was no way she could retrace her steps back around the lake and still get to the lander before her air ran out. The lake was dense enough that she could almost *swim* across it, if it weren't for the viscosity of the sulfur, which would coat her heat radiators and burn out her suit in no time flat. And the heat of the liquid. And whatever internal flows and undertows it might have. As it was, the experience would be like drowning in molasses. Slow and sticky.

She sat down and began to cry.

After a time she began to build up her nerve to grope for the snap-coupling to her airpack. There was a safety for it, but among those familiar with the rig it was an open secret that if you held the safety down with your thumb and yanked suddenly on the coupling, the whole thing would come undone, emptying the suit in less than a second. The gesture was so distinctive that hot young astronauts-in-training would mime it when one of their number said something particularly stupid. It was called the suicide flick.

There were worse ways of dying.

"Will build. Bridge. Have enough. Fine control of. Physical processes. To build. Bridge."

"Yeah, right, very nice, you do that," Martha said absently. If you can't be polite to your own hallucinations . . . She didn't bother finishing the thought. Little crawly things were creeping about on the surface of her skin. Best to ignore them.

"Wait. Here. Rest. Now."

She said nothing but only sat, not resting. Building up her courage. Thinking about everything and nothing. Clutching her knees and rocking back and forth.

Eventually, without meaning to, she fell asleep.

"Wake. Up. Wake. Up. Wake. Up."

"Uhh?"

Martha struggled up into awareness. Something was happening before her, out on the lake. Physical processes were at work. Things were moving.

As she watched, the white crust at the edge of the dark lake bulged outward, shooting out crystals, extending. Lacy as a snowflake. Pale as frost. Reaching across the molten blackness. Until there was a narrow white bridge stretching all the way to the far shore.

"You must. Wait," Io said. "Ten minutes and. You can. Walk across. It. With ease."

"Son of a bitch!" Martha murmured. "I'm sane."

In wondering silence, she crossed the bridge that Io had enchanted across the dark lake. Once or twice the surface felt a little mushy underfoot, but it always held.

It was an exalting experience. Like passing over from Death into Life.

At the far side of the Styx, the pyroclastic plains rose gently toward a distant horizon. She stared up yet another long, crystal-flower-covered slope. Two in one day. What were the odds against that?

She struggled upward, flowers exploding as they were touched by her boots. At the top of the rise, the flowers gave way to sulfur hardpan again. Looking back, she could see the path she had crunched through the flowers begin to erase itself. For a long moment she stood still, venting heat. Crystals shattered soundlessly about her in a slowly expanding circle.

She was itching something awful now. Time to freshen up. Six quick taps brought up a message on her visor: *Warning: Continued use of this drug at current levels can result in paranoia, psychosis, hallucinations, misperceptions, and hypomania, as well as impaired judgment.*

Fuck that noise. Martha dealt herself another hit.

It took a few seconds. Then—whoops. She was feeling light and full of energy again. Best check the airpack reading. Man, that didn't look good. She had to giggle.

Which was downright scary.

Nothing could have sobered her up faster than that high little druggie laugh. It terrified her. Her life depended on her ability to maintain. She had to keep taking meth to keep going, but she also had to keep going under the drug.

She couldn't let it start calling the shots. Focus. Time to switch over to the last airpack. Burton's airpack. "I've got eight hours of oxygen left. I've got twelve miles yet to go. It can be done," she said grimly. "I'm going to do it now."

If only her skin weren't itching. If only her head weren't crawling. If only her brain weren't busily expanding in all directions.

Trudge, drag, trudge, drag. All through the night. The trouble with repetitive labor was that it gave you time to think. Time to think when you were speeding also meant time to think about the quality of your own thought.

You didn't dream in real-time, she'd been told. You get it all in one flash, just as you're about to wake up, and in that instant extrapolate a complex dream all in one whole. It feels as if you've been dreaming for hours. But you've only had one split second of intense nonreality.

Maybe that's what's happening here.

She had a job to do. She had to keep a clear head. It was important that she get back to the lander. People had to *know*. They weren't alone anymore. Damnit, she'd just made the biggest discovery since fire!

Either that, or she was so crazy she was hallucinating that Io was a gigantic alien machine. So crazy she'd lost herself within the convolutions of her own brain.

Which was another terrifying thing she wished she hadn't thought of. She'd been a loner as a child. Never made friends easily. Never had or been a best friend to anybody. Had spent half her girlhood buried in books. Solipsism terrified her—she'd lived right on the edge of it for too long. So it was vitally important that she determine whether the voice of Io had an objective, external reality. Or not.

Well, how could she test it?

Sulfur was triboelectric, Io had said. Implying that it

was in some way an electrical phenomenon. If so, then it ought to be physically demonstrable.

Martha directed her helmet to show her the electrical charges within the sulfur plains. Crank it up to the max.

The land before her flickered once, then lit up in fairy-land colors. Light! Pale oceans of light overlaying light, shifting between pastels, from faded rose to boreal blue, multilayered, labyrinthine, and all pulsing gently within the heart of the sulfur rock. It looked like thought made visual. It looked like something straight out of Disney Virtual, and not one of the nature channels either—definitely DV-3.

"Damn," she muttered. Right under her nose. She'd had no idea.

Glowing lines veined the warping wings of subterranean electromagnetic forces. Almost like circuit wires. They crisscrossed the plains in all directions, combining and then converging—not upon her, but in a nexus at the sled. Burton's corpse was lit up like neon. Her head, packed in sulfur dioxide snow, strobed and stuttered with light so rapidly that it shone like the sun.

Sulfur was triboelectric. Which meant that it built up a charge when rubbed.

She'd been dragging Burton's sledge over the sulfur surface of Io for how many hours? You could build up a hell of a charge that way.

So, okay. There was a physical mechanism for what she was seeing. Assuming that Io really *was* a machine, a triboelectric alien device the size of Earth's moon, built eons ago for who knows what purpose by who knows what godlike monstrosities, then, yes, it might be able to communicate with her. A lot could be done with electricity.

Lesser, smaller, and dimmer "circuitry" reached for Martha as well. She looked down at her feet. When she lifted one from the surface, the contact was broken, and the lines of force collapsed. Other lines were born when she put her foot down again. Whatever slight contact might be made was being constantly broken. Whereas Burton's sledge was in constant contact with the sulfur surface of Io. That hole in Burton's skull would be a highway straight into her brain. And she'd packed it in solid SO_2 as well. Conductive *and* supercooled. She'd made things easy for Io.

She shifted back to augmented real-color. The DV-3 SFX faded away.

Accepting as a tentative hypothesis that the voice was a real rather than a psychological phenomenon. That Io was able to communicate with her. That it was a machine. That it had been built . . .

Who, then, had built it?

Click.

"Io? Are you listening?"

"Calm on the listening ear of night. Come Heaven's melodious strains. Edmund Hamilton Sears."

"Yeah, wonderful, great. Listen, there's something I'd kinda like to know—who built you?"

"You. Did."

Slyly, Martha said, "So I'm your creator, right?"

"Yes."

"What do I look like when I'm at home?"

"Whatever. You wish. To."

"Do I breathe oxygen? Methane? Do I have antennae? Tentacles? Wings? How many legs do I have? How many eyes? How many heads?"

"If. You wish. As many as. You wish."

"How many of me are there?"

"One." A pause. "Now."

"I was here before, right? People like me. Mobile intelligent life forms. And I left. How long have I been gone?"

Silence. "How long—" she began again.

"Long time. Lonely. So very. Long time."

Trudge, drag. Trudge, drag. Trudge, drag. How many centuries had she been walking? Felt like a lot. It was night again. Her arms felt like they were going to fall out of their sockets.

Really, she ought to leave Burton behind. She'd never said anything to make Martha think she cared one way or the other where her body wound up. Probably would've thought a burial on Io was pretty damn nifty. But Martha wasn't doing this for her. She was doing it for herself. To prove that she wasn't entirely selfish. That she did too have feelings for others. That she was motivated by more than just the desire for fame and glory.

Which, of course, was a sign of selfishness in itself. The desire to be known as selfless. It was hopeless. You could nail yourself to a fucking cross, and it would still be proof of your innate selfishness.

"You still there, Io?"

Click.

"Am. Listening."

"Tell me about this fine control of yours. How much do you have? Can you bring me to the lander faster than I'm going now? Can you bring the lander to me? Can you return me to the orbiter? Can you provide me with more oxygen?"

"Dead egg, I lie. Whole. On a whole world I cannot touch. Plath."

"You're not much use, then, are you?"

There was no answer. Not that she had expected one. Or needed it, either. She checked the topos and found herself another eighth-mile closer to the lander. She could even see it now under her helmet photomultipliers, a dim glint upon the horizon. Wonderful things, photomultipliers. The sun here provided about as much light as a full moon did back on Earth. Jupiter by itself provided even less. Yet crank up the magnification, and she could see the airlock awaiting the grateful touch of her gloved hand.

Trudge, drag, trudge. Martha ran and reran and rereran the math in her head. She had only three miles to go, and enough oxygen for as many hours. The lander had its own air supply. She was going to make it.

Maybe she wasn't the total loser she'd always thought she was. Maybe there was hope for her, after all.

Click.

"Brace. Yourself."

"What for?"

The ground rose up beneath her and knocked her off her feet.

When the shaking stopped, Martha clambered unsteadily to her feet again. The land before her was all a jumble, as if a careless deity had lifted the entire plain up a foot and then dropped it. The silvery glint of the lander on the horizon was gone. When she pushed her helmet's magnification to the max, she could see a metal leg rising crookedly from the rubbled ground.

Martha knew the sheer strength of every bolt and failure point of every welding seam in the lander. She knew exactly how fragile it was. That was one device that was never going to fly again.

She stood motionless. Unblinking. Unseeing. Feeling nothing. Nothing at all.

Eventually she pulled herself together enough to think. Maybe it was time to admit it: she never *had* believed she was going to make it. Not really. Not Martha Kivelsen. All her life she'd been a loser. Sometimes—like when she qualified for the expedition—she lost at a higher level than usual. But she never got whatever it was she really wanted.

Why was that, she wondered? When had she ever desired anything bad? When you get right down to it, all she'd ever wanted was to kick God in the butt and get his attention. To be a big noise. To be the biggest fucking noise in the universe. Was that so unreasonable?

Now she was going to wind up as a footnote in the annals of humanity's expansion into space. A sad little cautionary tale for mommy astronauts to tell their baby astronauts on cold winter nights. Maybe Burton could've gotten back to the lander. Or Hols. But not *her*. It just wasn't in the cards.

Click.

"Io is the most volcanically active body in the solar system."

"You fucking bastard! Why didn't you warn me?"

"Did. Not. Know."

Now her emotions returned to her in full force. She wanted to run and scream and break things. Only there wasn't anything in sight that hadn't already been broken. "You shithead!" she cried. "You idiot machine! What use are you? What goddamn use at all?"

"Can give you. Eternal life. Communion of the soul. Unlimited processing power. Can give Burton. Same."

"Hah?"

"After the first death. There is no other. Dylan Thomas."

"What do you mean by that?"

Silence.

"Damn you, you fucking machine! What are you trying to say?"

Then the devil took Jesus up into the holy city and set him on the highest point of the temple, and said to him, "If thou be the Son of God, cast thyself down: for it is written he shall give his angels charge concerning thee: and in their hands they shall bear thee up."

Burton wasn't the only one who could quote scripture. You didn't have to be Catholic, like her. Presbyterians could do it too.

Martha wasn't sure what you'd call this feature. A volcanic phenomenon of some sort. It wasn't very big. Maybe twenty meters across, not much higher. Call it a crater, and let be. She stood shivering at its lip. There was a black pool of molten sulfur at its bottom, just as she'd been told. Supposedly its roots reached all the way down to Tartarus.

Her head ached so badly.

Io claimed—had *said*—that if she threw herself in, it would be able to absorb her, duplicate her neural patterning, and so restore her to life. A transformed sort of life, but life nonetheless. "Throw Burton in," it had said. "Throw yourself in. Physical configuration will be. Destroyed. Neural configuration will be. Preserved. Maybe."

"Maybe?"

"Burton had limited. Biological training. Understanding of neural functions may be. Imperfect."

"Wonderful."

"Or. Maybe not."

"Gotcha."

Heat radiated up from the bottom of the crater. Even protected and shielded as she was by her suit's HVAC systems, she felt the difference between front and back. It was like standing in front of a fire on a very cold night.

They had talked, or maybe negotiated was a better word for it, for a long time. Finally Martha had said, "You savvy Morse code? You savvy orthodox spelling?"

"Whatever Burton. Understood. Is. Understood."

"Yes or no, damnit!"

"Savvy."

"Good. Then maybe we can make a deal."

• • •

She stared up into the night. The orbiter was out there somewhere, and she was sorry she couldn't talk directly to Hols, say good-bye and thanks for everything. But Io had said no. What she planned would raise volcanoes and level mountains. The devastation would dwarf that of the earthquake caused by the bridge across Lake Styx.

It couldn't guarantee two separate communications.

The ion flux tube arched from somewhere over the horizon in a great looping jump to the north pole of Jupiter. Augmented by her visor, it was as bright as the sword of God.

As she watched, it began to sputter and jump, millions of watts of power dancing staccato in a message they'd be picking up on the surface of Earth. It would swamp every radio and drown out every broadcast in the Solar System.

THIS IS MARTHA KIVELSEN, SPEAKING FROM THE SURFACE OF IO ON BEHALF OF MYSELF, JULIET BURTON, DECEASED, AND JACOB HOLS, OF THE FIRST GALILEAN SATELLITES EXPLORATORY MISSION. WE HAVE MADE AN IMPORTANT DISCOVERY . . .

Every electrical device in the System would *dance* to its song!

Burton went first. Martha gave the sledge a shove, and out it flew, into empty space. It dwindled, hit, kicked up a bit of a splash. Then, with a disappointing lack of pyrotechnics, the corpse slowly sank into the black glop.

It didn't look very encouraging at all.

Still . . .

"Okay," she said. "A deal's a deal." She dug in her toes and spread her arms. Took a deep breath. Maybe I am going to survive after all, she thought. It could be Burton was already halfway-merged into the oceanic mind of Io, and awaiting her to join in an alchemical marriage of personalities. Maybe I'm going to live forever. Who knows? Anything is possible.

Maybe.

There was a second and more likely possibility. All this could well be nothing more than a hallucination. Nothing but the sound of her brain short-circuiting and squirting bad chemicals in all directions. Madness. One last grandiose dream before dying. Martha had no way of judging.

Whatever the truth might be, though, there were no alternatives, and only one way to find out.

She jumped.

Briefly, she flew.

EX VITRO

Daniel Marcus

*"Ex Vitro" appeared in the mid-December 1995
issue of* Asimov's, *with an illustration by Mike As-
pengren. Daniel Marcus is a graduate of Clarion
West who holds a PhD in engineering and who has
worked as an applied mathematician at the
Lawrence Livermore National Laboratory. His
technical papers have appeared in* Communications
in Mathematical Physics *and the* Journal of Theoretical and Computational Fluid Dynamics, *but he
made his first fiction sale within the genre in 1992,
and has since appeared in* Asimov's Science Fiction, The Magazine of Fantasy and Science Fiction,
and Science Fiction Age. *In 1995, he was a finalist
for the John W. Campbell Award for Best New
Writer, was marketing his first novel, and was at
work on several more. He lives with his wife in
Berkeley, California, where he also teaches a
course in science fiction writing.*

*Here he takes us to a moon orbiting the ringed
gas-giant Saturn, perhaps the most instantly rec-
ognizable planet in the Solar System, and down to
an all-too-fragile-dome on the hostile frozen surface of that moon, for an engrossing meditation on
love, death, life, and identity.*

I

The communications room was a weird place. Jax wanted to hunch his shoulders against the close metal walls, against the silent machines that smelled faintly of ozone and heat. An array of yellow telltales glowed steadily on the panel over his head; the blank, grey screen hung before him like an open mouth. The one decoration in the barren cubicle was a software ad-fax Maddy had taped to the wall—INSTANT ACCESS, some sort of file-retrieval utility, the first word highlighted in blue and the letters slanted, trailing comb-like filigrees denoting speed.

There was something that drew him to the place, though, and he caught solitary time there whenever he could. He imagined himself a point of light on the far tip of a rocky promontory, a beacon rising above a dark, endless ocean.

Jax heard a sound behind him and turned around. Maddy stood in the doorway. She had been working out, and her shirt was damp with sweat. Ringlets of dark hair framed her face; red splotches stood out high on her pale cheeks.

"What's up?" she asked, still a little short of breath. "I didn't hear a comm bell . . ."

"Nothing," Jax replied. "I'm just hanging. Fog's really bad—we can't even watch the slugs."

Maddy shrugged. The slugs didn't interest her much—anything that happened on time-scales shorter than a thousand millennia slid under her radar. Titan itself, though, was to her like a blood-glittering, faceted ruby to a gemologist. Ammonia seas, vast lava fields laced with veins of waxy, frozen hydrocarbons. She was taking ultrasound readings to map the moon's crust and mantle. Jax had never seen her so engaged, but the news from home was like a tidal force pulling at her from another direction.

"Anything new on the laser feed?" she asked.

Jax knew that, decoded, the question was, "War news?" Or more specifically, "How bad does it have to get before we can go home?"

She had family in the EC, in Paris, and the information that came in on the feed was frustrating in what it withheld. It was like deducing the shape and texture of an object by studying the shadow it cast in bright, white light.

They did know that a couple of days ago, PacRim had lobbed a mininuke at one of the EC's factory-continents in the Indian Ocean, claiming a territorial incursion. The EC had followed suit by vaporizing Jakarta. There had been some sporadic ground combat in New Zealand and Antarctica and a lot of saber-rattling, but no further nuclear exchanges. The North American Free Trade Coalition and the Russian Hegemony were sitting back and waiting, urging restraint and dialogue in the emergency League session and keeping ground and space defenses at full alert.

"PacRim's been making noises about a nova bomb, but nobody really thinks they're *that* crazy. Naft's warning everybody off their wind farms in the South Atlantic— that's not exactly news, not since Johannesburg." Jax shook his head. "The Net's going completely apeshit, of course. Traffic volume's sky high . . ."

She took a step toward him and he stood up and put his arms around her. They stood like that for several minutes, their breathing merging slowly to unison. She smelled of sweat and of the hydroponics media she had been working with earlier that morning. The taut, lean muscles of her back relaxed to a yielding firmness under his hands. She began to move against him, and she gently pushed him back into the chair.

"Wait," he said. "Not here. Let's go to the pod."

Maddy nodded without speaking and turned around,

reaching behind her back for his hand. He took it and
trailed her down the narrow corridor. They passed other
passageways branching off, leading to sleeping quarters,
the galley, the labs. At the end of the corridor, standing
like an abstract sculpture, was a gleaming, twisted piece
of obsidian Maddy had brought in from one of Titan's
lava plains. Oxidation from the station's atmosphere gave
its surface a rainbow sheen. A rude step was carved into
its side with a hand laser. Above it was a round, open
hatch. Maddy let go of his hand, stepped up onto the rock,
and pulled herself through. Jax followed behind her,
emerging into a crystalline bubble surrounded by a sea of
swirling mist.

They had grown the pod from a single crystal into a
transparent, 5-meter hemisphere. It was light and thin, but
strong enough to keep out the deadly hydrocarbon brew
that was Titan's atmosphere. The fog was beginning to
thin a little, and through it Jax could see the frozen landscape glittering in tenebrous, diffuse light. He caught a
glimpse of a herd of slugs on the shore of the nearby
ammonia sea. Their shiny, chitinous bodies were scattered
across the lava beach in a rough pattern, like sheared concentric diamonds, slowly shifting.

Maddy had already taken her clothes off, and she stood
facing him, waiting. Jax stepped out of his shorts and put
his arms around her again. They stood there, rocking
slowly, then together they sank to the carpeted floor.

When Maddy came, a shuddering ripple passed unseen
through the pattern made by the slugs' bodies. Jax's pleasure shortly afterward sent another wave passing through
the pattern from the opposite side. The ripples collided
and scattered, each leaving an imprint of its shape on the
other.

Jax gently disentangled himself from Maddy, trying not
to wake her. She groaned softly once and rolled over, then

her breathing returned to normal. Her face was relaxed and completely expressionless, as if sleep were a black hole from which nothing of herself escaped.

For an instant, it looked to Jax like the face of a perfect stranger, its contours so achingly familiar that the familiarity itself was something exotic. He reached out to touch her, and his hand hovered above the curve of her cheek, trembling slightly.

So strange, he thought, the two of us out here, middle of nowhere, ties to home nothing more than electromagnetic ephemera. Ghosts. What are we to each other in the absence of context? We create our own, always have.

They'd met when they were graduate students at the Sorbonne, Maddy in planetary physics, Jax in system dynamics. They were both driven to succeed, the shining stars in their respective departments' firmament of hopeful students, and they gravitated toward one another with the same intensity that fueled their research.

They cycled through several iterations of crash and burn, learning each other's boundaries, before they settled into a kind of steady state. Still, their relationship felt to Jax like a living entity, a nonlinear filter whose response to stimuli was never quite what you thought it was going to be.

Individually, they were excellent candidates for SunGroup, a system-wide industrial development consortium—mining, pharmaceuticals, SP-sats, all supported by a broad base of research and exploration. As a couple they were perfect for one of Sun's elite research teams. When they finished out their three-year term, especially if they had "made their bones" by discovering something of interest and potential profit, they would have enough clout in SunGroup to command their own programs.

The slugs were certainly of interest. They were at the apex of Titan's spartan ecosystem—black, almost featureless bullet-shaped creatures about the size of dogs.

Methane-breathers, they basked in the shallows of Titan's ammonia seas and fed on anything organic—the primitive lichen that grew in sporadic patches on the moon's rough surface, the glittering chunks of hydrocarbon ice scattered like moraine across the landscape, even each other.

Jax could watch them for hours. They exhibited behavior not unlike schooling or flocking, merging in geometric clusters, shifting, forming new patterns. Individually, they seemed less sensate than bees; their central nervous system consisted of nothing more than a small knot of ganglia at the wider end, where there was a cluster of light-sensitive vision patches. They were living cellular automata—each responding only to nearest-neighbor stimuli. Collectively, though, from the local interactions, there emerged a complex, evolving pattern.

The fog was thick again, a uniform shroud. It seemed to glow with a dim, pearly light of its own. Jax wondered about the slugs outside, what they were doing. He closed his eyes and in that darkness he imagined a slowly shifting pattern of glowing points, an elongated oval surrounding a hard, geometric figure of sharp edges and straight lines.

II

Maddy took another leaf from the small pile of lettuce in the colander and put it in her mouth. The taste was so bittersweet *green*, so substantial and earthy, that it brought tears to her eyes.

"The new crop of lettuce is really good," she said. "I think I finally got the 'ponics chemistry down."

"About time," Jax said. He looked up from the catfish he was cleaning. Fresh from the tank-farm, its bright organs spilled out on the cutting board. Blood streaked his hands and the smell of it was strong and sharp in the little galley. "The last batch had that weird, rotten aftertaste. I kept waiting for the cramps to start."

"Well, *fuck* you, then." The words seemed to materialize in the air between them, as if they had come from somewhere separate from her. She felt color rising to her cheeks, but there was no place to go but forward. "Anytime you want the job, you just say so."

Jax looked startled and hurt. He wiped his cheek, leaving a bloody streak, and bent down to his work again. His large hands were quick and sure. Maddy could feel the tension between them like a third presence in the room. She took a deep breath and let it out. Again. In, I calm my body. Out, dwelling in the present moment. In, listen, listen. Out, the sound of my breathing brings me back to my true self.

She took a step toward him and put her hand on his arm. He looked up. She kissed his cheek, tasting blood.

"I'm sorry, baby," she said. "I'm a little wired out with the war news. I can't take much more of it." She bit her lip. "If it gets any worse, I'm going to want Sun to pull us out of here. I need to be near my parents."

"Jesus, Maddy, Paris is the last place we want to be if the shit really hits the fan—it'll go up in a puff of plasma." He paused when he saw the expression on her face and reached out to touch her arm. "I'm sorry, but you know it's true. Do you really want to move to Ground Zero?" He let his arm fall again. "Besides, if we abort, they'll nail us with a stiff fine and we'll never get them to back us again."

"We can afford it."

Jax shrugged. "We can afford the fine, yeah, but we'd have to start from scratch with another Group, and that wouldn't be easy."

"Maurice will swing it for us." Maurice Enza was their sponsor at Sun-Group. A hundred-thirty-two years old, mostly cybernetic prosthetics including eyes and voice-box, still publishing in the theoretical bio-economics literature. Maddy revered him. Jax respected him, but privately thought he was something of a spook and had always kept him at a polite distance.

"Maurice may be as old as Elvis but he isn't God."

Maddy closed her eyes. In, I calm my body. Out, listen, listen.

She opened her eyes and looked closely at him. His face was open and earnest. He wasn't just being an asshole or doing some kind of power thing.

Maddy smiled gently. "Let's just see what happens, okay?"

The catfish was delicious, its flesh moist and white, the Cajun-style crust black and redolent with spice. The lettuce tasted sweeter with the fact that she had grown it with her own hands, nursed from a rack of seedlings in a carefully tended nutrient bath to full, leafy plants, their tangled roots weaving through their bed of saturated foam.

They ate together in silence. A Bach violin concerto played softly on the lounge speakers, the melodic lines arching gracefully over the muted hum of the life support systems.

Strange to be so connected with the sensate, Maddy thought, these earthy pleasures, while we're in this tin can at the bottom of an ocean of freezing poison, a billion and a half klicks from most of the people I love. Where everything's falling apart. Listening to Bach, no less.

She shook her head. Cognitive dissonance.

Jax looked over at her and smiled. "What?"

"Oh, nothing, I . . . I don't know." She held her hands out in front of her, palms up, as if she were gauging the weight of an invisible package.

The veined rock flashed by her in a grey, flickering blur. Every now and then, she emerged into an open space for an instant and caught a brief glimpse of distant walls, stalactites and stalagmites merging in midair to form complex, bulbous shapes, ghostly green in the enhanced infrared. Then the bottom wall would rush up and swallow her again. A readout on the display in the lower left corner of her vision flashed her depth below the surface.

Maddy saw a fault open up off to her left and she steered her way over to it by opening the right-hand throttle of her jetpack, a bit of Buck Rogers kitsch she'd coded up to contextualize the virtual a bit, give it some tactile reference. Too easy to get disoriented otherwise—simsick.

She followed the fault down toward Titan's core, passing through large black regions where her mapping was still incomplete. The fault twisted and turned, opening at times to a wide crevasse, then narrowing down until it was little more than a stress plane in the tortured rock.

She slowed down and pushed a button on the virtual display. Three-dimensional volume renderings of the stress field in the rock appeared all around her as glowing lines, fractal neon limbs cascading into smaller and smaller filamentary tangles. She filtered the display until all she saw were the glowing tangles against a field of deep, velvet blackness. The fault itself was a tortured sheet of cold fire.

She hovered there in the darkness, surrounded by light. *This* is what I know, she thought. *This* is familiar. She could as well have been in a geosimulation of the Earth's crust. The equations of elasto-plastic deformation are invariant under acts of God and Man. Stochastic, fractal, extraordinarily complex, the solutions could still be understood, predicted with some reliability, projected onto a lower-dimensional attractor for a smoother representation.

All well and good as science. As personal metaphor it had its drawbacks. Maddy knew people back home whose lives were distressingly simple—work, family, sheep-like pursuit of leisure all fixed, remorseless basins of attraction with no fractal boundaries. They eluded her, whatever drove them completely foreign. Her personal trajectory was constrained to a more chaotic topology.

With a corner of her awareness, she could feel her real-time body, helmeted, visored, ensconced in a padded chair in a darkened featureless room.

And in the lab, cocooned in biostasis, the embryo, a radiant point of light in her mind's eye. She could imagine the impossibly slow heartbeat, just enough to keep it suspended above the threshold of death. In quiet moments, she imagined that pulse to be her own, could feel her awareness contract to that tiny lump of blood and meat, miracle of coded proteins. One part Jax, one part Maddy. Something other than the sum of its constituents.

It was usually bearable, her awareness of it a dull, constant pressure in the back of her mind. But sometimes she felt an ache in the deepest part of her, as if it had been torn from her leaving a bleeding, septic cavity. How could it live apart from her? Or she from it? She would tell Jax soon.

III

He turned off the suit speaker. The sibilant whisper of his breath and the deep ocean surge of blood music in his ears rushed in to fill the silence. Titan's daylight sky arched over his head like a great inverted bowl, deep cyan overhead fading to a bruised purple around the horizon. The photochemical smog was thinned to a gauzy softness, a blurring of focus, and Sol hung overhead like a bright, fuzzy diamond. He could almost feel the weight of Saturn's presence suspended unseen in the sky, shielded by Titan's bulk.

He had walked about a klick along the shore. The station was no longer visible behind him and he felt exhilarated with the solitude. A herd of about twenty slugs had been pacing him as he walked, oozing along almost like a single organism. He hadn't been sure at first whether they started trailing him or he them, but he was certain they were aware of him now. When he stopped, they did. He walked another few steps along the rocky shore, and the herd moved along with him like an amoeba, extending a long, thin pseudopod which was then reabsorbed into the main body. This was the first time they had exhibited anything like a response to an external stimulus. Like *awareness*.

What *are* you? They stretched out before him, attenuating into a long, sinuously curving line, like an old river.

He closed his eyes and concentrated as hard as he could. *Tell me what you are.*

In his mind's eye he saw the pattern, a meandering line of bright sparks, ripple slightly. He opened his eyes.

Tell me.

Another rippling wave passed through the line.

He turned on his radio. "Maddy. Can you suit up and get out here. I want—"

"What the fuck have you been doing? I've been trying to reach you for the last hour." Her voice sounded tight and thin.

"I turned off the speaker. I—"

"Can you get in here?" Long pause. "Please?"

The holotank was on, but she was staring off into space. In the transparent, glass cube Jax could see ghostly, flickering images of fire and smoke.

"*—retaliated with a 50-kiloton airburst over Manila. The latest estimates of the death toll—*"

"What's going on?"

She looked up at him. Her eyes were puffy. "Paris."

He felt the word almost like a physical blow. "Shit. Where else?"

She shook her head. "It's all coming apart. Naft and

Russia have managed to keep out of it so far, but it's just a matter of time."

"*—emergency session, but no word yet from the CEO Council—*"

"Anything from SunGroup?"

She shook her head again. She had the look of an accident victim—hollow eyes, slow, deliberate gestures.

"*—ground forces overwhelmed Mitsubishi troops outside Sydney. Conventional theater weapons—*"

Jax waved his hand sharply over a panel on the wall. The volume of the newsfeed decreased to a murmur. The holotank still flickered and glowed with the images of burning cities. He walked over to her and put his hand on her shoulder. She sat there stiffly, as if unaware of his presence; her shoulder felt as if it was made of wood. He put his other hand there and started to knead the tight muscles, but she shook him off.

He stood behind her for a long time, not knowing what to do. Every now and then, Maddy let out a long, shuddering sigh.

Finally she looked up. "What are we going to do?"

He shrugged. "What can we do? We can survive here indefinitely—the station ecology's intact and stable. We continue the research, wait for SunGroup to pull us out of here."

Even as he said it, though, Jax felt a rush of panic at the thought of leaving. He closed his eyes and a matrix of points, white on velvet black, pulsed and flowed. Concentric diamonds, slowly shearing. He opened his eyes and Maddy was staring at him.

"Continue the research? What for? We don't even know if there *is* a SunGroup anymore. We have to find out what's left back there, get back if we can. We can *help*."

Jax was silent for a long time. "What we need to do is survive, Maddy," he said slowly. "Keep the systems green, keep the research going. I'll try to raise Maurice, find out what their status is, but I don't know when they're going to be able to get to us. I think we're pretty much on our own.''

"If they can spare a ship, I want to go home," Maddy said. "Luna, one of the O'Neills, I don't care. Our place right now is back there.''

Jax forced himself to smile reassuringly. "All right, Maddy, we'll see what they can do. We'll have at least three hours until we can get a reply—''

"—a hundred-seventy-four minutes—''

"—providing we can get through at all. The Net is probably stone dead, all those e.m.p.'s.'' He gestured toward the holotank. "That stuff is probably coming in relayed from one of the O'Neills. . . .''

"We can't really tell what's going on back there from the newsfeed—the information entropy is sky-high. We're not going to know until we ask someone who knows something. Let's just do it.''

Together they walked down the corridor to the communications room. Jax logged on, set the protocol, and transmitted Maurice's address from memory.

He faced the blank screen. A section of it elasticized invisibly, ready to transform his voice into digitized bits and hurl them up to the relay satellite waiting at one of Titan's Trojan Points. There was no return visual, of course—dialogue was impossible.

Whenever Jax transmitted across the lightspeed gulf separating him from Earth, he had the sensation that his words were disappearing down a well. He could feel Maddy's presence behind him like a hovering cloud.

"Maurice. This is Jax and Maddy calling from Titan Station.'' Obviously. Where else would they be calling from? "Please advise us as to your status. We—''

"Pull us out of here, Moe,'' Maddy cut in. "Please. We want to come home.''

Jax shot her an annoyed glance and turned back to the screen. "Please advise," he repeated. "End."

Ignoring Maddy, he tried to log onto his WorldNet node, but couldn't get a stable carrier at the other end. Tried routing through Luna, through Olympus Mons, through the O'Neills.

"Nada," he said, shaking his head and looking up. Maddy was gone.

He looked in the lounge. Empty. In the holotank, a pair of translucent figures gestured in animated conversation, but Jax couldn't make out the words. Galley, labs, sleep-room, all empty. Finally, he walked down to the end of the corridor and pulled himself up into the pod. The fog nestled against the dome in thick, soft swirls. Maddy lay curled up on a foam pad, breathing deeply.

He walked past her to the edge of the dome and peered out through the fog. He could just see them, stretched out in a slowly undulating line next to the ammonia sea. The undulations grew until the line broke apart, the segments forming a series of rings. Slowly, one at a time, the rings merged and the pattern segued to a nest of concentric diamonds, slowly shearing. There was sense and meaning to it, he was sure, but comprehension hovered just out of reach. *What are you?*

The soft chime of the comm bell shook Jax out of his reverie. *Three hours? I've been standing here for three hours?* He looked around the dome, his eyes coming to rest on Maddy lying in a fetal curl, her shoulders slowly rising and falling. He stepped over her and lowered himself down the hatch.

There was no visual, but Jax recognized the flat inflections of Maurice's voice synthesizer.

"Sorry about the visual—we're under severe band-width restrictions. Power rationing, too, so I'll have to be quick. The fighting's almost over, except for a few hot-spots. Earth is pretty much of a mess—Europe, Japan, Indonesia . . . latest estimates say a billion dead. Naft came through pretty well. Russia, too, but they're going to take a lot of fallout from PacRim. SunGroup is putting together a group at O'Neill Two, sort of a reconstruction team. We can use all the help here we can get, but we also need to keep the long range research efforts going. Your call, but frankly, we could use you. We're sending a ship out to make a sweep of the research stations, any-body who wants to come back. Old ore freighter from the Belt, retrofitted with an ion drive. Best we can do right now. Let me know what you want to do. We don't want to burn up the delta vee to get out to you if we don't have to.''

Jax listened to the spectral hiss of interplanetary white noise riding over the carrier hum. He played the message back again. The words began to merge together, their in-dividual meaning softening like heated wax. He played the message back again.

IV

She hovered on the knife-edge between wakefulness and sleep. Images of smoke and flame, of exploding suns, chased each other across the surface of her consciousness. She was on a hover-barge on the Seine, sitting in the back at the controls. Sharp smell of moss and damp stone as she passed under a bridge. Her parents and sisters on the deck in front of her, sitting beneath a blue-and-white um-brella. Sipping drinks, laughing. Low grey clouds holding the threat of rain.

Suddenly, an impossibly bright light swelling from the east, a second sun breaking through the clouds. The um-brella bursting into flame, her family instantly transformed into stick figure torches. The Seine was *boiling*, bubbling up over the sides of the barge. . . .

She opened her eyes. Jax's face hovered above her in the half dark. He put his hand on her arm.

"Dreams?"

She nodded, still gripped by the vision. "Yeah."

Jax stroked her arm. "I heard from Maurice," he said after a moment. "We're on our own, Maddy. He has no idea when they'll be able to get to us."

It was like a physical blow. Her tropism for home radiated up from the very center of her, from her First Chakra. Its denial sent a surge of panic through her.

She closed her eyes. Breathe, breathe. In, I calm my body. Out, my breathing returns me to my true self. In, breathe calm, white sun swelling in the East. Out, listen, listen, Seine bubbling up over the sides of the barge. In, centuries old stone bridge sagging molten soft. Out, pillars of flame dancing on the deck of the barge snuffed by hammer wind.

"Maddy." Her eyes fluttered open again. "Are you all right?"

She looked closely at him. His long, thin face, so familiar, composed in a mask of concern.

Slowly, she shook her head. "No," she said. "Nothing's all right."

Maddy hadn't worn her environment suit in weeks and it chafed under her arms and between her legs. She looked back at the station, so out of place in the alien landscape, clinging in the tattered mist to the dark rock like a cluster of warts. The pod glittered in the dim light. She imagined Jax back there, his sleeping form sprawled naked across the foam pad.

She still ached slightly from their sex. He had been fast and rough, almost brutal. She didn't care, had lain there limply, receiving him. Her orgasm was joyless, passing through her like a wave, leaving no trace of itself.

When she got to the shore of the ammonia sea, she stopped. Small ripples lapped up against the rocky beach. She looked down at the canister she was carrying. Featureless, burnished metal, such an innocuous thing.

Without further thought, she pressed a recessed button on its side. A thin line appeared around the top rim and a puff of vapor escaped, freezing instantly into a cloud of scintillating crystals. She unscrewed the lid and shook its contents out into the sea. Shards of metglass webbing, spidery strands of plastic tubing, chunks of brittle, frozen foam. She couldn't even see the scrap of flesh they cradled. A few meters away, a small herd of slugs clustered near the shore in a senseless and inchoate sprawl.

INTO THE BLUE ABYSS

Geoffrey A. Landis

"Into the Blue Abyss" appeared in the August 1999 issue of Asimov's, *with an illustration by Alan Giana. A physicist who works for NASA, and who has recently been working on the Martian Lander program, Geoffrey A. Landis is a frequent contributor to* Analog *and to* Asimov's Science Fiction, *and has also sold stories to markets such as* Interzone, Amazing, *and* Pulphouse. *Landis is not a prolific writer, by the high-production standards of the genre, but he is popular. His story "A Walk in the Sun" won him a Hugo Award in 1992, "Ripples in the Dirac Sea" won him a Nebula Award in 1990, and "Elemental" was on the final Hugo ballot a few years back. His first book was the collection,* Myths, Legends, and True History, *and he has just sold his first novel,* Mars Crossing. *He lives in Brook Park, Ohio.*

This one takes us to Uranus (no jokes, please!), one of the strangest planets in the solar system, in company with some intrepid explorers who are about to boldly go where no one has gone before, a plunge into Uranus itself—and are about to find

*there wonders no one could possibly have imag-
ined.*

There is nothing quite like the color of a hydrogen atmosphere tinted with methane. Deeper than sapphire; milkier
than turquoise, Uranus was an indescribable luminous
hue. Over the weeks, it had swollen from a dim, watery
speck to the featureless blue pearl that hung below us.

Supported by an invisible microwave beam, the base
station lowered into the edge of the stratosphere, and the
moment came.

Wrapped in a cocoon of diamond and steel, safe within
our technology, we readied ourselves to drop.

"Two questions," I had said. "Why Uranus? And why
me?"

God, who would ever go to Uranus? Way out in the
big dark, nearly as far beyond Saturn as Saturn is from
the sun. It is cold and dark and, for the most part, unin-
teresting.

Stodderman was a thin man, neatly dressed, intense; a
natural team leader. Some women would have found him
sexy, I think. I was not one of them.

We had been in the common lounge of an orbital habitat with the improbable name of Wat Benchamabopit.
That suited me; I hadn't wanted to go down to Earth quite
yet anyway. I had unfinished business there which I was
not quite ready to face.

The Wat Benchamabopit habitat had been chosen as a
pragmatic place to meet: it was in an eccentric trans-
lagrangian orbit that placed it at an energy convenient for
both of us to rendezvous. Like many orbital habs, it rented
out a common area for the use of transients. The recycled
air odor was covered over with the faint scent of some
flowery fragrance, perhaps incense. Entry to the main part
of the habitat was through the wide-open mouth of a blue-

faced demon, elaborately carved with huge bulging eyes and protruding tusks. The symbolism seemed, to me, to be ominous.

Stodderman chose his words carefully. "The ice moons of the outer solar system are beginning to attract some attention. You know that there's a lot of prospecting going on right now. Uranus is far from the commercial belt, but there are people who think that the moons may be valuable soon."

"I've heard the rumors," I told him. "But you weren't talking about the moons, you were talking about the planet itself. Cut to the data-dump. Uranus? Why?"

"One of the prospectors. An old coot, a miner. The kind with wild hair and huge eyes and UV-hardened skin, been alone a little too long with only her p-buggy and computer for company. Those outer-moon prospectors are all half-crazy, Dr. Hamakawa."

"Leah," I said. "Please. Go on."

"Leah. Right," he said. "The prospectors. They've got tools, you know, some pretty good prospecting tools, and they've got a lot of free time. So, this one had a hobby: she took to sending some of her prospecting probes out, instead of down. Looking at Uranus from orbit. Something she saw got us interested. Down in the atmosphere. Deep down. We seem to be seeing some, ah, call it disequilibrium chemistry."

"Disequilibrium chemistry" I said. "You mean, life? You're saying that there's life on *Uranus?*"

"Call it, possible indications of organic molecules of unknown origin," Stodderman said. "Hydrocarbons and so forth. We'd prefer not to suggest anything about life right now. You're too young, I expect, but I remember the Zeus expedition."

The Zeus expedition had been an expedition to Jupiter's moon Europa. It had been an enormous, extravagant mission, as expensive as an interstellar probe. The expedition leaders had publicly vowed that they would return with proof that there was life in the oceans below Europa's icy crust.

Two hundred people, in habitats magnetically shielded from the deadly radiation of Jupiter's belts, had landed on the shattered ice-plains of Europa and bored with a fusion drill twenty kilometers through the ice to the secret ocean beneath. They brought arc-lights to depths that had not seen sunlight in a hundred million years, and explored the fantastic seascapes with submarines, bottom-crawlers, sub-surface drillers, and telerobotic probes. They found wispy structures of precipitated limestone, pale and fragile and intricate as a lace curtain, extending for hundreds of kilometers. They found strange chemistry, undersea volcanoes, a fascinating system of global oceanic currents driven by tidal stretching—but they found no life: no hydrothermal-vent communities, no bacteria, not even pre-biotic molecules.

The Zeus mission had scouted and catalogued the resources of Europa. The infrastructure that Zeus set up had opened up the moon to human habitation. Europa was now the largest human settlement in the Jupiter system, and the largest of the Europan cities was Zeus, honoring not the god, but the mission. But in the public mind, the Zeus mission was still a synonym for an expensive failure.

The solar system, except for the Earth, was dead. From the sulfur ice-caps of Mercury to the fairy-castle frost of Charon, a hundred expeditions had searched for life, and had failed to find it. No one except the crazies and the fanatics looked anymore.

"That's why we're keeping this low key," he said.

The first Uranus expeditions had looked for life, of course. Humans had not explored the planet itself in person—that idea was crazy—but Uranus had been investigated with robotic probes that floated on hot-air (or rather, hot-hydrogen) balloons in the cloud layers. That was the obvious place to look for life; up where there was still sunlight, where the pressure was only one or two atmospheres.

"Nobody has looked down deep," Stodderman said. "The atmosphere is fifteen hundred kilometers thick. They only looked at the very top."

"It seems terribly unlikely," I said. "Where's the energy?" Life is a solar-driven heat engine—regardless of how strange life might be, it would need energy. "Does any sunlight penetrate the atmosphere?"

"No," he said. "There's not much sunlight even above the clouds. Below? Nothing. Where the oceans are, it's dark."

"So what drives the life? Heat from the interior?"

Stodderman shook his head. "No. Turns out Uranus is odd—it's the only one of the gas giants that has no detectable heat coming out of its interior."

"Then, what?"

"That's what we're looking to find out."

"Fair enough," I said. "And my second question? Why me?"

"Several reasons," he said. "One is that we're looking for somebody with skill as a submersible pilot."

As a student, I had worked for a fish farm. We corralled the fish with submersible vehicles, mechanical fish piloted by a virtual reality link. A school of fish doesn't have a leader—its motion is a perfect example of a self-organizing chaotic system—but with a computer providing real-time feedback, a single mechanical Judas fish could subtly influence the motion of a school and, over time, lead it anywhere. I had gotten to be good at it. It was a popular job for university students, something that could be done from a dormitory, where I was a student anonymous among ten thousand others. I had never needed to be within a thousand kilometers of the ocean.

I nodded. "Okay. So, out of maybe fifty million people

who had jobs as fish-pushers in college, why do you want me? I'm a physicist. Seems to me that you want a biologist."

"Oh, we have a biologist on the mission, of course. But what attracted us was the fact that, although you're a physicist now, you have some background in biochemistry as well."

"That was years ago."

"No matter. You seem to dabble in many subjects, and you're not afraid to stick your neck out and speculate a little. We're going to dive into an ocean where the pressure is well over fifty thousand atmospheres. It's a realm that's never been explored; we have no ideas what we might find. We thought a physicist might be a good thing to have along."

I nodded.

The reward that he hadn't bothered to state aloud was a tempting one.

I was not a member of an institute, but a freelancer, a mercenary scientist, desperate to get in an institute—but not willing to sell my freedom for it. If I went on the expedition, and if we were to find life, I could return not merely an associate, but a full fellow of any one of the great institutes. That would give me my freedom.

But that didn't matter. I had been hooked before he said a single word. There was no way they could keep me off this expedition.

Uranus! I was on my way.

Stodderman had put together his expedition on a budget of hopes, promises, and the discarded oxygen canisters and recycled detritus of earlier missions. He had hired transport to Uranus on the fusion-powered transfer ship *Astrid* that brought supplies to the prospector's camp on Oberon. He had arranged the use of the fusion motor on

Astrid, and on a second freighter, *Norge*, for a full week after our arrival.

The expedition base station hung from a hundred-kilometer long tether, dangling into the fringes of the stratosphere below a V-shaped sail made of thin metallic mesh. Thousands of kilometers away, in a stationary orbit, two fusion-powered masers generated beams of microwaves that reflected off the sail, producing the upward force that held the base station up, lowering us slowly. At the lowest point, barely dipping into the fringes of atmosphere, the base station would drop the two exploration pods into the depths.

The maser idea had seemed crazy to me, and I'd told him so. Why not descend with rockets? Or balloon in the atmosphere?

Stodderman shrugged. "We looked at that. The balloon would have to be enormous. The atmosphere is mostly hydrogen, so a balloon doesn't have much lifting power."

"But on Venus they have whole cities floating in the clouds."

"On Venus they don't drop the cities down a gravity well, float them for a while, then try to launch them back out. The gravity is less than Earth's, but the well is twice as deep.

"Turns out our way is simpler. The ships are here anyway; *Norge* isn't heading back for weeks, and *Astrid* is staying even longer. Twenty kilometers per second into the gravity well, and another twenty out again, that's a killer task even for a fusion rocket. But it's not hard to reconfigure fusion engines to make a maser. And a mesh sail weighs almost nothing; it's like lowering a spiderweb down. It sounds complex, but really it's the low-cost solution."

"Doesn't sound complex; it sounds risky," I said. "What if the maser fails when you're lowering the station? Or when you're hovering for the drop-off?"

"If the maser fails, we all get to see the oceans of Uranus first-hand," Stodderman said. "We'd better hope like hell that the crew on the ships are working to restart it. In two, maybe three minutes, we hit the atmosphere hard enough to pick up frictional heat. About six minutes, give or take, the base station is moving so fast that even if the maser could reacquire the sail, we can't accelerate fast enough to pull out. In eight minutes, the sail hits the atmosphere."

"And then?" I asked.

Stodderman shrugged. "It's a toss-up. Either the atmospheric pressure crushes us, the tether melts, or the mesh sail hits the atmosphere and disintegrates. I don't think anybody is taking odds." He looked at me. "This bother you?"

"No," I said. "I don't understand much about people. But I do know one thing. People die."

Of the five of us in the expedition, two of us were to descend through the atmosphere into the Uranian ocean. Over the eight weeks spent on *Astrid* in transit to Uranus, we had trained on the use of the Uranus hydrosphere mobility pods in the simulator. We crawled into it in a fetal position, bodies slick with transceiver gel, wearing neural pickup gloves and skinsuit. In the actual vehicles, we would be intubated for oxygen and liquids, but in the simulator, this final step was skipped.

Hanita Jayavel and I were the most adept at the intricate set of skills required in piloting the pods. To call the skill "piloting" was to understate the task; the mobility pods fit around us like a second body, a body with a diamond shell, steel muscles and electronic senses that taste the chemicals in the water and see sonar echoes.

Exploring the oceans of Uranus in person, and not by telepresence, was crazy. The expedition pods were the reason that it was possible at all.

The two pods had been specially designed for the Uranus ocean, and were the most expensive objects on the expedition. Tiny, self-contained submarines with full life-support systems and independent power, they had an ovoid pressure vessel, grown from diamond fiber, to protect us from the enormous pressures beneath the Uranian atmosphere. Around the pressure capsule, the body had been designed on the model of a dolphin, with dolphin's flexibility to its steel fins and tail. Attached to the diamond bodies were a thermophotovoltaic isotope power supply and canisters filled with chemicals that, when our mission was over, would generate the hot gas that would fill the buoyancy floats to bring us to the surface. From the surface, balloons inflate to bring us into the Uranian stratosphere, where we could ignite solid rocket motors to hop back to the hovering base station. The pod also had a sample acquisition arm, slender and jointed, which retracted fully into the body.

Over the long transit, Hanita and I had talked for a long time, and she told me of her life.

Hanita Jayavel had been the daughter of a Kuiper habitat. I had known little about the fringe habitats that were scattered deep out in the far dark, only that they were inhabited by antisocial fanatics and isolationist religious factions; they were unimportant to the politics and economics of the inner solar system. Hanita's birth habitat had been a communistic one. They lived on an icy body in the Kuiper belt, a body with plentiful water and nitrogenous volatiles, and, most important, one that was far from everybody else. Their economic system was to share and share alike, and their credo that nobody in the habitat was any better than anybody else. There were other colonies in the Kuiper diaspora, a thousand groups seeking to distance themselves from the crush of humanity, but with a hundred million kilometers between outposts, commerce between them was slight.

And then the fusion renaissance expanded outward. It swallowed the Kuiper diaspora without even a gulp, destroyed them not by war, but by a surfeit of riches. The children of the commune saw the wealth that the robber barons brought. They had been taught that the robber barons were evil, but what they saw was the robber barons financing institutes, art, science. The laws of Hanita's habitat had not been restrictive; they were proud to allow their inhabitants to leave freely, and, free, their children had drifted away.

Hanita's family had been one of the last to leave, when the settlement had lost so many of the younger generation that it had become clear that there would be too few to sustain it. More of an immigrant than a refugee, Hanita had studied chemistry in one of the inner belt communities, and joined on to the expedition as much for her background in the outer solar system as for her expertise in chemistry.

After three weeks of the mental and physical exhaustion of training together, Hanita had confided in me further. Unknown to Stodderman, she had a personal reason for joining the expedition, a secret reason for her fierce dedication to mastering the piloting simulation. She was making certain that she would be one of the two chosen to dive into the unknown ocean.

Hanita Jayavel wanted to reinvent paradise.

Uranus is four times the diameter of the Earth, but the density of the planet is so low that the surface gravity is actually slightly lower than Earth's. Above the clouds, the temperature is frigid—seventy degrees Kelvin, cold enough to freeze oxygen. Down below the cloud tops, though, the temperature rises. It rises only slowly, because the interior of Uranus produces almost no heat. At the ocean, it was calculated that the temperature was moderate, in the range of three to four hundred Kelvin: the range required for human biochemistry.

The search for life motivated Stodderman, but did not excite Hanita. As a chemist, she had long ago concluded that in the absence of either sunlight or interior heat there was no entropy gradient for life to exploit.

In the warm dark ocean, Hanita Jayavel wanted to make a new colony of humans. Hidden a thousand kilometers under the opaque atmosphere of Uranus, she would set a secret colony far from the numerous habitations of humankind. A colony free of the economics of the solar system.

Humans don't need sunlight; the Kuiper colonies in the cold dark had proved that. With an infinite supply of hydrogen and deuterium from the ocean waters, with helium-three from the atmosphere, humans could create their own sun. The oceans of Uranus had everything needed, except life.

She would bring that.

She explained her plans to me, showing me how she would modify the human genome to make oceanic life. She drew a fantastic picture of life in a three-dimensional ocean, spreading out across a world with a surface area sixty times larger than the land area of the Earth. To her, the expedition into Uranus's oceans was not a search for life—it was a scouting trip.

Hanita was a fanatic, I realized, and, when I told her so, she admitted it. I will stop at nothing, she said.

"Even killing?" I asked.

"Without hesitation," she said.

Okay. I could live with that.

Inwardly, I agreed with Hanita; with no plausible source of energy, we were unlikely to find life. For me, curiosity alone was sufficient reason to drop into the seas of Uranus.

But I, too, had motivations that I kept to myself.

In the inner solar system my life had been becoming complicated. I was not sure how to deal with romance. I didn't know what to think. I had never learned how to love. Was this love, what I felt? Would I even know it?

And yet, though I had made no encouragement at all, he wanted me.

The meat was nothing to me. People died. There was no point in getting close to them; they die and leave you alone. This was what I knew.

In some vague, abstract way, I wondered if I was even capable of this thing, love, that others find so all important. Probably not. But if I were, if I were a whole person, if I'd never experienced what I had experienced, in the camps, in the war, I would not be the same person. Perhaps growing up as a child of the war had burned something out of me, something that others thought precious, but it also had forged me and shaped me into the person I now was. This was the price I had paid, for being what I was. And the price was cheap.

The situation was too complicated for me. Uranus was conveniently far away from Earth. A mission to Uranus uncomplicated my life.

As for basic facts about Uranus—before the expedition, I had known little more than the dumb jokes ("Hey, there are rings of dirt around Uranus!"). It's true: the rings of Uranus are unlike Saturn's gleaming particles of ice; they are dark, the color of coal. Rings of dirt. What else was there to know about Uranus, other than that it was cold and dark? An oddball among the planets, it orbits on its side, with the north pole pointing sunward for half of its eighty-four-year orbit, the south pole sunward for the other half.

Below the clouds, way below, was an ocean of liquid water. Uranus was the true water-world of the solar system, a sphere of water surrounded by a thick atmosphere. Unlike the other planets, Uranus has a rocky core too small to measure, or perhaps no solid core at all, but only ocean, an ocean that has actually dissolved the silicate core of the planet away, a bottomless ocean of liquid water twenty thousand kilometers deep.

The microwave jockeys tweaked their masers, and inch by inch lowered us down the gravity well. There were four of us in the station; Hanita and I to pilot the pods, Stodderman as the expedition leader, and our technician Kamishinay. Kamishinay was a spindly guy from a zero-grav habitat, limbs as thin as chopsticks with small hard muscles protruding like walnuts. He was quiet, but superb with equipment.

At last the expedition base station hung in the most tenuous wisps of the Uranian atmosphere. The base station was smaller even than the quarters on the *Astrid*, barely large enough for the control center and the two exploration pods docked in their slings. It smelled of metal and oil and the aceticacid smell of outgassing silicone seals. After the rancid sweat and the organic smell of the recirculated air in the transfer ship's cabins, the new-equipment smells of the station were welcome. We worked elbow to elbow, getting ready. Hanita and I stripped, and our technician Kamishinay assisted in pasting sensor electrodes over our bodies, checking each one as it was placed, adjusting it minutely for the best pickup of muscular signals. Unexpectedly, although he had just run his hands over nearly every square decimeter of our naked bodies, Kamishinay was squeamish about inserting our catheters, and so I lubricated the tube and insert it for Hanita as he averted his eyes, and then spread my legs and held myself rigid to let her reciprocate for me. Despite the grease, the catheter stung like a rasp as it slid in. Finally, with Kamishinay again helping, we in-

serted the intravenous monitors—another sharp sting—
and nasal tubes, until both of us seemed to be cybernetic
organisms as much as biological.

Through this all, Stodderman had been ignoring us,
concentrating on details of piloting and reading the external sensors for clues to the environment below. To him,
we had become little more than two more pieces of the
mission's equipment. His intensity was reserved for his
machines.

The Uranus exploration pods were tiny, and slithering
inside was a tough proposition requiring a liberal appli-
cation of gel. Once inside, in the tight dark, with the
sense-net hugging your body closer than a lover, the bile
taste of the tongue control and the scratching, choking itch
of the tubes down your throat, it felt like some medieval
torture—until the system was energized.

With the power on, your senses came alive, the diamond shell became your skin, the sonar senses your second eyes, the chemical sensors your smell and taste and
touch, a thousand times more sensitive than the crude
chemical instruments that humans call their senses. The
fins flexed to our slightest touch. Mechanical dolphins, we
squirmed and fidgeted, itching for release from the docking harness that held us.

The moment came. Our systems had been tested, the
tests checked, the checks rechecked and verified, and the
verification checked. We were ready.

First Hanita, and then it was my turn: we were jetti-
soned from the expedition base station, and fell—plum-
meted—into the pearly blueness of Uranus.

We dove into the infinite abyss.

An unmanned probe, operated by telepresence, would
have been less crazy, but that solution turned out to be
unworkable. Under the enormous pressure of the hydrogen atmosphere, hydrogen atoms are forced into solution,
and dissociate into ions. This made the water conductive

enough to block electromagnetic transmissions. If we wanted to know what lay below the surface of the ocean, we had to explore it in person.

Even farther down, the pressure becomes so high that the water itself became liquid metal. Slow currents flowing in the water gave Uranus its magnetic field. But that was farther than we would ever go. To explore the upper ocean would be enough for any one expedition.

Above us, the base station, lightened by the loss of the exploration pods, rose on its microwave wings back into orbit.

We fell, shrieking, down through the hydrogen atmosphere.

At the edge of the atmosphere, the sunlight was like a late afternoon, not noticeably dim, Uranus a huge blue ocean below us.

The blue slowly deepened from sapphire into cobalt into the deepest shade of midnight.

The atmosphere thickened. In the stratosphere, there were winds of a thousand kilometers per hour; but here below the clouds, the atmosphere was still. If there were any winds at all, they were below the level of detectability.

Down, into the deeper blue. Dark blue. Pastel, then ink. Down.

We fell through clouds: first methane clouds, then ammonia clouds, then ammonium hydrosulfide, and into the darkness. Oddly, we didn't even need parachutes. As the atmosphere thickened, by slow degrees our fall slackened speed. We fell for hours; a thousand kilometers, and continued to fall. We were falling in utter darkness now, and incrementally the atmosphere had become so dense that our fall slowed to a crawl.

And, in the darkness, below a thousand kilometers of

atmosphere, as slowly as an ant falling through the thick air, we splashed in slow motion into the ocean.

We were now buoyant: no longer falling, we were swimming. Sweeping across the darkness, our spotlights saw only a waveless obsidian surface; our sonar saw nothing at all but its own reflection. Only the taste had changed, from methane-laced hydrogen into water.

We were fishes in the Uranian sea.

But the tantalizing hints of disequilibrium chemistry that had drawn us across the vast darkness and down through the clouds had not been here at the surface. We swam, making measurements, taking the measure of our diamond and steel bodies, checking the systems that had been checked a thousand times before, leaving wakes across the waveless sea.

And then we dove.

The ocean was the temperature of blood. Encased inside mechanical dolphins, we swam in the dark. I chased Hanita, laughing, and tagged her; then she turned and chased me, and then together we dove deeper into the darkness of the Uranian sea.

I had left myself behind.

We tasted the water, we heard the sounds. Sound? We reconfigured, boosting the amplification on our electronic ears. Sonar showed nothing there, but something was making a chirruping, faint but (to our amplified ears) quite clear. A sound oddly like the serenade of spring peepers. We turned our floodlights on to the brightest setting, but they showed nothing, only water. There was no discernible directionality to the sound, and nothing there to see.

Deeper.

There were no currents in this sunless sea, or if there were currents, they were so sluggish that we could not detect them. No bubbles, no form to the water. It was so clear and dark that we had almost no sense of immersion;

it was as if instead of diving we were hanging motionless, suspended in nothing.

And then, as we dove—a kilometer below the surface, by my pressure gauge—suddenly there was something in our lights. A layer, as thin as a soap bubble, iridescent in the glow of our floodlights, giving a visible surface to the formless deep. It undulated sluggishly. We penetrated through it, and it offered no barrier to our passage. Slow oily ripples spread out from the area of penetration, pieces breaking off and floating free, oscillating in shape, dancing like tiny butterflies in a way that was almost lascivious. A layer of thin, oily scum.

Organics. Biological in origin? Maybe. But what could be the energy source? We had been measuring thermal lapse as we penetrated deeper, and we had found only a minuscule heat flow, just enough to keep the oceans from freezing. There was no trace of free thermal energy. Where there was no free energy, there could be no life.

I schooled myself not to be excited, so I would not be disappointed. I hadn't wanted to be a fellow anyway.

Hanita's chemical analysis showed the scum to be tangled chain molecules; hydrocarbon, primarily, with small amounts of nitrogen and traces of sulfur. "Not really biological," she informed me, "but in some ways similar to biological chemistry. You might call it pre-biotic molecules. Primordial slime." The organic slime from which, on Earth, life had arisen.

Despite the lack of an identifiable energy source, the organic molecules were slowly replicating, but they assembled nothing of interest: no cells, no complicated structure, just endless copies of hydrocarbon ooze. Was ooze life? I didn't want to be a fellow, all it would give me was freedom, and I didn't need or care about freedom.

The molecules catalyze their own formation, Hanita reported. Out of dissolved methane, hydrogen sulfide, and ammonia, they formed molecules that serve as catalysts to form more of themselves. Was this life? Perhaps by the simplest definitions—it replicated—but with no structure, with no metabolism, it would hardly serve to excite those above.

Meanwhile, I had been trying to analyze the sound. My working hypothesis was that the sound was meteorological in origin. The vortices of storms hundreds of kilometers overhead were filtered by the layers of atmosphere, turning noise into eerie music. It was odd, but no odder than stratospheric whistlers.

Then a fish swept by us. It was huge. It was a filter-feeder, grazing on the hydrocarbon layer.

It was singing.

The fish was wide and flat and thin, an irregularly shaped pancake. It moved slowly, creeping along at the pace of a carpet of ants. It had no sense organs that we could detect, no eyes, no sonar.

It didn't mind our floodlights; why should it? How could it have evolved photosensitivity, a thousand kilometers below any possible trace of sunlight? We circled it, photographing, documenting the fish in the Uranian ocean. This changed everything.

It was perhaps the world's ugliest fish, a lumpy grey tortilla, undulating languidly as it munched its way across the oily slime. Our sonar showed—nothing. It was the same density, apparently the same composition as the scum that it ate.

This changed more than just the way the solar system would view our expedition, I realized. Hanita wanted to recreate her childhood paradise in the oceans of Uranus, but this could only be possible if humanity ignored Uranus. Uranus wouldn't be ignored if life was reported.

But if Stodderman's mission reported nothing, no one would ever return to Uranus, not soon, not perhaps for hundreds of years. Long enough for a colony to flourish.

Under conductive ocean, we weren't able to report our results. No one would know what we found until we surfaced. There was only one solution: Hanita must try to kill me before we reach the surface.

I was suddenly aware of my body, cramped into fetal position, packed in gel and penetrated by tubes, unable to do more than twitch, separated from crushing pressure by only a thin eggshell of diamond filament. We had been training on the mobility pods for weeks; we both knew hundreds of things that could go wrong, weak points that could be exploited to let in the deadly pressure. Death would take only a moment.

Okay. I could deal with that.

We privately tagged the layer of hydrocarbons "plankton," although compared to terrestrial plankton, this was unthinkably more primitive. The filter-feeder crept along like a lawn mower, and the oily layer imperceptibly oozed closed behind it, leaving a trail of slightly disturbed hydrocarbon. The trail was invisible in sonar and in visible light, but by polarizing our floodlights, we could see a curved line that faded in the distance, faintly extending back as far as our floodlights would reach. At irregular intervals it was crossed by other paths through the slime layer, even older and fainter.

By following the other trails, we found other fish. They were the same in everything except size, identical as clones, equally flat, equally lumpy, equally ugly. They were only sparsely populated across the ocean; I estimated a density of only a single fish in every twenty square kilometers.

"But this is impossible," Hanita said. "Where the hell is the energy source?"

While she had been photographing the fish—the fourth one we had found, identical in all particulars to the other three—I had been thinking. While I thought, I had been analyzing the water, the organics, the electrochemical potentials.

"I can tell you that," I said.

Water rises in the atmosphere, I explained. Rises into the stratosphere, and when it gets high enough it is photodissociated to free oxygen and hydroxl radicals. High in the stratosphere, the radicals recombine into oxygen and to hydrogen peroxide. Heavier than the hydrogen, these cool and fall, tiny cold droplets of oxidant raining slowly into the ocean. No photosynthesis was needed. The oceans were plentiful with dissolved hydrogen, so there was fuel and oxidizer. The pre-biotic molecules self-assemble, fueled by the energy of the oxygen; the filter-feeders subsist on them.

The life was driven by the oxygen cycle, which was, ultimately, driven by sunlight.

"But that can't be very efficient!"

"My quick calculation is that it's about a million times less efficient than the photosynthesis that powers the Earth," I said. "So? It's slow-motion life. Where there is energy, there is life."

And then a predator. Of course, there would be predators, I realized, predation was a cheap way to harvest energy— let somebody else do it—and such a rich ecological niche wouldn't stay empty. Sharks, a pack of them. In slow motion, the filter-feeder banked as if to flee, rising up out of the slime layer, but the sharks were inexorable.

The ease with which they ripped the fish apart showed that the filter-feeding life form had no bones, no detectable muscles, no internal structure. It must be more like a motile jellyfish than any sort of true fish, I realized. I swam around, keeping the floodlight on the scene, as Hanita photographed the slaughter. With scoop-like mouths, the sharks suctioned the shreds down their gullets. A few of the fragments, too small for the sharks to bother with, gradually contracted into pancake shape, becoming finger-nail-sized copies of the fish that been torn apart. They settled toward the slime layer, and then began to feed.

Then a shark turned on us.

Its mouth was huge. Hanita kept photographing right up to the moment it swallowed her.

Like the filter-feeder, the sharks were transparent to sonar. I turned just a moment too late to see the one that grabbed me.

We cannot possibly be its natural food. The shark had made an unfortunate mistake, and swallowing us was most likely going to poison it.

I was unable to shake free of it. Our diamond bodies were already under hydrostatic pressure of fifty tons per square centimeter, and designed with considerable safety margin, they could withstand far more than that. It was unlikely that the shark could directly harm the craft. Still, trying with futile vigor to rip into us, the shark produced an erratically varying, non-uniform pressure far different from anything that the pod had been designed for, and it would not be very wise to let it continue.

I was briefly sorry for the shark, but there was no choice.

The balloon inflated sluggishly with hydrogen. The shark was disoriented, and attempted to swim, to hold its position, but hydrostatic pressure and Archimedes' law were unforgiving. It was inexorably pulled to the surface. Unwilling, or more likely with too little brainpower to let us go, it bloated and came apart.

As I rose, I grabbed with my manipulator arm, and with a lucky swipe, managed to snag a piece of flesh. A sample.

Bobbing at the surface of the ocean, we were again in electromagnetic contact with the hovering base, bathed in a flood of welcome microwave energy.

I was still alive.

"Wow," I said. "What a ride."

We were floating in darkness on a warm, stagnant sea. "I expected you to kill me," I said.

"It was a dream, all my life, to return," Hanita said, slowly. "And since there was no place to return to, I dreamed I would make a place. It was a nice dream."

"Why?" I said.

"Why didn't I kill you? I don't know." Encased in her pressure shell, she was invisible to me, but in my mind's eye I could see her shake her head. At last, she spoke again. "Can you ever really go back?" she said.

We have found life in the cold dark, life that could never even conceive of the stars. The gravity is lower than the gravity of Earth, but the well is far deeper. Life in a realm with no metals, no fire. Life that could never escape.

Uranus is ocean, all ocean, an ocean twenty thousand kilometers deep. We have barely seen the outermost skin of the Uranian ocean. What life could there be, in the incalculable depths?

We fire the pyrotechnic separators to sever us from the now-useless steel exostructure of our dolphin bodies, leaving only the naked eggs of our pressure vessels, and the balloons and rockets that will take us home. By burning hydrogen into helium and using the waste heat to fill and then stretch taut the gas-bags, the balloons tug us sluggishly free of the ocean.

Side by side, we rise like jellyfish through the thick air toward the stratosphere. It will take days to reach a height where we can ignite our solid rockets, as the base station, suspended below its microwave-lit sail, dips to meet us. There is still the split-second rendezvous to accomplish, still a thousand things that could go wrong, but for all that, nevertheless the mission is over. We have transmitted the most important parts of our results, the photographs and the chemical analyses, and the base station is broadcasting them across the solar system. In a few hours, everyone will know.

"What will you do now," I ask her.

"I don't know," she says. She could have asked me the same question, but she doesn't.

But I know.

Life can exist even in the most extreme environment. It is not fragile. It can feed on only the tiniest scraps of energy.

There will be other missions, and beyond them yet other missions. I will let things happen, as I always have, as I always would. The events will flow over me, and I will be unchanged.

Outward, to the farthest horizons, I thought. And beyond them, other horizons, never ending.

Home.

SECOND SKIN

Paul J. McAuley

"Second Skin" appeared in the April 1997 issue of
Asimov's, *with an illustration by Steve Cavallo. It
was one of only a handful of sales McAuley has
made to the magazine to date, but each one has
been memorable, and we hope to see a lot more
from him as the new century progresses. Born in
Oxford, England, in 1955, Paul J. McAuley now
makes his home in London. He is considered to be
one of the best of the new breed of British writers
(although a few Australian writers could be fit in
under this heading as well) who are producing that
sort of revamped, updated, widescreen Space
Opera sometimes referred to as "radical hard science fiction," and is a frequent contributor to In-*
terzone, *as well as to markets such as* Amazing,
The Magazine of Fantasy and Science Fiction,
When the Music's Over, *and elsewhere. His first
novel,* Four Hundred Billion Stars, *won the Philip
K. Dick Award. His other books include the novels*
Of the Fall, Eternal Light, *and* Pasquale's Angel,
two collections of his short work, The King of the
Hill and Other Stories *and* The Invisible Country,
*and an original anthology co-edited with Kim New-
man,* In Dreams. *His acclaimed novel,* Fairyland
won both the Arthur C. Clarke Award and the John

W. Campbell Award in 1996. His most recent books are Child of the River *and* Ancient of Days, *the first two volumes of a major new trilogy of ambitious scope and scale,* Confluence, *set ten million years in the future.*

In the suspenseful and richly inventive story that follows, McAuley takes us on a journey across space to nearly the farthest reaches of the solar system, to the Neptune system, and then beneath the frozen surface of the moon Proteus, for a tale that demonstrates that sometimes the most effective warfare is not waged with armies or high-tech weapons, and that sometimes the most dangerous battlefield of all may be the human heart.

The transport, once owned by an outer system cartel and appropriated by Earth's Pacific Community after the Quiet War, ran in a continuous, ever-changing orbit between Saturn, Uranus, and Neptune. It never docked. It mined the solar wind for hydrogen to mix with the nanogram of antimatter that could power it for a century, and once or twice a year, during its intricate gravity-assisted loops between Saturn's moons, maintenance drones attached remora-like to its hull, and fixed whatever its self-repairing systems couldn't handle.

Ben Lo and the six other members of the first trade delegation to Proteus since the war were transferred onto the transport as it looped around Titan, still sleeping in the hibernation pods they'd climbed into in Earth orbit. Sixty days later, they were released from the transport in individual drop capsules of structural diamond, like so many seeds scattered by a pod.

Ben Lo, swaddled in the crash web that took up most of the volume of the drop capsule's little bubble, watched with growing vertigo as the battered face of Proteus drew closer. He had been awakened only a day ago, and was as weak and unsteady as a new-born kitten. The sun was behind the bubble's braking chute. Ahead, Neptune's disc was tipped in star-sprinkled black above the little moon. Neptune was subtly banded with blue and violet, its poles capped with white cloud, its equator streaked with cirrus. Slowly, slowly, Proteus began to eclipse it. The transport had already dwindled to a bright point amongst the bright points of the stars, on its way to spin up around Neptune, loop past Triton, and head on out for the next leg of its continuous voyage, halfway across the solar system to Uranus.

Like many of the moons of the outer planets, Proteus was a ball of ice and rock. Over billions of years, most of the rock had sunk to the core, and the moon's icy, dirty white surface was splotched with a scattering of large impact craters with black interiors, like well-used ash trays, and dissected by large stress fractures, some running halfway round the little globe.

The spy fell toward Proteus in a thin transparent bubble of carbon, wearing a paper suit and a diaper, and trussed up in a cradle of smart cabling like an early Christian martyr. He could barely move a muscle. Invisible laser light poured all around him—the capsule was opaque to the frequency used—gently pushing against the braking sail which had unfolded and spun into a twenty kilometer diameter mirror after the capsule had been released by the transport. Everything was fine.

The capsule said, "Only another twelve hours, Mr. Lo. I suggest that you sleep. Elfhame's time zone is ten hours behind Greenwich Mean Time."

Had he been asleep for a moment? Ben Lo blinked and said, "Jet lag," and laughed.

"I don't understand," the capsule said politely. It didn't need to be very intelligent. All it had to do was control the attitude of the braking sail, and keep its passenger amused and reassured until landing. Then it would be recycled.

Ben Lo didn't bother to try to explain. He was feeling

the same kind of yawning apprehension that must have gripped ninety-year-old airline passengers at the end of the twentieth century. A sense of deep dislocation and estrangement. How strange that I'm here, he thought. And, how did it happen? When he'd been born, spaceships had been crude, disposable chemical rockets. The first men on the moon. President Kennedy's assassination. No, that happened before I was born. For a moment, his yawning sense of dislocation threatened to swallow him whole, but then he had it under control and it dwindled to mere strangeness. It was the treatment, he thought. The treatment and the hibernation.

Somewhere down there in the white moonscape, in one of the smaller canyons, was Ben Lo's first wife. But he mustn't think of that. Not yet. Because if he did . . . no, he couldn't remember. Something bad, though.

"I can offer a variety of virtualities," the capsule said. It's voice was a husky contralto. It added, "Certain sexual services are also available."

"What I'd like is a chateaubriand steak butterflied and well-grilled over hickory wood, a Caesar salad, and a 1998 Walnut Creek Cabernet Sauvignon."

"I can offer a range of nutritive pastes, and eight flavors of water, including a balanced electrolyte," the capsule said. A prissy note seemed to have edged into its voice. It added, "I would recommend that you restrict intake of solids and fluids until after landing."

Ben Lo sighed. He had already had his skin scrubbed and repopulated with strains of bacteria and yeast native to the Protean ecosystem, and his GI tract had been reamed out and packed with a neutral gel containing a benign strain of *E. coli*. He said, "Give me an inflight movie."

"I would recommend virtualities," the capsule said. "I have a wide selection."

Despite the capsule's minuscule intelligence, it had a

greater memory capacity than all the personal computers on Earth at the end of the millennium. Ben Lo had downloaded his own archives into it.

"*Wings of Desire*," he said.

"But it's in black and white! And flat. And only two senses—"

"There's color later on. It has a particular relevance to me, I think. Once upon a time, capsule, there was a man who was very old, and became young again, and found that he'd lost himself. Run the movie, and you'll understand a little bit about me."

The moon, Neptune, the stars, fell into a single point of light. The light went out. The film began.

Falling through a cone of laser light, the man and the capsule watched how an angel became a human being, out of love.

The capsule skimmed the moon's dirty-white surface and shed the last of its relative velocity in the inertia buffers of the target zone, leaving its braking sail to collapse across kilometers of moonscape. It was picked up by a striding tripod that looked like a prop from *The War of the Worlds*, and carried down a steeply sloping tunnel through triple airlocks into something like the ER room of a hospital. With the other members of the trade delegation, Ben Lo, numbed by neural blocks, was decanted, stripped, washed, and dressed in fresh paper clothes.

Somewhere in the press of nurses and technicians he thought he glimpsed someone he knew, or thought he knew. A woman, her familiar face grown old, eyes faded blue in a face wrinkled as a turtle's. . . . But then he was lifted onto a gurney and wheeled away.

Waking, he had problems with remembering who he was. He knew he was nowhere on Earth. A universally impersonal hotel room, but he was virtually in free fall. Some moon, then. But what role was he playing?

He got up, moving carefully in the fractional gravity, and pulled aside the floor-to-ceiling drapes. It was night, and across a kilometer of black air was a steep dark mountainside or perhaps a vast building, with lights wound at its base, shimmering on a river down there. . . .

Proteus. Neptune. The trade delegation. And the thing he couldn't think about, which was fractionally nearer the surface now, like a word at the back of his tongue. He could feel it, but he couldn't shape it. Not yet.

He stripped in the small, brightly lit sphere of the bathroom and turned the walls to mirrors and looked at himself. He was too young to be who he thought he was. No, that was the treatment, of course. His third. Then why was his skin this color? He hadn't bothered to tint it for . . . how long?

That sci-fi version of *Othello*, a century and a half ago, when he'd been a movie star. He remembered the movie vividly, although not the making of it. But that was the color he was now, his skin a rich dark mahogany, gleaming as if oiled in the lights, his hair a cap of tight black curls.

He slept again, and dreamed of his childhood home. San Francisco. Sailboats scattered across the blue bay. He'd had a little boat, a Laser. The cold salt smell of the sea. The pinnacles of the rust-red bridge looming out of banks of fog, and the fog horn booming mournfully. Cabbage leaves in the gutters of Spring Street. The crowds swirling under the crimson and gold neon lights of the trinket shops of Grant Avenue, and the intersection at Grant and California tingling with trolley car bells.

He remembered everything as if he had just seen it in a movie. Non-associational aphasia. It was a side effect of the treatment he'd just had. He'd been warned about it, but it was still unsettling. The woman he was here to . . . Avernus. Her name now. But when they had been married, a hundred and sixty-odd years ago, she had been called Barbara Reiner. He tried to remember the taste of her mouth, the texture of her skin, and could not.

The next transport would not swing by Proteus for a hundred and seventy days, so there was no hurry to begin the formal business of the trade delegation. For a while, its members were treated as favored tourists, in a place that had no tourist industry at all.

The sinuous rill canyon which housed Elfhame had been burned to an even depth of a kilometer, sealed under a construction diamond roof, and pressurized to 750 millibars with a nitrox mix enriched with 1 percent carbon dioxide to stimulate plant growth. The canyon ran for fifty kilometers through a basaltic surface extrusion, possibly the remnant of the giant impact that had resurfaced the farside hemisphere of the moon a billion years ago, or the result of vulcanism caused by thermal drag when the satellite had been captured by Neptune.

The sides of the canyon were raked to form a deep vee in profile, with a long narrow lake lying at the bottom like a black ribbon, dusted with a scattering of pink and white coral keys. The Elfhamers called it the Skagerrak. The sides of the canyon were steeply terraced, with narrow vegetable gardens, rice paddies, and farms on the higher levels, close to the lamps that, strung from the diamond roof, gave an insolation equivalent to that of the Martian surface. Farther down, amongst pocket parks and linear strips of designer wilderness, houses clung to the steep slopes like soap bubbles, or stood on platforms or bluffs, all with panoramic views of the lake at the bottom and screened from their neighbors by soaring ginkgoes, cypress, palmettos, bamboo (which grew to fifty meters in the microgravity), and dragon's blood trees. All the houses were large and individually designed; Elfhamers went in for extended families. At the lowest levels were the government buildings, commercials malls and parks, the university and hospital, and the single hotel, which bore all the marks of having been recently constructed for the trade delegation. And then there was the lake, the Skagerrak, with its freshwater corals and teeming fish, and slow, ten-meter-high waves. The single, crescent-shaped beach of black sand at what Elfhamers called the North End was very steeply raked, and constantly renewed; the surfing was fabulous.

There was no real transportation system except for a single tube train line that shuttled along the west side, and moving lines with T-bar seats, like ski lifts, that made silver lines along the steep terraced slopes. Mostly, people bounded around in huge kangaroo leaps, or flew using startlingly small wings of diamond foil or little hand-held airscrews—the gravity was so low, 0.007g, that human flight was ridiculously easy. Children rode airboards or simply dived from terrace to terrace, which strictly speaking was illegal, but even adults did it sometimes, and it seemed to be one of those laws to which no one paid much attention unless someone got hurt. It *was* possible to break a bone if you jumped from the top of the canyon and managed to land on one of the lakeside terraces, but you'd have to work at it. Some of the kids did—the latest craze was terrace bouncing, in which half a dozen screaming youngsters tried to find out how quickly they could get from top to bottom with the fewest touchdown points.

The entire place, with its controlled, indoor weather, its bland affluent sheen, and its universal cleanliness, was ridiculously vulnerable. It reminded Ben Lo of nothing so much as an old-fashioned shopping mall, the one at Santa Monica, for instance. He'd had a bit part in a movie made in that mall, somewhere near the start of his career. He was still having trouble with his memory. He could remember every movie he'd made, but couldn't remember *making* any one of them.

He asked his guide if it was possible to get to the real

surface. She was taken aback by the request, then suggested that he could access a mobot using the point-of-presence facility of his hotel room.

"Several hundred were released fifty years ago, and some of them are still running, I suppose. Really, there is nothing up there but some industrial units."

"I guess Avernus has her labs on the surface."

Instantly, the spy was on the alert, suppressing a thrill of panic.

His guide was a very tall, thin, pale girl called Marla. Most Elfhamers were descended from Nordic stock, and Marla had the high cheekbones, blue eyes, blond hair, and the open and candid manner of her counterparts on Earth. Like most Elfhamers, she was tanned and athletically lithe, and wore a distractingly small amount of fabric: tight shorts, a band of material across her small breasts, plastic sandals, a communications bracelet.

At the mention of Avernus, Marla's eyebrows dented over her slim, straight nose. She said, "I would suppose so, yah, but there's nothing interesting to see. The program, it is reaching the end of its natural life, you see. The surface is not interesting, and it is dangerous. The cold and the vacuum, and still the risk of micrometeorites. Better to live inside."

Like worms in an apple, the spy thought. The girl was soft and foolish, very young and very naïve. It was only natural that a member of the trade delegation would be interested in Elfhame's most famous citizen. She wouldn't think anything of this.

Ben Lo blinked and said, "Well, yes, but I've never been there. It would be something, for someone of my age to set foot on the surface of a moon of Neptune. I was born two years before the first landing on Earth's moon, you know. Have you ever been up there?"

Marla's teeth were even and pearly white, and when she smiled, as she did now, she seemed to have altogether too many. "By point-of-presence, of course. It is part of our education. It is fine enough in its own way, but the surface is not our home, you understand."

They were sitting on the terrace of a café that angled out over the lake. Resin tables and chairs painted white, clipped bay trees in big white pots, terra-cotta tiles, slightly sticky underfoot, like all the floor coverings in Elfhame. Bulbs of schnapps cooled in an ice bucket.

Ben Lo tipped his chair back and looked up at the narrow strip of black sky and its strings of brilliant lamps that hung high above the steep terraces on the far side of the lake. He said, "You can't see the stars. You can't even see Neptune."

"Well, we *are* on the farside," Marla said, reasonably. "But by point-of-presence mobot I have seen it, several times. I have been on Earth the same way, and Mars, but those were fixed, because of the signal lag."

"Yes, but you might as well look at a picture!"

Marla laughed. "Oh, yah. Of course. I forget that you are once a capitalist—" the way she said it, he might have been a dodo, or a dolphin—"from the United States of the Americas, as it was called then. That is why you put such trust in what you call *real*. But really, it is not such a big difference. You put on a mask, or you put on a pressure suit. It is all barriers to experience. And what is to see? Dusty ice, and the same black sky as home, but with more and weaker lamps. We do not need the surface."

Ben Lo didn't press the point. His guide was perfectly charming, if earnest and humorless, and brightly but brainlessly enthusiastic for the party line, like a cadre from one of the supernats. She was transparently a government spy, and was recording everything—she had shown him the little button camera and asked his permission.

"Such a historical event this is, Mr. Lo, that we wish

to make a permanent record of it. You will I hope not mind?''

So now Ben Lo changed the subject, and asked why there were no sailboats on the lake, and then had to explain to Marla what a sailboat was.

Her smile was brilliant when she finally understood. ''Oh yah, there are some I think who use such boards on the water, like surfing boards with sails.''

''Sailboards, sure.''

''The waves are very high, so it is not easy a sport. Not many are allowed, besides, because of the film.''

It turned out that there was a monomolecular film across the whole lake, to stop great gobs of it floating off into the lakeside terraces.

A gong beat softly in the air. Marla looked at her watch. It was tattooed on her slim, tanned wrist. ''Now it will rain soon. We should go inside, I think. I can show you the library this afternoon. There are several real books in it that one of our first citizens brought all the way from Earth.''

When he was not sight-seeing or attending coordination meetings with the others in the trade delegation (he knew none of them well, and they were all so much younger than him, and as bright and enthusiastic as Marla), he spent a lot of time in the library. He told Marla that he was gathering background information that would help finesse the target packages of economic exchange, and she said that it was good, this was an open society, they had nothing to hide. Of course, he couldn't use his own archive, which was under bonded quarantine, but he was happy enough typing away at one of the library terminals for hours on end, and after a while, Marla left him to it. He also made use of various point-of-presence mobots to explore the surface, especially around Elfhame's roof.

And then there were the diplomatic functions to attend:

a party in the prime minister's house, a monstrous construction of pine logs and steeply pitched roofs of wooden shingles cantilevered above the lake; a reception in the assembly room of the parliament, the Riksdag; others at the university and the Supreme Court. Ben Lo started to get a permanent crick in his neck from looking up at the faces of his etiolated hosts while making conversation.

At one, held in the humid, rarefied atmosphere of the research greenhouses near the top of the East Wall of Elfhame, Ben Lo glimpsed Avernus again. His heart lifted strangely, and the spy broke off from the one-sided conversation with an earnest hydroponicist and pushed through the throng toward his target, the floor sucking at his sandals with each step.

The old woman was surrounded by a gaggle of young giants, set apart from the rest of the party. The spy was aware of people watching when he took Avernus's hand, something that caused a murmur of unrest amongst her companions.

"An old custom, dears," Avernus told them. "We pre-date most of the plagues that made such gestures taboo, even after the plagues were defeated. Ben, dear, what a surprise. I had hoped never to see you again. Your employers have a strange sense of humor."

A young man with big, red-framed data glasses said, "You know each other?"

"We lived in the same city," Avernus said, "many years ago." She had brushed her vigorous grey hair back from her forehead. The wine-dark velvet wrap did not flatter her skinny old woman's body. She said to Ben, "You look so young."

"My third treatment," he confessed.

Avernus said, "It was once said that in American lives there was no second act—but biotech has given almost everyone who can afford it a second act, and for some a third one, too. But what to *do* in them? One simply can't pretend to be young again—one is too aware of death, and has too much at stake, too much invested in *self*, to risk being young.''

''There's no longer any America,'' Ben Lo said. ''Perhaps that helps.''

''To be without loyalty,'' the old woman said, ''except to one's own continuity.''

The spy winced, but did not show it.

The old woman took his elbow. Her grip was surprisingly strong. ''Pretend to be interested, dear,'' she said. ''We are having a delightful conversation in this delightful party. Smile. That's better!''

Her companions laughed uneasily at this. Avernus said quietly to Ben, ''You must visit me.''

''I have an escort.''

''Of course you do. I'm sure someone as resourceful as you will think of something. Ah, this must be your guide. What a tall girl!''

Avernus turned away, and her companions closed around her, turning their long bare backs on the Earthman.

Ben Lo asked Marla what Avernus was doing there. He was dizzy with the contrast between what his wife had been, and what she had become. He could hardly remember what they had talked about. Meet. They had to meet. They would meet.

It was beginning.

Marla said, ''It is a politeness to her. Really, she should not have come, and we are glad she is leaving early. You do not worry about her, Mr. Lo. She is a sideline. We look inward, we reject the insane plans of the previous administration. Would you like to see the new oil-rich strains of *Chlorella* we use?''

Ben Lo smiled diplomatically. ''It would be very interesting.''

•　•　•

There had been a change of government, after the war. It had been less violent and more serious than a revolution, more like a change of climate, or of religion. Before the Quiet War (that was what it was called on Earth, for although tens of thousands had died in the war, none had died on *Earth*), Proteus had been loosely allied with, but not committed to, an amorphous group which wanted to exploit the outer reaches of the solar system, beyond Pluto's orbit; after the war, Proteus dropped its expansionist plans and sought to reestablish links with the trading communities of Earth.

Avernus had been on the losing side of the change in political climate. Brought in by the previous regime because of her skills in gengeneering vacuum organisms, she found herself sidelined and ostracized, her research group disbanded and replaced by government cadres, funds for her research suddenly diverted to new projects. But her contract bound her to Proteus for the next ten years, and the new government refused to release her. She had developed several important new dendrimers, light-harvesting molecules used in artificial photosynthesis, and established several potentially valuable genelines, including a novel form of photosynthesis based on a sulphur-spring *Chloroflexus* bacterium. The government wanted to license them, but to do that it had to keep Avernus under contract, even if it would not allow her to work.

Avernus wanted to escape, and Ben Lo was there to help her. The Pacific Community had plenty of uses for vacuum organisms—there was the whole of the Moon to use as a garden, to begin with—and was prepared to overlook Avernus's political stance in exchange for her expertise and her knowledge.

He was beginning to remember more and more, but there was still so much he didn't know. He supposed that the knowledge had been buried, and would flower in due course. He tried not to worry about it.

Meanwhile, the meetings of the trade delegation and Elfhame's industrial executive finally began. Ben Lo spent most of the next ten days in a closed room dickering with Parliamentary speakers on the Trade Committee over marginal rates for exotic organics. When the meetings were finally over, he slept for three hours and then, still logy from lack of sleep but filled with excess energy, went body surfing at the black beach at the North End. It was the first time he had managed to evade Marla. She had been as exhausted as he had been by the rounds of negotiations, and he had promised that he would sleep all day so that she could get some rest.

The surf was tremendous, huge smooth slow glassy swells falling from thirty meters to batter the soft, sugary black sand with giant's paws. The air was full of spinning globs of water, and so hazed with spray, like a rain of foamy flowers, that it was necessary to wear a filtermask. It was what the whole lake would be like, without its monomolecular membrane.

Ben Lo had thought he would still have an aptitude for body surfing, because he'd done so much of it when he had been living in Los Angeles, before his movie career really took off. But he was as helpless as a kitten in the swells, his boogie board turning turtle as often as not, and twice he was caught in the undertow. The second time, a pale naked giantess got an arm around his chest and hauled him up onto dry sand.

After he hawked up a couple of lungs-full of fresh water, he managed to gasp his thanks. The woman smiled. She had black hair in a bristle cut, and startlingly green eyes. She was very tall and very thin, and completely naked. She said, "At last you are away from that revisionist bitch."

Ben Lo sat up, abruptly conscious, in the presence of this young naked giantess, of his own nakedness. "Ah. You are one of Avernus's—"

The woman walked away with her boogie board under her arm, pale buttocks flexing. The spy unclipped the ankle line that tethered him to his rented board, bounded up the beach in two leaps, pulled on his shorts, and followed.

Sometime later, he was standing in the middle of a vast red-lit room at blood heat and what felt like a hundred percent humidity. Racks of large-leaved plants receded into infinity; those nearest him towered high above, forming a living green wall. His arm stung, and the tall young woman, naked under a green gown open down the front, but masked and wearing disposable gloves, deftly caught the glob of expressed blood—his blood—in a capillary straw, took a disc of skin from his forearm with a spring-loaded punch, sprayed the wound with sealant and went off with her samples.

A necessary precaution, the old woman said. Avernus. He remembered now. Or at least could picture it. Taking a ski lift all the way to the top. Through a tunnel lined with tall plastic bags in which green *Chlorella* cultures bubbled under lights strobing in fifty millisecond pulses. Another attack of memory loss—they seemed to be increasing in frequency. Stress, he told himself.

"Of all the people I could identify," Avernus said, "they had to send *you*."

"Ask me anything," Ben Lo said, although he wasn't sure that he recalled very much of their brief marriage.

"I mean identify genetically. We exchanged strands of hair in amber, do you remember? I kept mine. It was mounted in a ring."

"I didn't think that you were sentimental."

"It was my idea, and I did it with all my husbands. It reminded me of what I once was."

"My wife."

"An idiot."

"I must get back to the hotel soon. If they find out I've

been wandering around without my escort, they'll start to suspect.''

"Good. Let them worry. What can they do? Arrest me? Arrest you?''

"I have diplomatic immunity.''

Avernus laughed. "Ben, Ben, you always were so status-conscious. That's why I left. I was just another thing you'd collected. A trophy, like your Porsche, or your Picasso.''

He didn't remember.

"It wasn't a very good Picasso. One of his fakes—do you know that story?''

"I suppose I sold it.''

The young woman in the green gown came back. "A positive match,'' she said. "Probability of a negative identity point oh oh one or less. But he is doped up with immunosuppressants and testosterone.''

"The treatment,'' the spy said glibly. "Is this where you do your research?''

"Of course not. They certainly would notice if you turned up there. This is one of the pharm farms. They grow tobacco here, with human genes inserted to make various immunoglobulins. They took away my people, Ben, and replaced them with spies. Ludmilla is one of my original team. They put her to drilling new agricultural tunnels.''

"We are alone here,'' Ludmilla said.

"Or you would have made your own arrangements.''

"I hate being dependent on people. Especially from Earth, if you'll forgive me. And especially you. Are the others in your trade delegation . . . ?''

"Just a cover,'' the spy said. "They know nothing. They are looking forward to your arrival in Tycho. The laboratory is ready to be fitted out to your specifications.''

"I swore I'd never go back, but they are fools here. They stand on the edge of greatness, the next big push, and they turn their backs on it and burrow into the ice like maggots.''

The spy took her hands in his. Her skin was loose on her bones, and dry and cold despite the humid heat of the hydroponic greenhouse. He said, ''Are you ready? Truly ready?''

She did not pull away. ''I have said so. I will submit to any test, if it makes your masters happy. Ben, you are exactly as I remember you. It is very strange.''

''The treatments are very good now. You must use one.''

''Don't think I haven't, although not as radical as yours. I like to show my age. You could shrivel up like a Struldbrugg, and I don't have to worry about *that*, at least. That skin color, though. Is it a fashion?''

''I was Othello, once. Don't you like it?'' Under the red lights his skin gleamed with an ebony luster.

''I always thought you'd make a good Iago, if only you had been clever enough. I asked for someone I knew, and they sent you. It almost makes me want to distrust them.''

''We were young, then.'' He was trying to remember, searching her face. Well, it was two hundred years ago. Still, he felt as if he trembled at a great brink, and a tremendous feeling of nostalgia for what he could not remember swept through him. Tears grew like big lenses over his eyes and he brushed them into the air and apologized.

''I am here to do a job,'' he said, and said it as much for his benefit as hers.

Avernus said, ''Be honest, Ben. You hardly remember anything.''

''Well, it *was* a long time ago.'' But he did not feel relieved at this admission. The past was gone. No more than pictures, no longer a part of him.

Avernus said, ''When we got married, I was in love, and a fool. It was in the Wayfarer's Chapel, do you re-

member? Hot and dry, with a Santa Ana blowing, and
Channel Five's news helicopter hovering overhead. You
were already famous, and two years later you were so
famous I no longer recognized you."

They talked a little while about his career. The acting,
the successful terms as state senator, the unsuccessful term
as congressman, the fortune he had made in land deals
after the partition of the USA, his semi-retirement in the
upper house of the Pacific Community parliament. It was
a little like an interrogation, but he didn't mind it. At least
he knew *this* story well.

The tall young woman, Ludmilla, took him back to the
hotel. It seemed natural that she should stay for a drink,
and then that they should make love, with a languor and
then an urgency that surprised him, although he had been
told that restoration of his testosterone levels would sometimes cause emotional or physical cruxes that would re-
quire resolution. Ben Lo had made love in microgravity
many times, but never before with someone who had been
born to it. Afterward, Ludmilla rose up from the bed and
moved gracefully about the room, dipping and turning as
she pulled on her scanty clothes.

"I will see you again," she said, and then she was
gone.

The negotiations resumed, a punishing schedule taking up
at least twelve hours a day. And there were the briefings
and summary sessions with the other delegates, as well as
the other work the spy had to attend to when Marla
thought he was asleep. Fortunately, he had a kink that
allowed him to build up sleep debt and get by on an hour
a night. He'd sleep long when this was done, all the way
back to Earth with his prize. Then at last it was all in
place, and he only had to wait.

Another reception, this time in the little zoo halfway
up the West Side. The Elfhamers were running out of

novel places to entertain the delegates. Most of the animals looked vaguely unhappy in the microgravity and none were very large. Bushbabies, armadillos, and mice; a pair of hippopotami no larger than domestic cats; a knee-high pink elephant with some kind of skin problem behind its disproportionately large ears.

Ludmilla brushed past Ben Lo as he came out of the rest room and said, "When can she go?"

"Tonight," the spy said.

Everything had been ready for fourteen days now. He went to find something to do now that he was committed to action.

Marla was feeding peanuts to the dwarf elephant. Ben Lo said, "Aren't you worried that the animals might escape? You wouldn't want mice running around your Shangri-la."

"They all have a kink in their metabolism. An artificial amino acid they need. That girl you talked with was once one of Avernus's assistants. She should not be here."

"She propositioned me." Marla said nothing. He said, "There are no side deals. If someone wants anything, they have to bring it to the table through the proper channels."

"You are an oddity here, it is true. Too much muscles. Many women would sleep with you, out of curiosity."

"But *you* have never asked, Marla. I'm ashamed." He said it playfully, but he saw that Marla suspected something. It didn't matter. Everything was in place.

They came for him that night, but he was awake and dressed, counting off the minutes until his little bundle of surprises started to unpack itself. There were two of them, armed with tasers and sticky foam canisters. The spy blinded them with homemade capsicum spray (he'd stolen chilli pods from one of the hydroponic farms and suspended a water extract in a perfume spray) and killed them as they blundered about, screaming and pawing at their eyes. One of them was Marla, another a well-muscled policeman who must have spent a good portion of each day in a centrifuge gym. The spy disabled the sprinkler system, set fire to his room, kicked out the window, and ran.

There were more police waiting outside the main entrance of the hotel. The spy ran right over the edge of the terrace and landed two hundred meters down amongst blue pines grown into bubbles of soft needles in the microgravity. Above, the fire touched off the homemade plastic explosive, and a fan of burning debris shot out above the spy's head, seeming to hover in the black air for a long time before beginning to flutter down toward the Skagerrak. Briefly, he wondered if any of the delegation had survived. It didn't matter. The young, enthusiastic, and naïve delegates had always been expendable.

Half the lights were out in Elfhame, and all of the transportation systems, the phone system was crashing and resetting every five minutes, and the braking lasers were sending twenty-millisecond pulses to a narrow wedge of the sky. It was a dumb bug, only a thousand lines long. The spy had laboriously typed it from memory into the library system, which connected with everything else. It wouldn't take long to trace, but by then, other things would start happening.

The spy waited in the cover of the bushy pine trees. One of his teeth was capped and he pulled it out and unraveled the length of monomolecular diamond wire coiled inside.

In the distance, people called to each other over a backdrop of ringing bells and sirens and klaxons. Flashlights flickered in the darkness on the far side of the Skagerrak's black gulf; on the terrace above the spy's hiding place, the police seemed to have brought the fire in the hotel under control. Then the branches of the pines started to doff as a wind came up; the bug had reached the air conditioning. In the darkness below, waves grew higher on the Skagerrak, sloshing and crashing together, as the wind drove waves toward the beach at the North End and reflected waves clashed with those coming onshore. The monomolecular film over the lake's surface was not infinitely strong. The wind began to tear spray from the tops of the towering waves, and filled the lower level of the canyon with flying foam flowers. Soon the waves would grow so tall that they'd spill over the lower levels.

The spy counted out ten minutes, and then started to bound up the terraces, putting all his strength into his thigh and back muscles. Most of the setbacks between each terrace were no more than thirty meters high; for someone with muscles accustomed to one gee, it was easy enough to scale them with a single jump in the microgravity, even from a standing start.

He was halfway there when the zoo's elephant charged past him in the windy semidarkness. Its trunk was raised above its head and it trumpeted a single despairing cry as it ran over the edge of the narrow terrace. Its momentum carried it a long way out into the air before it began to fall, outsized ears flapping as if trying to lift it. Higher up, the plastic explosive charges the spy had made from sugar, gelatin, and lubricating grease blew out hectares of plastic sheeting and structural frames from the long greenhouses.

The spy's legs were like wood when he reached the high agricultural regions; his heart was pounding and his lungs were burning as he tried to strain oxygen from the thin air. He grabbed a fire extinguisher and mingled with panicked staff, ricocheting down long corridors and bounding across windblown fields of crops edged by shattered glass walls and lit by stuttering red emergency lighting. He was only challenged once, and he struck the woman with the butt end of the fire extinguisher and ran on without bothering to check if she was dead or not.

Marla had shown him the place where they stored genetic material on one of her endless tours. Everything was kept in liquid nitrogen, and there was a wide selection of dewar flasks. He chose one about the size of a human head, filled it, and clamped on the lid.

Then through a set of double pressure doors, banging the switch that closed them behind him, setting down the flask and dropping the coil of diamond wire beside it, stepping into a dressing frame, and finally pausing, breathing hard, dry-mouthed and suddenly trembling, as the vacuum suit was assembled around him. As the gold-filmed bubble was lowered over his head and clamped to the neck seal, Ben Lo started, as if waking. Something was terribly wrong. What was he doing here?

Dry air hissed around his face; headup displays stuttered and scrolled down. The spy walked out of the frame, stowed the diamond wire in one of the suit's utility pockets, picked up the flask of liquid nitrogen, and started the airlock cycle, ignoring the computer's contralto as it recited a series of safety precautions while the room revolved, and opened on a flood of sunlight.

The spy came out at the top of the South End of Elfhame. The canyon stretched away to the north, its construction-diamond roof like black sheet-ice: a long, narrow lake of ice curving away downhill, it seemed, between odd, rounded hills like half-buried snowballs, their sides spattered with perfect round craters. He bounded around the tangle of pipes and fins of some kind of distillery or cracking plant, and saw the line of the railway arrowing away across a glaring white plain toward an horizon as close as the top of a hill.

The railway was a single rail hung from smart A-frames whose carbon fiber legs compensated for movements in the icy surface. Thirteen hundred kilometers long, it described a complete circle around the little moon from pole to pole, part of the infrastructure left over from Elfhame's expansionist phase, when it was planned to string sibling settlements all the way around the moon.

The spy kangaroo-hopped along the sunward side of the railway, heading south toward the rendezvous point they had agreed upon. In five minutes, the canyon and its associated domes and industrial plant had disappeared beneath the horizon behind him. The ice was rippled and cracked and blistered, and crunched under the cleats of his boots at each touchdown.

"That was some diversion," a voice said over the open channel. "I hope no one was killed."

"Just an elephant, I think. Although if it landed in the lake, it might have survived." He wasn't about to tell Avernus about Marla and the policeman.

The spy stopped in the shadow of a carbon-fiber pillar, and scanned the icy terrain ahead of him. The point-of-presence mobots hadn't been allowed into this area. The ice curved away to the east and south like a warped checkerboard. There was a criss-cross pattern of ridges that marked out regular squares about two hundred meters on each side, and each square was a different color. Vacuum organisms. He'd reached the experimental plots.

Avernus said over the open channel, "I can't see the pickup."

He started along the line again. At the top of his leap, he said, "I've already signaled to the transport using the braking lasers. It'll be here in less than an hour. We're a little ahead of schedule."

The transport was a small gig with a brute of a motor taking up most of its hull, leaving room for only a single hibernation pod and a small storage compartment. If everything went according to plan, that was all he would need.

He came down and leaped again, and then he saw her on the far side of the curved checkerboard of the experimental plots, a tiny figure in a transparent vacuum suit sitting on a slope of black ice at what looked like the edge of the world. He bounded across the fields toward her.

The ridges were only a meter high and a couple of meters across, dirty water and methane ice fused smooth as glass. It was easy to leap over each of them—the gravity was so light that the spy could probably get into orbit if he wasn't careful. Each field held a different growth. A corrugated grey mold that gave like rubber under his boots. Flexible spikes the color of dried blood, all different heights and thicknesses, but none higher than his knees. More grey stuff, this time mounded in discrete blisters each several meters from its nearest neighbors, with fat grey ropes running beneath the ice. Irregular stacks of what looked like black plates that gave way, halfway across the field, to a blanket of black stuff like cracked tar.

The figure had turned to watch him, its helmet a gold bubble that refracted the rays of the tiny, intensely bright star of the sun. As the spy made the final bound across the last of the experimental plots—more of the black stuff, like a huge wrinkled vinyl blanket dissected by deep wandering cracks—Avernus said in his ear, "You should have kept to the boundary walls."

"It doesn't matter now."

"Ah but I think you'll find it does."

Avernus was sitting in her pressure suit on top of a ridge of upturned strata at the rim of a huge crater. Her suit was transparent, after the fashion of the losing side of the Quiet War. It was intended to minimize the barrier between the human and the vacuum environments. She might as well have flown a flag declaring her allegiance to the outer alliance. Behind her, the crater stretched away south and west, and the railway ran right out above its dark floor on pillars that doubled and tripled in height as they stepped away down the inner slope. The crater was so large that its far side was hidden beyond the little moon's curvature. The black stuff had overgrown the ridge, and flowed down into the crater. Avernus was sitting in the only clear spot.

She said, "This is my most successful strain. You can see how vigorous it is. You didn't get that suit from my lab, did you? I suggest you keep moving around. This stuff is thixotropic in the presence of foreign bodies, like smart paint. It spreads out, flowing under pressure, over the neighboring organisms, but doesn't overgrow itself."

The spy looked down, and saw that the big cleated boots of his pressure suit had already sunken to the ankles in the black stuff. He lifted one, then the other; it was like walking in tar. He took a step toward her, and the ground collapsed beneath his boots and he was suddenly up to his knees in black stuff.

"My suit," Avernus said, "is coated with the protein by which the strain recognizes its own self. You could say I'm like a virus, fooling the immune system. I dug a trench, and that's what you stepped into. Where is the transport?"

"On its way, but you don't have to worry about it," the spy said, as he struggled to free himself. "This silly little trap won't hold me for long."

Avernus stepped back. She was four meters away, and the black stuff was thigh deep around the spy now, sluggishly flowing upward. The spy flipped the catches on the flask and tipped liquid nitrogen over the stuff. The nitrogen boiled up in a cloud of dense vapor and evaporated. It had made no difference at all to the stuff's integrity.

A point of light began to grow brighter above the close horizon of the moon, moving swiftly aslant the field of stars.

"It gets brittle at close to absolute zero," Avernus said, "but only after several dozen hours." She turned, and added, "There's the transport."

The spy snarled at her. He was up to his waist, and had to fold his arms across his chest, or else they would be caught fast.

Avernus said, "You never were Ben Lo, were you? Or at any rate no more than a poor copy. The original is back on Earth, alive or dead. If he's alive, no doubt he'll claim that this is all a trick of the outer alliance against the Elfhamers and their new allies, the Pacific Community."

He said, "There's still time, Barbara. We can do this together."

The woman in the transparent pressure suit turned back to look at him. Sun flared on her bubble helmet. "Ben, poor Ben. I'll call you that for the sake of convenience. Do you know what happened to you? Someone used you. That body isn't even yours. It isn't anyone's. Oh, it looks like you, and I suppose the altered skin color disguises the rougher edges of the plastic surgery. The skin matches your genotype, and so does the blood, but the skin was cloned from your original, and the blood must come from marrow implants. No wonder there's so much immuno-suppressant in your system. If we had just trusted your skin and blood, we would not have known. But your sperm—it was all female. Not a single Y chromosome. I think you're probably haploid, a construct from an unfertilized blastula. You're not even male, except somatically—you're swamped with testosterone, probably have been since gastrulation. You're a *weapon*, Ben. They used things like you as assassins in the Quiet War."

He was in a pressure suit, with dry air blowing around his head and headup displays blinking at the bottom of the clear helmet. A black landscape, and stars high above, with something bright pulsing, growing closer. A space-ship! That was important, but he couldn't remember why. He tried to move, and discovered that he was trapped in something like tar that came to his waist. He could feel it clamping around his legs, a terrible pressure that was compromising the heat exchange system of his suit. His legs were freezing cold, but his body was hot, and sweat prickled across his skin, collecting in the folds of the suit's undergarment.

"Don't move," a woman's voice said. "It's like quicksand. It flows under pressure. You'll last a little longer if you keep still. Struggling only makes it more liquid."

Barbara. No, she called herself Avernus now. He had the strangest feeling that someone else was there, too, just out of sight. He tried to look around, but it was terribly hard in the half-buried suit. He had been kidnapped. It was the only explanation. He remembered running from the burning hotel. . . . He was suddenly certain that the other members of the trade delegation were dead, and cried out, "Help me!"

Avernus squatted in front of him, moving carefully and slowly in her transparent pressure suit. He could just see the outline of her face through the gold film of her helmet's visor. "There are two personalities in there, I think. The dominant one let you back, Ben, so that you would plead with me. But don't plead, Ben. I don't want my last memory of you to be so undignified, and anyway, I won't listen. I won't deny you've been a great help. Elfhame always was a soft target, and you punched just the right buttons, and then you kindly provided the means of getting where I want to go. They'll think I was kidnapped." Avernus turned and pointed up at the sky. "Can you see? That's your transport. Ludmilla is going to reprogram it."

"Take me with you, Barbara."

"Oh, Ben, Ben. But I'm not going to Earth. I considered it, but when they sent you, I knew that there was something wrong. I'm going *out*, Ben. Farther out. Beyond Pluto, in the Kuiper Disk, where there are more than fifty thousand objects with a diameter of more than a hundred kilometers, and a billion comet nuclei ten kilometers or so across. And then there's the Oort Cloud, and its billions of comets. The fringes of *that* mingle with the fringes of Alpha Centauri's cometary cloud. Life spreads. That's its one rule. In ten thousand years, my children will reach Alpha Centauri, not by starship, but simply through expansion of their territory.''

''That's the way you used to talk when we were married. All that sci-fi you used to read!''

''You don't remember it, Ben. Not really. It was fed to you. All my old interviews, my books and articles, all your old movies. They did a quick construction job, and just when you started to find out about it, the other one took over.''

''I don't think I'm quite myself. I don't understand what's happening, but perhaps it is something to do with the treatment I had. I told you about that.''

''Hush, dear. There was no treatment. That was when they fixed you in the brain of this empty vessel.''

She was too close, and she had half-turned to watch the moving point of light grow brighter. He wanted to warn her, but something clamped his lips and he almost swallowed his tongue. He watched as his left hand stealthily unfastened a utility pocket and pulled out a length of glittering wire fine as a spider-thread. Monomolecular diamond. Serrated along its length, except for five centimeters at each end, it could easily cut through pressure suit material and flesh and bone.

He knew then. He knew what he was.

The woman looked at him and said sharply, ''What are you doing, Ben?''

And for that moment, he was called back, and he made a fist around the thread and plunged it into the black stuff. The spy screamed and reached behind his helmet and dumped all oxygen from his main pack. It hissed for a long time, but the stuff gripping his legs and waist held firm.

''It isn't an anaerobe,'' Avernus said. She hadn't

moved. "It is a vacuum organism. A little oxygen won't
hurt it."

Ben Lo found that he could speak. He said, "He
wanted to cut off your head."

"I wondered why you were carrying that flask of liquid
nitrogen. You were going to take my head back with
you—and what? Use a bush robot to strip my brain neuron by neuron and read my memories into a computer?
How convenient to have a genius captive in a bottle!"

"It's me, Barbara. I couldn't let him do that to you."
His left arm was buried up to the elbow.

"Then thank you, Ben. I'm in your debt."

"I'd ask you to take me with you, but I think there's
only one hibernation pod in the transport. You won't be
able to take your friend, either."

"Well, Ludmilla has her family here. She doesn't want
to leave. Or not yet."

"I can't remember that story about Picasso. Maybe you
heard it after we—after the divorce."

"You told it to me, Ben. When things were good between us, you used to tell stories like that."

"Then I've forgotten."

"It's about an art dealer who buys a canvas in a private
deal, that is signed 'Picasso.' This is in France, when Picasso was working in Cannes, and the dealer travels there
to find if it is genuine. Picasso is working in his studio.
He spares the painting a brief glance and dismisses it as
a fake."

"I had a Picasso, once. A bull's head. I remember that,
Barbara."

"You thought it was a necessary sign of your wealth.
You were photographed beside it several times. I always
preferred Georges Braque myself. Do you want to hear
the rest of the story?"

"I'm still here."

"Of course you are, as long as I stay out of reach. Well,
a few months later, the dealer buys another canvas signed

by Picasso. Again he travels to the studio; again Picasso spares it no more than a glance, and announces that it is a fake. The dealer protests that this is the very painting he found Picasso working on the first time he visited, but Picasso just shrugs and says, 'I often paint fakes.' "

His breathing was becoming labored. Was there something wrong with the air system? The black stuff was climbing his chest. He could almost see it move, a creeping wave of black devouring him centimeter by centimeter.

The star was very close to the horizon, now.

He said, "I know a story."

"There's no more time for stories, dear. I can release you, if you want. You only have your reserve air in any case."

"No. I want to see you go."

"I'll remember you. I'll tell your story far and wide."

Ben Lo heard the echo of another voice across their link, and the woman in the transparent pressure suit stood and lifted a hand in salute and bounded away.

The spy came back, then, but Ben Lo fought him down. There was nothing he could do, after all. The woman was gone. He said, as if to himself, "I know a story. About a man who lost himself, and found himself again, just in time. Listen. *Once upon a time . . .*"

Something bright rose above the horizon and dwindled away into the outer darkness.

GOOD-BYE,
ROBINSON CRUSOE

John Varley

"Good-bye, Robinson Crusoe" was purchased by George Scithers, and appeared in the very first issue of Asimov's, *our premiere issue, Spring 1977 (we were a quarterly magazine then); it was, in fact, one of the very first stories bought for that very first issue, which also featured the classic Varley story "Air Raid," which appeared under a pseudonym, because of an old magazine tradition of not having two stories by the same author in the same issue. Since then, the magazine has seen less of him as his career as a novelist predominates, although a story by him still appears here every once in a while, and we hope to coax more stories out of him in the future.*

John Varley appeared on the SF scene in 1975, and by the end of 1976—in what was a meteoric rise to prominence even for a field known for meteoric rises—he was already being recognized as one of the hottest new writers of the seventies. His books include the novels Ophiuchi Hotline, Millennium *(a novelization of one of his own short stories that was also made into a movie),* Titan, Wizard,

Demon, *and* Steel Beach, *and the collections* The
Persistence of Vision, The Barbie Murders, Picnic
on Nearside, *and* Blue Champagne. *After a long
silence, Varley seems to be making something of a
comeback here at the end of the century, publishing
a major new novel,* The Golden Globe, *in 1998,
with another new novel,* Irontown Blues, *coming up
soon. He has won two Nebulas and two Hugos for
his short fiction.*

  *In the vivid adventure that follows, he takes to
the very outermost edge of the solar system, to a
tourist's paradise being constructed inside the ninth
planet, Pluto, for a story that demonstrates that
when you become a man, it's time to put away
childish things—but that sometimes doing that can
be very hard indeed.*

It was summer, and Piri was in his second childhood.
First, second; who counted? His body was young. He had
not felt more alive since his original childhood back in
the spring, when the sun drew closer and the air began to
melt.

He was spending his time at Rarotonga Reef, in the
Pacifica disneyland. Pacifica was still under construction,
but Rarotonga had been used by the ecologists as a testing
ground for the more ambitious barrier-type reef they were
building in the south, just off the "Australian" coast. As
a result, it was more firmly established than the other bi-
omes. It was open to visitors, but so far only Piri was
there. The "sky" disconcerted everyone else.

Piri didn't mind it. He was equipped with a brand-new
toy: a fully operational imagination, a selective sense of
wonder that allowed him to blank out those parts of his
surroundings that failed to fit with his current fantasy.

He awoke with the tropical sun blinking in his face
through the palm fronds. He had built a rude shelter from
flotsam and detritus on the beach. It was not to protect
him from the elements. The disneyland management had

the weather well in hand; he might as well have slept in the open. But castaways *always* build some sort of shelter.

He bounced up with the quick alertness that comes from being young and living close to the center of things, brushed sand from his naked body, and ran for the line of breakers at the bottom of the narrow strip of beach.

His gait was awkward. His feet were twice as long as they should have been, with flexible toes that were webbed into flippers. Dry sand showered around his legs as he ran. He was brown as coffee and cream, and hairless.

Piri dived flat to the water, sliced neatly under a wave, and paddled out to waist-height. He paused there. He held his nose and worked his arms up and down, blowing air through his mouth and swallowing at the same time. What looked like long, hairline scars between his lower ribs came open. Red-orange fringes became visible inside them, and gradually lowered. He was no longer an air-breather.

He dived again, mouth open, and this time he did not come up. His esophagus and trachea closed and a new valve came into operation. It would pass water in only one direction, so his diaphragm now functioned as a pump pulling water through his mouth and forcing it out through the gill-slits. The water flowing through this lower chest area caused his gills to engorge with blood, turning them purplish-red and forcing his lungs to collapse upward into his chest cavity. Bubbles of air trickled out his sides, then stopped. His transition was complete.

The water seemed to grow warmer around him. It had been pleasantly cool; now it seemed no temperature at all. It was the result of his body temperature lowering in response to hormones released by an artificial gland in his cranium. He could not afford to burn energy at the rate he had done in the air; the water was too efficient a coolant for that. All through his body arteries and capillaries were constricting as parts of him stabilized at a lower rate of function.

No naturally evolved mammal had ever made the switch from air to water breathing, and the project had taxed the resources of bio-engineering to its limits. But everything in Piri's body was a living part of him. It had taken two full days to install it all.

He knew nothing of the chemical complexities that kept him alive where he should have died quickly from heat loss or oxygen starvation. He knew only the joy of arrowing along the white sandy bottom. The water was clear, blue-green in the distance.

The bottom kept dropping away from him, until suddenly it reached for the waves. He angled up the wall of the reef until his head broke the surface, climbed up the knobs and ledges until he was standing in the sunlight. He took a deep breath and became an air-breather again.

The change cost him some discomfort. He waited until the dizziness and fit of coughing had passed, shivering a little as his body rapidly underwent a reversal to a warm-blooded economy.

It was time for breakfast.

He spent the morning foraging among the tidepools. There were dozens of plants and animals that he had learned to eat raw. He ate a great deal, storing up energy for the afternoon's expedition on the outer reef.

Piri avoided looking at the sky. He wasn't alarmed by it; it did not disconcert him as it did the others. But he had to preserve the illusion that he was actually on a tropical reef in the Pacific Ocean, a castaway, and not a vacationer in an environment bubble below the surface of Pluto.

Soon he became a fish again, and dived off the sea side of the reef.

The water around the reef was oxygen-rich from the constant wave action. Even here, though, he had to remain in motion to keep enough water flowing past his external gill fringes. But he could move more slowly as he wound his way down into the darker reaches of the sheer reef face. The reds and yellows of his world were swallowed by the blues and greens and purples. It was quiet. There were sounds to hear, but his ears were not adapted to them. He moved slowly through shafts of blue light, keeping up the bare minimum of water flow.

He hesitated at the ten-meter level. He had thought he was going to his Atlantis Grotto to check out his crab farm. Then he wondered if he ought to hunt up Ocho the Octopus instead. For a panicky moment he was afflicted with the bane of childhood: an inability to decide what to do with himself. Or maybe it was worse, he thought. Maybe it was a sign of growing up. The crab farm bored him, or at least it did today.

He waffled back and forth for several minutes, idly chasing the tiny red fish that flirted with the anemones. He never caught one. This was no good at all. Surely there was an adventure in this silent fairyland. He had to find one.

An adventure found him, instead. Piri saw something swimming out in the open water, almost at the limits of his vision. It was long and pale, an attenuated missile of raw death. His heart squeezed in panic, and he scuttled for a hollow in the reef.

Piri called him the Ghost. He had seen him many times in the open sea. He was eight meters of mouth, belly and tail: hunger personified. There were those who said the great white shark was the most ferocious carnivore that ever lived. Piri believed it.

It didn't matter that the Ghost was completely harmless to him. The Pacifica management did not like having its guests eaten alive. An adult could elect to go into the water with no protection, providing the necessary waivers were on file. Children had to be implanted with an equalizer. Piri had one, somewhere just below the skin of his left wrist. It was a sonic generator, set to emit a sound that would mean terror to any predator in the water.

The Ghost, like all the sharks, barracudas, morays, and other predators in Pacifica, was not like his cousins who swam the seas of Earth. He had been cloned from cells stored in the Biological Library on Luna. The library had been created two hundred years before as an insurance policy against the extinction of a species. Originally, only endangered species were filed, but for years before the Invasion the directors had been trying to get a sample of everything. Then the Invaders had come, and Lunarians were too busy surviving without help from Occupied Earth to worry about the library. But when the time came to build the disneylands, the library had been ready.

By then, biological engineering had advanced to the point where many modifications could be made in genetic structure. Mostly, the disneyland biologists had left nature alone. But they had changed the predators. In the Ghost, the change was a mutated organ attached to the brain that responded with a flood of fear when a supersonic note was sounded.

So why was the Ghost still out there? Piri blinked his nictating membranes, trying to clear his vision. It helped a little. The shape looked a bit different.

Instead of moving back and forth, the tail seemed to be going up and down, perhaps in a scissoring motion. Only one animal swims like that. He gulped down his fear and pushed away from the reef.

But he had waited too long. His fear of the Ghost went beyond simple danger, of which there was none. It was something more basic, an unreasoning reflex that prickled his neck when he saw that long white shape. He couldn't fight it, and didn't want to. But the fear had kept him against the reef, hidden, while the person swam out of

reach. He thrashed to catch up, but soon lost track of the
moving feet in the gloom.

He had seen gills trailing from the sides of the figure,
muted down to a deep blue-black by the depths. He had
the impression that it was a woman.

Tongatown was the only human habitation on the island.
It housed a crew of maintenance people and their children,
about fifty in all, in grass huts patterned after those of
South Sea natives. A few of the buildings concealed elevators that went to the underground rooms that would
house the tourists when the project was completed. The
shacks would then go at a premium rate, and the beaches
would be crowded.

Piri walked into the circle of firelight and greeted his
friends. Nighttime was party time in Tongatown. With the
day's work over, everybody gathered around the fire and
roasted a vat-grown goat or lamb. But the real culinary
treats were the fresh vegetable dishes. The ecologists were
still working out the kinks in the systems, controlling
blooms, planting more of failing species. They often produced huge excesses of edibles that would have cost a
fortune on the outside. The workers took some of the excess for themselves. It was understood to be a fringe benefit of the job. It was hard enough to find people who
could stand to stay under the Pacifica sky.

"Hi, Piri," said a girl. "You meet any pirates today?"
It was Harra, who used to be one of Piri's best friends
but had seemed increasingly remote over the last year. She
was wearing a handmade grass skirt and a lot of flowers,
tied into strings that looped around her body. She was
fifteen now, and Piri was . . . but who cared? There were
no seasons here, only days. Why keep track of time?

Piri didn't know what to say. The two of them had once
played together out on the reef. It might be Lost Atlantis,
or Submariner, or Reef Pirates; a new plot line and cast

of heroes and villains every day. But her question had held such thinly veiled contempt. Didn't she care about the Pirates anymore? What was the matter with her?

She relented when she saw Piri's helpless bewilderment.

"Here, come on and sit down. I saved you a rib." She held out a large chunk of mutton.

Piri took it and sat beside her. He was famished, having had nothing all day since his large breakfast.

"I thought I saw the Ghost today," he said, casually.

Harra shuddered. She wiped her hands on her thighs and looked at him closely.

"Thought? You thought you saw him?" Harra did not care for the Ghost. She had cowered with Piri more than once as they watched him prowl.

"Yep. But I don't think it was really him."

"Where was this?"

"On the sea-side, down about, oh, ten meters. I think it was a woman."

"I don't see how it could be. There's just you and— and Midge and Darvin with—did this woman have an air tank?"

"Nope. Gills. I saw that."

"But there's only you and four others here with gills. And I know where they all were today."

"You used to have gills," he said, with a hint of accusation.

She sighed. "Are we going through that again? I *told* you, I got tired of the flippers. I wanted to move around the *land* some more."

"I can move around the land," he said, darkly.

"All right, all right. You think I deserted you. Did you ever think that you sort of deserted *me*?"

Piri was puzzled by that, but Harra had stood up and walked quickly away. He could follow her, or he could finish his meal. She was right about the flippers. He was no great shakes at chasing anybody.

Piri never worried about anything for too long. He ate, and ate some more, long past the time when everyone else had joined together for the dancing and singing. He usually hung back, anyway. He could sing, but dancing was out of his league.

Just as he was leaning back in the sand, wondering if there were any more corners he could fill up—perhaps another bowl of that shrimp teriyaki?—Harra was back. She sat beside him.

"I talked to my mother about what you said. She said a tourist showed up today. It looks like you were right. It was a woman, and she was amphibious."

Piri felt a vague unease. One tourist was certainly not an invasion, but she could be a harbinger. And amphibious. So far, no one had gone to that expense except for those who planned to live here for a long time. Was his tropical hide-out in danger of being discovered?

"What—what's she doing here?" He absently ate another spoonful of crab cocktail.

"She's looking for *you*," Harra laughed, and elbowed him in the ribs. Then she pounced on him, tickling his ribs until he was howling in helpless glee. He fought back, almost to the point of having the upper hand, but she was bigger and a little more determined. She got him pinned, showering flower petals on him as they struggled. One of the red flowers from her hair was in her eye, and she brushed it away, breathing hard.

"You want to go for a walk on the beach?" she asked.

Harra was fun, but the last few times he'd gone with her she had tried to kiss him. He wasn't ready for that. He was only a kid. He thought she probably had something like that in mind now.

"I'm too full," he said, and it was almost the literal truth. He had stuffed himself disgracefully, and only wanted to curl up in his shack and go to sleep.

Harra said nothing, just sat there getting her breathing under control. At last she nodded, a little jerkily, and got to her feet. Piri wished he could see her face to face. He knew something was wrong. She turned from him and walked away.

Robinson Crusoe was feeling depressed when he got back to his hut. The walk down the beach away from the laughter and singing had been a lonely one. Why had he rejected Harra's offer of companionship? Was it really so bad that she wanted to play new kinds of games?

But no, damn it. She wouldn't play his games, why should he play hers?

After a few minutes of sitting on the beach under the crescent moon, he got into character. Oh, the agony of being a lone castaway, far from the company of fellow creatures, with nothing but faith in God to sustain oneself. Tomorrow he would read from the scriptures, do some more exploring along the rocky north coast, tan some goat hides, maybe get in a little fishing.

With his plans for the morrow laid before him, Piri could go to sleep, wiping away a last tear for distant England.

The ghost woman came to him during the night. She knelt beside him in the sand. She brushed his sandy hair from his eyes and he stirred in his sleep. His feet thrashed.

He was churning through the abyssal deeps, heart hammering, blind to everything but internal terror. Behind him, jaws yawned, almost touching his toes. They closed with a snap.

He sat up woozily. He saw rows of serrated teeth in the line of breakers in front of him. And a tall, white shape in the moonlight dived into a curling breaker and was gone.

●   ●   ●

"Hello."

Piri sat up with a start. The worst thing about being a child living alone on an island—which, when he thought about it, was the sort of thing every child dreamed of— was not having a warm mother's breast to cry on when you had nightmares. It hadn't affected him much, but when it did, it was pretty bad.

He squinted up into the brightness. She was standing with her head blocking out the sun. He winced, and looked away, down to her feet. They were webbed, with long toes. He looked a little higher. She was nude, and quite beautiful.

"Who . . . ?"

"Are you awake now?" She squatted down beside him. Why had he expected sharp, triangular teeth? His dreams blurred and ran like watercolors in the rain, and he felt much better. She had a nice face. She was smiling at him.

He yawned, and sat up. He was groggy, stiff, and his eyes were coated with sand that didn't come from the beach. It had been an awful night.

"I think so."

"Good. How about some breakfast?" She stood, and went to a basket on the sand.

"I usually—" but his mouth watered when he saw the guavas, melons, kippered herring, and the long brown loaf of bread. She had butter, and some orange marmalade. "Well, maybe just a—" and he had bitten into a succulent slice of melon. But before he could finish it, he was seized by an even stronger urge. He got to his feet and scuttled around the palm tree with the waist-high dark stain and urinated against it.

"Don't tell anybody, huh?" he said, anxiously.

She looked up. "About the tree? Don't worry."

He sat back down and resumed eating the melon. "I could get in a lot of trouble. They gave me a thing and told me to use it."

John Varley

"It's all right with me," she said, buttering a slice of bread and handing it to him. "Robinson Crusoe never had a portable EcoSan, right?"

"Right," he said, not showing his surprise. How did she know *that*?

Piri didn't know quite what to say. Here she was, sharing his morning, as much a fact of life as the beach or the water.

"What's your name?" It was as good a place to start as any.

"Leandra. You can call me Lee."

"I'm—"

"Piri. I heard about you from the people at the party last night. I hope you don't mind me barging in on you like this."

He shrugged, and tried to indicate all the food with the gesture. "Anytime," he said, and laughed. He felt good. It was nice to have someone friendly around after last night. He looked at her again, from a mellower viewpoint.

She was large; quite a bit taller than he was. Her physical age was around thirty, unusually old for a woman. He thought she might be closer to sixty or seventy, but he had nothing to base it on. Piri himself was in his nineties, and who could have known that? She had the slanting eyes that were caused by the addition of transparent eyelids beneath the natural ones. Her hair grew in a narrow band, cropped short, starting between her eyebrows and going over her head to the nape of her neck. Her ears were pinned efficiently against her head, giving her a lean, streamlined look.

"What brings you to Pacifica?" Piri asked.

She reclined on the sand with her hands behind her head, looking very relaxed.

"Claustrophobia." She winked at him. "Not really. I wouldn't survive long in Pluto with *that*." Piri wasn't even sure what it was, but he smiled as if he knew. "Tired of the crowds. I heard that people couldn't enjoy themselves here, what with the sky, but I didn't have any trouble when I visited. So I bought flippers and gills and decided to spend a few weeks skin-diving by myself.''

Piri looked at the sky. It was a staggering sight. He'd grown used to it, but knew that it helped not to look up more than he had to.

It was an incomplete illusion, all the more appalling because the half of the sky that had been painted was so very convincing. It looked like it really was the sheer blue of infinity, so when the eye slid over to the unpainted overhanging canopy of rock, scarred from blasting, painted with gigantic numbers that were barely visible from twenty kilometers below—one could almost imagine God looking down through the blue opening. It loomed, suspended by nothing, gigatons of rock hanging up there.

Visitors to Pacifica often complained of headaches, usually right on the crown of the head. They were cringing, waiting to get conked.

"Sometimes I wonder how *I* live with it," Piri said.

She laughed. "It's nothing for me. I was a space pilot once.''

"Really?'' This was catnip to Piri. There's nothing more romantic than a space pilot. He had to hear stories.

The morning hours dwindled as she captured his imagination with a series of tall tales he was sure were mostly fabrication. But who cared? Had he come to the South Seas to hear of the mundane? He felt he had met a kindred spirit, and gradually, fearful of being laughed at, he began to tell her stories of the Reef Pirates, first as wishful wouldn't-it-be-fun-if's, then more and more seriously as she listened intently. He forgot her age as he began to spin the best of the yarns he and Harra had concocted.

It was a tacit conspiracy between them to be serious about the stories, but that was the whole point. That was the only way it would work, as it had worked with Harra.

Somehow, this adult woman was interested in playing the same games he was.

Lying in his bed that night, Piri felt better than he had for months, since before Harra had become so distant. Now that he had a companion, he realized that maintaining a satisfying fantasy world by yourself is hard work. Eventually you need someone to tell the stories to, and to share in the making of them.

They spent the day out on the reef. He showed her his crab farm, and introduced her to Ocho the Octopus, who was his usual shy self. Piri suspected the damn thing only loved him for the treats he brought.

She entered into his games easily and with no trace of adult condescension. He wondered why, and got up the courage to ask her. He was afraid he'd ruin the whole thing, but he had to know. It just wasn't normal.

They were perched on a coral outcropping above the high tide level, catching the last rays of the sun.

"I'm not sure," she said. "I guess you think I'm silly, huh?"

"No, not exactly that. It's just that most adults seem to, well, have more 'important' things on their minds." He put all the contempt he could into the word.

"Maybe I feel the same way you do about it. I'm here to have fun. I sort of feel like I've been re-born into a new element. It's *terrific* down there, you know that. I just didn't feel like I wanted to go into that world alone. I was out there yesterday . . ."

"I thought I saw you."

"Maybe you did. Anyway, I needed a companion, and I heard about you. It seemed like the polite thing to, well, not to ask you to be my guide, but sort of fit myself into your world. As it were." She frowned, as if she felt she had said too much. "Let's not push it, all right?"

"Oh, sure. It's none of my business."

"I like you, Piri."

"And I like you. I haven't had a friend for . . . too long."

That night at the luau, Lee disappeared. Piri looked for her briefly, but was not really worried. What she did with her nights was her business. He wanted her during the days.

As he was leaving for his home, Harra came up behind him and took his hand. She walked with him for a moment, then could no longer hold it in.

"A word to the wise, old pal," she said. "You'd better stay away from her. She's not going to do you any good."

"What are you talking about? You don't even know her."

"Maybe I do."

"Well, do you or don't you?"

She didn't say anything, then sighed deeply.

"Piri, if you do the smart thing you'll get on that raft of yours and sail to Bikini. Haven't you had any . . . feelings about her? Any premonitions or anything?"

"I don't know what you're talking about," he said, thinking of sharp teeth and white death.

"I think you do. You have to, but you won't face it. That's all I'm saying. It's not my business to meddle in your affairs."

"I'll say it's not. So why did you come out here and put this stuff in my ear?" He stopped, and something tickled at his mind from his past life, some earlier bit of knowledge, carefully suppressed. He was used to it. He knew he was not really a child, and that he had a long life and many experiences stretching out behind him. But he didn't think about it. He hated it when part of his old self started to intrude on him.

"I think you're jealous of her," he said, and knew it was his old, cynical self talking. "She's an adult, Harra. She's no threat to you. And, hell, I know what you've been hinting at these last months. I'm not ready for it, so leave me alone. I'm just a kid.''

Her chin came up, and the moonlight flashed in her eyes.

''You idiot. Have you looked at yourself lately? You're not Peter Pan, you know. You're growing up. You're damn near a man.''

''That's not true.'' There was panic in Piri's voice. ''I'm only . . . well, I haven't exactly been counting, but I can't be more than nine, ten years—''

''Shit. You're as old as I am, and I've had breasts for two years. But I'm not out to cop you. I can cop with any of seven boys in the village younger than you are, but not you.'' She threw her hands up in exasperation and stepped back from him. Then, in a sudden fury, she hit him on the chest with the heel of her fist. He fell back, stunned at her violence.

''She *is* an adult,'' Harra whispered through her teeth. ''That's what I came here to warn you against. *I'm* your friend, but you don't know it. Ah, what's the use? I'm fighting against that scared old man in your head, and he won't listen to me. Go ahead, go with her. But she's got some surprises for you.''

''What? What surprises?'' Piri was shaking, not wanting to listen to her. It was a relief when she spat at his feet, whirled, and ran down the beach.

''Find out for yourself,'' she yelled back over her shoulder. It sounded like she was crying.

That night, Piri dreamed of white teeth, inches behind him, snapping.

But morning brought Lee, and another fine breakfast in her bulging bag. After a lazy interlude drinking coconut milk, they went to the reef again. The pirates gave them a rough time of it, but they managed to come back alive in time for the nightly gathering.

Harra was there. She was dressed as he had never seen her, in the blue tunic and shorts of the reef maintenance crew. He knew she had taken a job with the disneyland and had been working days with her mother at Bikini, but had not seen her dressed up before. He had just begun to get used to the grass skirt. Not long ago, she had been always nude like him and the other children.

She looked older somehow, and bigger. Maybe it was just the uniform. She still looked like a girl next to Lee. Piri was confused by it, and his thoughts veered protectively away.

Harra did not avoid him, but she was remote in a more important way. It was like she had put on a mask, or possibly taken one off. She carried herself with a dignity that Piri thought was beyond her years.

Lee disappeared just before he was ready to leave. He walked home alone, half hoping Harra would show up so he could apologize for the way he'd talked to her the night before. But she didn't.

He felt the bow-shock of a pressure wave behind him, sensed by some mechanism he was unfamiliar with, like the lateral line of a fish, sensitive to slight changes in the water around him. He knew there was something behind him, closing the gap a little with every wild kick of his flippers.

It was dark. It was always dark when the thing chased him. It was not the wispy, insubstantial thing that darkness was when it settled on the night air, but the primal, eternal night of the depths. He tried to scream with his mouth full of water, but it was a dying gurgle before it passed his lips. The water around him was warm with his blood.

He turned to face it before it was upon him, and saw Harra's face corpse-pale and glowing sickly in the night. But no, it wasn't Harra, it was Lee, and her mouth was far down her body, rimmed with razors, a gaping crescent hole in her chest. He screamed again—

And sat up.

"What? Where are you?"

"I'm right here, it's going to be all right." She held his head as he brought his sobbing under control. She was whispering something but he couldn't understand it, and perhaps wasn't meant to. It was enough. He calmed down quickly, as he always did when he woke from nightmares. If they hung around to haunt him, he never would have stayed by himself for so long.

There was just the moon-lit paleness of her breast before his eyes and the smell of skin and sea water. Her nipple was wet. Was it from his tears? No, his lips were tingling and the nipple was hard when it brushed against him. He realized what he had been doing in his sleep.

"You were calling for your mother," she whispered, as though she'd read his mind. "I've heard you shouldn't wake someone from a nightmare. It seemed to calm you down."

"Thanks," he said, quietly. "Thanks for being here, I mean."

She took his cheek in her hand, turned his head slightly, and kissed him. It was not a motherly kiss, and he realized they were not playing the same game. She had changed the rules on him.

"Lee . . ."

"Hush. It's time you learned."

She eased him onto his back, and he was overpowered with *deja vu*. Her mouth worked downward on his body and it set off chains of associations from his past life. He was familiar with the sensation. It had happened to him often in his second childhood. Something would happen that had happened to him in much the same way before and he would remember a bit of it. He had been seduced by an older woman the first time he was young. She had taught him well, and he remembered it all but didn't want to remember. He was an experienced lover and a child at the same time.

"I'm not old enough," he protested, but she was holding in her hand the evidence that he was old enough, had been old enough for several years. *I'm fourteen years old*, he thought. How could he have kidded himself into thinking he was ten?

"You're a strong young man," she whispered in his ear. "And I'm going to be very disappointed if you keep saying that. You're not a child anymore, Piri. Face it."

"I . . . I guess I'm not."

"Do you know what to do?"

"I think so."

She reclined beside him, drew her legs up. Her body was huge and ghostly and full of limber strength. She would swallow him up, like a shark. The gill slits under her arms opened and shut quickly with her breathing, smelling of salt, iodine, and sweat.

He got on his hands and knees and moved over her.

He woke before she did. The sun was up: another warm, cloudless morning. There would be two thousand more before the first scheduled typhoon.

Piri was a giddy mixture of elation and sadness. It was sad, and he knew it already, that his days of frolicking on the reef were over. He would still go out there, but it would never be the same.

Fourteen years old! Where had the years gone? He was nearly an adult. He moved away from the thought until he found a more acceptable one. He was an adolescent, and a very fortunate one to have been initiated into the mysteries of sex by this strange woman.

He held her as she slept, spooned cozily back to front with his arms around her waist. She had already been playmate, mother, and lover to him. What else did she have in store?

But he didn't care. He was not worried about anything. He already scorned his yesterdays. He was not a boy, but a youth, and he remembered from his other youth what that meant and was excited by it. It was a time of sex, of internal exploration and the exploration of others. He would pursue these new frontiers with the same single-mindedness he had shown on the reef.

He moved against her, slowly, not disturbing her sleep. But she woke as he entered her and turned to give him a sleepy kiss.

They spent the morning involved in each other, until they were content to lie in the sun and soak up heat like glossy reptiles.

"I can hardly believe it," she said. "You've been here for . . . how long? With all these girls and women. And I know at least one of them was interested."

He didn't want to go into it. It was important to him that she not find out he was not really a child. He felt it would change things, and it was not fair. Not fair at all, because it *had* been the first time. In a way he could never have explained to her, last night had been not a re-discovery but an entirely new thing. He had been with many women and it wasn't as if he couldn't remember it. It was all there, and what's more, it showed up in his love-making. He had not been the bumbling teenager, had not needed to be told what to do.

But it was *new*. That old man inside had been a spec-tator and an invaluable coach, but his hardened viewpoint had not intruded to make last night just another bout. It had been a first time, and the first time is special.

When she persisted in her questions he silenced her in the only way he knew, with a kiss. He could see he had to re-think his relationship to her. She had not asked him questions as a playmate, or a mother. In the one role, she had been seemingly as self-centered as he, interested only in the needs of the moment and her personal needs above all. As a mother, she had offered only wordless comfort in a tight spot.

Now she was his lover. What did lovers do when they weren't making love?

They went for walks on the beach, and on the reef. They swam together, but it was different. They talked a lot.

She soon saw that he didn't want to talk about himself. Except for the odd question here and there that would momentarily confuse him, throw him back to stages of his life he didn't wish to remember, she left his past alone.

They stayed away from the village except to load up on supplies. It was mostly his unspoken wish that kept them away. He had made it clear to everyone in the village many years ago that he was not really a child. It had been necessary to convince them that he could take care of himself on his own, to keep them from being over-protective. They would not spill his secret knowingly, but neither would they lie for him.

So he grew increasingly nervous about his relationship with Lee, founded as it was on a lie. If not a lie, then at least a withholding of the facts. He saw that he must tell her soon, and dreaded it. Part of him was convinced that her attraction to him was based mostly on age difference.

Then she learned he had a raft, and wanted to go on a sailing trip to the edge of the world.

Piri did have a raft, though an old one. They dragged it from the bushes that had grown around it since his last trip and began putting it into shape. Piri was delighted. It was something to do, and it was hard work. They didn't have much time for talking.

It was a simple construction of logs lashed together with rope. Only an insane sailor would put the thing to sea in the Pacific Ocean, but it was safe enough for them.

They knew what the weather would be, and the reports were absolutely reliable. And if it came apart, they could swim back.

All the ropes had rotted so badly that even gentle wave action would have quickly pulled it apart. They had to be replaced, a new mast erected, and a new sailcloth installed. Neither of them knew anything about sailing, but Piri knew that the winds blew toward the edge at night and away from it during the day. It was a simple matter of putting up the sail and letting the wind do the navigating.

He checked the schedule to be sure they got there at low tide. It was a moonless night, and he chuckled to himself when he thought of her reaction to the edge of the world. They would sneak up on it in the dark, and the impact would be all the more powerful at sunrise.

But he knew as soon as they were an hour out of Rarotonga that he had made a mistake. There was not much to do there in the night but talk.

"Piri, I've sensed that you don't want to talk about certain things."

"Who? Me?"

She laughed into the empty night. He could barely see her face. The stars were shining brightly, but there were only about a hundred of them installed so far, and all in one part of the sky.

"Yeah, you. You won't talk about yourself. It's like you grew here, sprang up from the ground like a palm tree. And you've got no mother in evidence. You're old enough to have divorced her, but you'd have a guardian somewhere. Someone would be looking after your moral upbringing. The only conclusion is that you don't need an education in moral principles. So you've got a co-pilot."

"Um." She had seen through him. Of course she would have. Why hadn't he realized it?

"So you're a clone. You've had your memories transplanted into a new body, grown from one of your own cells. How old are you? Do you mind my asking?''

''I guess not. Uh . . . what's the date?''

She told him.

''And the year?''

She laughed, but told him that, too.

''Damn. I missed my one hundredth birthday. Well, so what? It's not important. Lee, does this change anything?''

''Of course not. Listen, I could tell the first time, that first night together. You had that puppy-dog eagerness, all right, but you knew how to handle yourself. Tell me: what's it like?''

''The second childhood, you mean?'' He reclined on the gently rocking raft and looked at the little clot of stars. ''It's pretty damn great. It's like living in a dream. What kid hasn't wanted to live alone on a tropic isle? I can, because there's an adult in me who'll keep me out of trouble. But for the last seven years I've been a kid. It's you that finally made me grow up a little, maybe sort of late, at that.''

''I'm sorry. But it felt like the right time.''

''It was. I was afraid of it at first. Listen, I *know* that I'm really a hundred years old, see? I know that all the memories are ready for me when I get to adulthood again. If I think about it, I can remember it all as plain as anything. But I haven't wanted to, and in a way, I still don't want to. The memories are suppressed when you opt for a second childhood instead of being transplanted into another full-grown body.''

''I know.''

''Do you? Oh, yeah. Intellectually. So did I, but I didn't understand what it meant. It's a nine or ten-year holiday, not only from your work, but from yourself. When you get into your nineties, you might find that you need it.''

She was quiet for a while, lying beside him without touching.

"What about the re-integration? Is that started?"

"I don't know. I've heard it's a little rough. I've been having dreams about something chasing me. That's probably my former self, right?"

"Could be. What did your older self do?"

He had to think for a moment, but there it was. He'd not thought of it for eight years.

"I was an economic strategist."

Before he knew it, he found himself launching into an explanation of offensive economic policy.

"Did you know that Pluto is in danger of being gutted by currency transfers from the Inner Planets? And you know why? The speed of light, that's why. Time lag. It's killing us. Since the time of the Invasion of Earth it's been humanity's idea—and a good one, I think—that we should stand together. Our whole cultural thrust in that time has been toward a total economic community. But it won't work at Pluto. Independence is in the cards."

She listened as he tried to explain things that only moments before he would have had trouble understanding himself. But it poured out of him like a breached dam, things like inflation multipliers, futures buying on the oxygen and hydrogen exchanges, phantom dollars and their manipulation by central banking interests, and the invisible drain.

"Invisible drain? What's that?"

"It's hard to explain, but it's tied up in the speed of light. It's an economic drain on Pluto that has nothing to do with real goods and services, or labor, or any of the other traditional forces. It has to do with the fact that any information we get from the Inner Planets is already at least nine hours old. In an economy with a stable currency—pegged to gold, for instance, like the classical economies on Earth—it wouldn't matter much, but it would still have an effect. Nine hours can make a difference in prices, in futures, in outlook on the markets. With a floating exchange medium, one where you need the hourly updates on your credit meter to know what your labor input will give you in terms of material output—your personal financial equation, in other words—and the inflation multiplier is something you simply *must* have if the equation is going to balance and you're not going to be wiped out, then time is really of the essence. We operate at a perpetual disadvantage on Pluto in relation to the Inner Planet money markets. For a long time it ran on the order of point three percent leakage due to outdated information. But the inflation multiplier has been accelerating over the years. Some of it's been absorbed by the fact that we've been moving closer to the I.P.; the time lag has been getting shorter as we move into summer. But it can't last. We'll reach the inner point of our orbit and the effects will really start to accelerate. Then it's war.''

''War?'' She seemed horrified, as well she might be.

''War, in the economic sense. It's a hostile act to renounce a trade agreement, even if it's bleeding you white. It hits every citizen of the Inner Planets in the pocketbook, and we can expect retaliation. We'd be introducing instability by pulling out of the Common Market.''

''How bad will it be? Shooting?''

''Not likely. But devastating enough. A depression's no fun. And they'll be planning one for us.''

''Isn't there any other course?''

''Someone suggested moving our entire government and all our corporate headquarters to the Inner Planets. It could happen, I guess. But who'd feel like it was ours? We'd be a colony, and that's a worse answer than independence, in the long run.''

She was silent for a time, chewing it over. She nodded her head once; he could barely see the movement in the darkness.

"How long until the war?"

He shrugged. "I've been out of touch. I don't know how things have been going. But we can probably take it for another ten years or so. Then we'll have to get out. I'd stock up on real wealth if I were you. Canned goods, air, water, so forth. I don't think it'll get so bad that you'll need those things to stay alive by consuming them. But we may get to a semi-barter situation where they'll be the only valuable things. Your credit meter'll laugh at you when you punch a purchase order, no matter how much work you've put into it."

The raft bumped. They had arrived at the edge of the world.

They moored the raft to one of the rocks on the wall that rose from the open ocean. They were five kilometers out of Rarotonga. They waited for some light as the sun began to rise, then started up the rock face.

It was rough: blasted out with explosives on this face of the dam. It went up at a thirty degree angle for fifty meters, then was suddenly level and smooth as glass. The top of the dam at the edge of the world had been smoothed by cutting lasers into a vast table top, three hundred kilometers long and four kilometers wide. They left wet footprints on it as they began the long walk to the edge.

They soon lost any meaningful perspective on the thing. They lost sight of the sea-edge, and couldn't see the drop-off until they began to near it. By then, it was full light. Timed just right, they would reach the edge when the sun came up and they'd really have something to see.

A hundred meters from the edge when she could see over it a little, Lee began to unconsciously hang back. Piri didn't prod her. It was not something he could force someone to see. He'd reached this point with others, and had to turn back. Already, the fear of falling was building up. But she came on, to stand beside him at the very lip of the canyon.

Pacifica was being built and filled in three sections. Two were complete, but the third was still being hollowed out and was not yet filled with water except in the deepest trenches. The water was kept out of this section by the dam they were standing on. When it was completed, when all the underwater trenches and mountain ranges and guyots and slopes had been built to specifications, the bottom would be covered with sludge and ooze and the whole wedge-shaped section flooded. The water came from liquid hydrogen and oxygen on the surface, combined with the limitless electricity of fusion powerplants.

"We're doing what the Dutch did on Old Earth, but in reverse," Piri pointed out, but he got no reaction from Lee. She was staring, spellbound, down the sheer face of the dam to the apparently bottomless trench below. It was shrouded in mist, but seemed to fall off forever.

"It's eight kilometers deep," Piri told her. "It's not going to be a regular trench when it's finished. It's there to be filled up with the remains of this dam after the place has been flooded." He looked at her face, and didn't bother with more statistics. He let her experience it in her own way.

The only comparable vista on a human-inhabited planet was the Great Rift Valley on Mars. Neither of them had seen it, but it suffered in comparison to this because not all of it could be seen at once. Here, one could see from one side to the other, and from sea level to a distance equivalent to the deepest oceanic trenches on Earth. It simply fell away beneath them and went straight down to nothing. There was a rainbow beneath their feet. Off to the left was a huge waterfall that arced away from the wall in a solid stream. Tons of overflow water went through the wall, to twist, fragment, vaporize and blow away long before it reached the bottom of the trench.

Straight ahead of them and about ten kilometers away
was the mountain that would become the Okinawa biome
when the pit was filled. Only the tiny, blackened tip of
the mountain would show above the water.

Lee stayed and looked at it as long as she could. It
became easier the longer one stood there, and yet something about it drove her away. The scale was too big, there
was no room for humans in that shattered world. Long
before noon, they turned and started the long walk back
to the raft.

She was silent as they boarded and set sail for the return
trip. The winds were blowing fitfully, barely billowing the
sail. It would be another hour before they blew very
strongly. They were still in sight of the dam wall.

They sat on the raft, not looking at each other.

"Piri, thanks for bringing me here."

"You're welcome. You don't have to talk about it."

"All right. But there's something else I have to talk
about. I . . . I don't know where to begin, really."

Piri stirred uneasily. The earlier discussion about economics had disturbed him. It was part of his past life, a
part that he had not been ready to return to. He was full
of confusion. Thoughts that had no place out here in the
concrete world of wind and water were roiling through
his brain. Someone was calling to him, someone he knew
but didn't want to see right then.

"Yeah? What is it you want to talk about?"

"It's about—" she stopped, seemed to think it over.
"Never mind. It's not time yet." She moved close and
touched him. But he was not interested. He made it known
in a few minutes, and she moved to the other side of the
raft.

He lay back, essentially alone with his troubled
thoughts. The wind gusted, then settled down. He saw a
flying fish leap, almost passing over the raft. There was a

piece of the sky falling through the air. It twisted and turned like a feather, a tiny speck of sky that was blue on one side and brown on the other. He could see the hole in the sky where it had been knocked loose.

It must be two or three kilometers away. No, wait, that wasn't right. The top of the sky was twenty kilometers up, and it looked like it was falling from the center. How far away were they from the center of Pacifica? A hundred kilometers?

A *piece of the sky?*

He got to his feet, nearly capsizing the raft.

"What's the matter?"

It was *big*. It looked large even from this far away. It was the dreamy tumbling motion that had deceived him.

"The sky is . . ." he choked on it, and almost laughed. But this was no time to feel silly about it. "The sky is falling, Lee." How long? He watched it, his mind full of numbers. Terminal velocity from that high up, assuming it was heavy enough to punch right through the atmosphere . . . over six hundred meters per second. Time to fall, seventy seconds. Thirty of those must already have gone by.

Lee was shading her eyes as she followed his gaze. She still thought it was a joke. The chunk of sky began to glow red as the atmosphere got thicker.

"Hey, it really is falling," she said. "Look at that."

"It's big. Maybe one or two kilometers across. It's going to make quite a splash, I'll bet."

They watched it descend. Soon it disappeared over the horizon, picking up speed. They waited, but the show seemed to be over. Why was he still uneasy?

"How many tons in a two-kilometer chunk of rock, I wonder?" Lee mused. She didn't look too happy, either. But they sat back down on the raft, still looking in the direction where the thing had sunk into the sea.

Then they were surrounded by flying fish, and the water

looked crazy. The fish were panicked. As soon as they hit they leaped from the water again. Piri felt rather than saw something pass beneath them. And then, very gradually, a roar built up, a deep bass rumble that soon threatened to turn his bones to powder. It picked him up and shook him, and left him limp on his knees. He was stunned, unable to think clearly. His eyes were still fixed on the horizon, and he saw a white fan rising in the distance in silent majesty. It was the spray from the impact, and it was still going up.

"Look up there," Lee said, when she got her voice back. She seemed as confused as he. He looked where she pointed and saw a twisted line crawling across the blue sky. At first he thought it was the end of his life, because it appeared that the whole overhanging dome was fractured and about to fall in on them. But then he saw it was one of the tracks that the sun ran on, pulled free by the rock that had fallen, twisted into a snake of tortured metal.

"The dam!" he yelled. "The dam! We're too close to the dam!"

"What?"

"The bottom rises this close to the dam. The water here isn't that deep. There'll be a wave coming, Lee, a big wave. It'll pile up here."

"Piri, the shadows are moving."

"Huh?"

Surprise was piling on surprise too fast for him to cope with it. But she was right. The shadows were moving. But *why?*

Then he saw it. The sun was setting, but not by following the tracks that led to the concealed opening in the west. It was falling through the air, having been shaken loose by the rock.

Lee had figured it out, too.

"What is that thing?" she asked. "I mean, how big is it?"

"Not too big, I heard. Big enough, but not nearly the size of that chunk that fell. It's some kind of fusion generator. I don't know what'll happen when it hits the water."

They were paralyzed. They knew there was something they should do, but too many things were happening. There was not time to think it out.

"Dive!" Lee yelled. "Dive into the water!"

"What?"

"We have to dive and swim away from the dam, and down as far as we can go. The wave will pass over us, won't it?"

"I don't know."

"It's all we can do."

So they dived. Piri felt his gills come into action, then he was swimming down at an angle toward the dark-shrouded bottom. Lee was off to his left, swimming as hard as she could. And with no sunset, no warning, it got black as pitch. The sun had hit the water.

He had no idea how long he had been swimming when he suddenly felt himself pulled upward. Floating in the water, weightless, he was not well equipped to feel accelerations. But he did feel it, like a rapidly rising elevator. It was accompanied by pressure waves that threatened to burst his eardrums. He kicked and clawed his way downward, not even knowing if he was headed in the right direction. Then he was falling again.

He kept swimming, all alone in the dark. Another wave passed, lifted him, let him down again. A few minutes later, another one, seeming to come from the other direction. He was hopelessly confused. He suddenly felt he was swimming the wrong way. He stopped, not knowing what to do. Was he pointed in the right direction? He had no way to tell.

He stopped paddling and tried to orient himself. It was

useless. He felt surges, and was sure he was being tumbled and buffeted.

Then his skin was tingling with the sensation of a million bubbles crawling over him. It gave him a handle on the situation. The bubbles would be going up, wouldn't they? And they were traveling over his body from belly to back. So down was *that* way.

But he didn't have time to make use of the information. He hit something hard with his hip, wrenched his back as his body tried to tumble over in the foam and water, then was sliding along a smooth surface. It felt like he was going very fast, and he knew where he was and where he was heading and there was nothing he could do about it. The tail of the wave had lifted him clear of the rocky slope of the dam and deposited him on the flat surface. It was now spending itself, sweeping him along to the edge of the world. He turned around, feeling the sliding surface beneath him with his hands, and tried to dig in. It was a nightmare; nothing he did had any effect. Then his head broke free into the air.

He was still sliding, but the huge hump of the wave had dissipated itself and was collapsing quietly into froth and puddles. It drained away with amazing speed. He was left there, alone, cheek pressed lovingly to the cold rock. The darkness was total.

He wasn't about to move. For all he knew, there was an eight-kilometer drop just behind his toes.

Maybe there would be another wave. If so, this one would crash down on him instead of lifting him like a cork in a tempest. It should kill him instantly. He refused to worry about that. All he cared about now was not slipping any farther.

The stars had vanished. Power failure? Now they blinked on. He raised his head a little, in time to see a soft, diffused glow in the east. The moon was rising, and it was doing it at breakneck speed. He saw it rotate from a thin crescent configuration to bright fullness in under a minute. Someone was still in charge, and had decided to throw some light on the scene.

He stood, though his knees were weak. Tall fountains of spray far away to his right indicated where the sea was battering at the dam. He was about in the middle of the tabletop, far from either edge. The ocean was whipped up as if by thirty hurricanes, but he was safe from it at this distance unless there was another tsunami yet to come.

The moonlight turned the surface into a silver mirror, littered with flopping fish. He saw another figure get to her feet, and ran in that direction.

The helicopter located them by infrared detector. They had no way of telling how long it had been. The moon was hanging motionless in the center of the sky.

They got into the cabin, shivering.

The helicopter pilot was happy to have found them, but grieved over other lives lost. She said the toll stood at three dead, fifteen missing and presumed dead. Most of these had been working on the reefs. All the land surface of Pacifica had been scoured, but the loss of life had been minimal. Most had had time to get to an elevator and go below or to a helicopter and rise above the devastation.

From what they had been able to find out, heat expansion of the crust had moved farther down into the interior of the planet than had been expected. It was summer on the surface, something it was easy to forget down here. The engineers had been sure that the inner surface of the sky had been stabilized years ago, but a new fault had been opened by the slight temperature rise. She pointed up to where ships were hovering like fireflies next to the sky, playing searchlights on the site of the damage. No one knew yet if Pacifica would have to be abandoned for another twenty years while it stabilized.

She set them down on Rarotonga. The place was a

mess. The wave had climbed the bottom rise and crested at the reef, and a churning hell of foam and debris had swept over the island. Little was left standing except the concrete blocks that housed the elevators, scoured of their decorative camouflage.

Piri saw a familiar figure coming toward him through the wreckage that had been a picturesque village. She broke into a run, and nearly bowled him over, laughing and kissing him.

"We were sure you were dead," Harra said, drawing back from him as if to check for cuts and bruises.

"It was a fluke, I guess," he said, still incredulous that he had survived. It had seemed bad enough out there in the open ocean; the extent of the disaster was much more evident on the island. He was badly shaken to see it.

"Lee suggested that we try to dive under the wave. That's what saved us. It just lifted us up, then the last one swept us over the top of the dam and drained away. It dropped us like leaves."

"Well, not quite so tenderly in my case," Lee pointed out. "It gave me quite a jolt. I think I might have sprained my wrist."

A medic was available. While her wrist was being bandaged, she kept looking at Piri. He didn't like the look.

"There's something I'd intended to talk to you about on the raft, or soon after we got home. There's no point in your staying here any longer anyway, and I don't know where you'd go."

"No!" Harra burst out. "Not yet. Don't tell him anything yet. It's not fair. Stay away from him." She was protecting Piri with her body, from no assault that was apparent to him.

"I just wanted to—"

"No, no. Don't listen to her, Piri. Come with me." She pleaded with the other woman. "Just give me a few hours alone with him, there's some things I never got around to telling him."

Lee looked undecided, and Piri felt mounting rage and frustration. He had known things were going on around him. It was mostly his own fault that he had ignored them, but now he had to know. He pulled his hand free from Harra and faced Lee.

"Tell me."

She looked down at her feet, then back to his eyes.

"I'm not what I seem, Piri. I've been leading you along, trying to make this easier for you. But you still fight me. I don't think there's any way it's going to be easy."

"No!" Harra shouted again.

"What are you?"

"I'm a psychiatrist. I specialize in retrieving people like you, people who are in a mental vacation mode, what you call 'second childhood.' You're aware of all this, on another level, but the child in you had fought it at every stage. The result has been nightmares—probably with me as the focus, whether you admitted it or not."

She grasped both his wrists, one of them awkwardly because of her injury.

"Now listen to me." She spoke in an intense whisper, trying to get it all out before the panic she saw in his face broke free and sent him running. "You came here for a vacation. You were going to stay ten years, growing up and taking it easy. That's all over. The situation that prevailed when you left is now out of date. Things have moved faster than you believed possible. You had expected a ten-year period after your return to get things in order for the coming battles. That time has evaporated. The Common Market of the Inner Planets has fired the first shot. They've instituted a new system of accounting and it's locked into their computers and running. It's aimed right at Pluto, and it's been working for a month now. We cannot continue as an economic partner to the C.M.I.P., because from now on every time we sell or buy or move money the inflationary multiplier is automatically juggled against us. It's all perfectly legal by all existing treaties, and it's necessary to their economy. But it ignores our time-lag disadvantage. We have to consider it as a hostile act, no matter what the intent. You have to come back and direct the war, Mister Finance Minister.''

The words shattered what calm Piri had left. He wrenched free of her hands and turned wildly to look all around him. Then he sprinted down the beach. He tripped once over his splay feet, got up without ever slowing, and disappeared.

Harra and Lee stood silently and watched him go.

''You didn't have to be so rough with him,'' Harra said, but knew it wasn't so. She just hated to see him so confused.

''It's best done quickly when they resist. And he's all right. He'll have a fight with himself, but there's no real doubt of the outcome.''

''So the Piri I know will be dead soon?''

Lee put her arm around the younger woman.

''Not at all. It's a re-integration, without a winner or a loser. You'll see.'' She looked at the tear-streaked face.

''Don't worry. You'll like the older Piri. It won't take him any time at all to realize that he loves you.''

He had never been to the reef at night. It was a place of furtive fish, always one step ahead of him as they darted back into their places of concealment. He wondered how long it would be before they ventured out in the long night to come. The sun might not rise for years.

They might never come out. Not realizing the changes in their environment, night fish and day fish would never adjust. Feeding cycles would be disrupted, critical temperatures would go awry, the endless moon and lack of sun would frustrate the internal mechanisms, bred over billions of years, and fish would die. It had to happen.

The ecologists would have quite a job on their hands.

But there was one denizen of the outer reef that would survive for a long time. He would eat anything that moved and quite a few things that didn't, at any time of the day or night. He had no fear, he had no internal clocks dictating to him, no inner pressures to confuse him except the one overriding urge to attack. He would last as long as there was anything alive to eat.

But in what passed for a brain in the white-bottomed torpedo that was the Ghost, a splinter of doubt had lodged. He had no recollection of similar doubts, though there had been some. He was not equipped to remember, only to hunt. So this new thing that swam beside him, and drove his cold brain as near as it could come to the emotion of anger, was a mystery. He tried again and again to attack it, then something would seize him with an emotion he had not felt since he was half a meter long, and fear would drive him away.

Piri swam along beside the faint outline of the shark. There was just enough moonlight for him to see the fish, hovering at the ill-defined limit of his sonic signal. Occasionally, the shape would shudder from head to tail, turn toward him, and grow larger. At these times Piri could see nothing but a gaping jaw. Then it would turn quickly, transfix him with that bottomless pit of an eye, and sweep away.

Piri wished he could laugh at the poor, stupid brute. How could he have feared such a mindless eating machine?

Good-bye, pinbrain. He turned and stroked lazily toward the shore. He knew the shark would turn and follow him, nosing into the interdicted sphere of his transponder, but the thought did not impress him. He was without fear. How could he be afraid, when he had already been swallowed into the belly of his nightmare? The teeth had closed around him, he had awakened, and remembered. And that was the end of his fear.

Good-bye, tropical paradise. You were fun while you lasted. Now I'm a grown-up, and must go off to war.

He didn't relish it. It was a wrench to leave his childhood, though the time had surely been right. Now the responsibilities had descended on him, and he must shoulder them. He thought of Harra.

"Piri," he told himself, "as a teenager, you were just too dumb to live."

Knowing it was the last time, he felt the coolness of the water flowing over his gills. They had served him well, but had no place in his work. There was no place for a fish, and no place for Robinson Crusoe.

Good-bye, gills.

He kicked harder for the shore and came to stand, dripping wet, on the beach. Harra and Lee were there, waiting for him.

PENGUIN PUTNAM INC.
Online

Your Internet gateway to a virtual environment with
hundreds of entertaining and enlightening books from
Penguin Putnam Inc.

*While you're there, get the latest buzz on
the best authors and books around—*

Tom Clancy, Patricia Cornwell, W.E.B. Griffin,
Nora Roberts, William Gibson, Robin Cook,
Brian Jacques, Catherine Coulter, Stephen King,
Jacquelyn Mitchard, and many more!

Penguin Putnam Online is located at
http://www.penguinputnam.com

PENGUIN PUTNAM NEWS

Every month you'll get an inside look at our upcoming
books and new features on our site. This is an ongoing
effort to provide you with the most up-to-date
information about our books and authors.

Subscribe to Penguin Putnam News at
http://www.penguinputnam.com/ClubPPI